RIVER GOLD

A NORTHERN LAKES MYSTERY

Award-Winning Series
NORTHERN LAKES MYSTERIES

FIGURE EIGHT
SPIDER LAKE
BOUGH CUTTER
MUSKY RUN
RIVER GOLD

Read more from Jeff Nania and
sign-up for email updates at
feetwetwriting.com

@jeffnaniaauthor   @jeffnania

JEFF NANIA
RIVER GOLD

A NORTHERN LAKES MYSTERY

Feet Wet Writing

Feet Wet Writing
Portage, Wisconsin 53901
feetwetwriting.com

Copyright © 2025 Jeff Nania and Feet Wet, LLC

Art and Design: Chris Nania and Terry Rydberg

First Printing June 2025
Printed in the United States of America

All rights reserved. This book or any portion thereof may not be reproduced or used in any manner whatsoever without the express written permission of the author except for the use of brief quotations in a book review. Contact office@feetwetwriting.com for permission requests.

For more information or to contact the author visit feetwetwriting.com.

Library of Congress Control Number: 2025937380

ISBN: 978-1-960681-12-6 (Paperback)
ISBN: 978-1-960681-13-3 (Ebook)
ISBN: 978-1-960681-14-0 (Hardcover)
ISBN: 978-1-960681-15-7 (Large Print)
ISBN: 978-1-960681-16-4 (Audio)

This book is a work of fiction. Any references to historical events, real people, or real places are used fictitiously. Other names, characters, place, and events are products of the author's imagination, and any resemblance to actual events or place or person, living or dead, is entirely coincidental.

For the rugged citizens who have the courage to fight for the preservation of our natural resources for the next generation

ACKNOWLEDGMENTS

I hope you enjoy reading *River Gold*. It would have never been written without the support of my family, friends, and an adequate supply of split dried ash. I can't thank you enough for your support.

We work diligently to make sure the technical details of the story are correct. Any mistakes are mine and mine alone. Thanks to our advisers, Sheriff's Captain Tanya Molony, Sheriff's Lieutenant JJ Molony, ME and FBI Special Agent Kent Miller, Michael Cooper DVM, historian James B. Kennedy and Wisconsin State Patrol John Schick. Our loyal early readers slog through unedited text and provide valuable feedback: The Huffakers, Marilyn Davis, Karin O'Malley, Julie Barnaby, Valerie Biel, and Joy Ribar.

Thank you to my wife, Victoria, who leads production and marketing with an amazing team, including editors Shannon Booth and Mark Rydberg, and designers Terry Rydberg and Chris Nania.

Let me say it again, my friends and family have made me rich in every way that matters.

Thanks again to Tommye Heinemann for keeping the tradition of Spider Lake alive so we can pass it on to the next generation.

PROLOGUE

Two ten-year-old boys, Jay John and his buddy Wyatt, lived with their parents along the Namekagon River. The waters, woods, and wetlands were the playground of local youngsters. There was no shortage of adventure in the backcountry. Building forts, playing pirates, and climbing higher in trees than their parents would care to see kept them thoroughly occupied.

They were good kids who loved to explore—especially when not sanctioned by Mom or Dad. Over the last few days the boys had hatched a plan, carefully squirreling away needed supplies in quantities no one would notice. They hid homemade wax and sawdust fire starters, fishhooks, fishing line, and anything else they could think of behind the garage in an old steel ash can with a tight-fitting lid. Two letters in zipped plastic bags were part of their master plan.

Jay John and Wyatt often earned "walking around money" helping a neighbor. Their most recent job was shoveling a foot of chicken manure out of the coop, wheelbarrowing it to the compost pile, and mixing it in. It was hard work, but the boys kept at it. The neighbor paid the boys with cash and brand-new, made in the USA Leathermans. Each multi-tool—with knife and saw blades, pliers, and assorted screwdrivers—was just the right size to fit in their jeans pocket.

That night, after dinner, the co-conspirators met behind the garage and transferred their secret supplies into old canvas backpacks. As they were finishing up, Jay John noticed two rusty traps hanging from a nail on the garage wall and threw them in with the rest of their gear, just in case the fish weren't biting. They hid the packs behind an old stump on what they called the school road.

The next morning, each told their parents they had volunteered to show up at school early to help with some chores. They were helpful boys, so no questions were asked. Along the way, they grabbed the packs and ran down the school road, stopping once to hide them in the bushes.

Mrs. Johnson met them at the door. They handed her the letters that explained why they would be absent for the day. As she started questioning them, other students began flooding through the doorway, and the boys slipped out, heading back on the school road.

At just the right time, they looked over their shoulder and jumped onto the river trail, known only to bears, wolves, deer, and local kids. The boys were home free, having fooled parents and teachers alike. Their "can't fail plan" would put them on the river, enjoying a day of fishing while the other kids worked on math and spelling.

The boys came to the place where a big white pine had fallen over a narrow spot in the river. They set up camp near a pool of clear, deep water at a bend. It was full of fish, so they expected no trouble catching lunch. Eating, however, was not their main objective. They'd heard that this pool contained a huge fish, far bigger than all the rest. Jay John's dad told him that the Namekagon River was known to have sturgeon, and that must be what folks were talking about.

They wedged a long, skinny pole into the crack of a giant rock slab that served as a fire ring. The boys had eaten breakfast and weren't hungry, but they were so excited to use their new tools that they built a fire and opened two cans of beans. They sat on the rock, backs resting on the white pine, and examined every feature of their Leathermans. It was then they realized they had forgotten to bring spoons. So they used their knife blades to whittle two pieces of wood into usable utensils. Beans consumed, the boys got down to catching that monster fish.

They set up fishing gear and shinnied out on the fallen pine. Once positioned over the deepest part of the river, they looped themselves together with rope, using bowline knots. They rigged up hand lines with hooks and worms and dropped them into the cold, clear water. Jay John's worm barely hit the water before he hooked a fish. Wyatt hooked another at almost the same time. Both were brook trout, the kind of fish Jay John's grandpa always went for in the upper Namekagon. The trout were brought to hand and skewered on a sharp branch. They caught one more small fish, and with lunch secured, they moved on to their master plan.

They hauled out their secret weapon—a five-aught hook and hundred-pound test line borrowed from Jay John's dad's tackle box. They baited the hook with a glob of worms and the head of the small fish and tied the line around a big branch.

The boys took their lunch of trout and leftover beans to the fire ring. They hung the cans of beans over the fire and roasted the trout on sticks. They called their lunch "beans and brookies." There was nothing better. Bellies full, they lay back against the pine. Suddenly Jay John glanced at the heavy line and jumped up. The line was taut and jerking hard. Whatever it was, it was a monster. The line held fast, and as the boys pulled it in, they were surprised to find it came easily.

After three or four feet, they wondered: *Had the fish gotten off?*

They were about to give up hope when the line again stretched taut, burning their fingers. *What to do?* If they untied the line from the tree, the fish might haul them into the river. They decided to leave the line tied and go down to the water's edge to catch a glimpse of this monster. The boys were expert climbers and descended the slippery rocks with ease. They lay down side by side, looking into the deep water. The sun was at just the right angle, revealing a behemoth, longer than either of the boys and probably outweighing them both.

They slapped palms, determined to land the biggest fish either had ever seen. They started back to their line when something in a little crevice caught Wyatt's eye. A shiny gold fishing lure? Jay John grabbed it and slipped it into his pocket. It was then their plans were interrupted by a big booming voice.

It was Jay John's father. Caught unawares, the boys scrambled to explain their way out of their predicament, each talking over the other. "You boys get yourselves back here," said Jay John's dad. "We need to get you on safe ground."

With the boys on solid footing, Jay John's father crawled out on the log to see what they had. It was indeed a sturgeon, big-bodied and probably over a hundred years old. He pulled on the line, which was the last straw for the sturgeon. It whipped its head and dove to the bottom of the river, line broken.

With the fish gone, the boys remembered the fishing lure. Jay John pulled it out of his pocket and handed it to his dad.

"This is no fishing lure," he said. "This is a gold coin."

The boys were awestruck. They had come for fish and had struck gold.

"Real gold?" they asked.

"Looks that way to me. We'll take it to town and find out for sure," said Jay John's father.

The coin was, in fact, gold. It had the name "Napoleon III

Empereur" with the image of a wreath around a man's head. The boys' find made the front page in the paper. Treasure hunters and historians called it the Lost Boys' coin. But when the interviewer of a local TV show called it by that name, Jay John and Wyatt were quick to point out they knew exactly where they were.

CHAPTER 1

I can't believe how the chips in my life have fallen. Some drifted down like autumn leaves floating gently to land at my feet. Others were thrown by tornadic winds driving me relentlessly forward into inescapable circumstances, spinning me in a vortex, waiting to be thrown out where things changed forever, lives lost, hearts broken. From these things, I can never escape. They will always be a part of me.

There is, however, another side to this: the day fair winds of opportunity blow my way. I muster courage, reach out, and take hold. With luck, I'm whisked off on breezes of happy memories and good things to come.

My life's path has traveled along a figure eight—coming back to familiar places but at different times in my life. When Uncle Nick and Aunt Rose willed me their cabin, they gave me a new chance when I needed it most.

Grand adventures of exploring the endless wilderness with my uncle filled the summer days of my childhood. Aunt Rose taught me not just to like but to love wild blueberry pie. Around the end of July and the beginning of August, she would send us out to pick.

We'd gather our buckets and hand rakes, scrub them clean in the lake, and travel by land and sea to secret locations where the berries thrived. I liked the water travel best, never knowing what I would encounter around the next bend. We loaded our gear and lunch cooler in the old canoe and paddled off. First stop would be Bear Meadow, named by locals because it was a favorite spot for humans and bears alike. When I asked Uncle Nick why he went knowing there were bears, he said, "Johnny, it's the best blueberry patch in the county. Bears or not, Aunt Rose's blueberry pie is worth the risk."

Lowbush blueberries grew all over Wisconsin, but the best grew in the north country. Bear Meadow was covered with these low-growing plants that spread across the ground. We quickly began picking for the pail and ourselves.

The real work started, however, when we arrived home with buckets full. Blueberry jam, blueberry maple syrup, blueberries for the freezer. But most importantly, blueberry pie. Around the cabin, blueberry pie was appropriate for breakfast, lunch, dinner, and in-between snacks.

Those wonderful, youthful days were the happiest of my life. Until now, that is. I love living in the cabin and never tire of the view of the lake. From sweet summer breezes to butt-deep snow, there is no place better to spend the rest of my days. The grass will never be green enough on the other side. I have found my home, but the genuine joy in my life comes from elsewhere.

After our share of trials and tribulations, I convinced the love of my life to marry me. I remember happily thinking when Julie Carlson said, "I do," in front of God and what seemed like the entire population of Namekagon County, there was no backing out.

We had lived together for some time, but waking up on the first day of our married life, we both felt the increased responsibility that came with every decision. One of the first was putting a honeymoon on hold. With our careers all-encompassing, we carved out quality time on the water, hiking the back trails, or enjoying good books on rainy days.

As might be expected, there were bumps in the road with shared decision-making. A couple of days after the ceremony, I was sitting at our picnic table with my proverbial cup of coffee, looking out at the lake. Julie walked out of the cabin, and for the millionth time, I was struck by how beautiful she was.

I like to think I'm making progress in my journey of evolving into a twenty-first-century man. During wedding planning, however, I clearly fell short. Len Bork, a thirty-year veteran as a Musky Falls police officer and Martha's husband, advised me to steer clear of preparations unless asked. I absorbed that premarital advice as well as I could, but good intentions were not enough. So, when Julie joined me at the picnic table, I thought my greeting was fine. "Mrs. Cabrelli, you look lovely."

She gave me a laughing smile and asked, "Who is Mrs. Cabrelli?"

"You are, honey," I laughed. "Don't you remember? We just got married."

"Oh, I remember our wedding very well. I also remember we talked about this," she replied.

"I know we did," I said, "and I thought I won. You were going to be Julie Cabrelli."

"You won? I have got some news for you. Our marriage will not be like the score of a football game. Besides, I think John Carlson has a wonderful Scandihoovian ring to it."

"Scandi-what?"

"Scandihoovian."

Ethnicity is a funny thing and has every chance of quickly

becoming unfunny. It's the butt of a gazillion jokes and has lit the fuse of bloody battles. Humor is often lost when the joke is delivered from one ethnicity to another. Then again, it's hilarious for people to tell jokes involving their own ethnicity. Last year, Julie and I attended the annual lutefisk dinner to raise money for charities in Musky Falls. My Italian taste buds have tried their best to be a lutefisk fan but have not yet made it. In the serving line, Donny Hahn, the chief cook, cornered me and said, "Hey, Sheriff, I'm going to give ya an extra portion so you can soak up a little more Norwegian now dat you threw a rope around dat Julie Carlson."

When you're getting married, there's a certain ownership that goes with obvious ethnicity, like names and how you look. Even if people didn't know my name, one look and they might suspect that I am of southern Mediterranean descent with dark hair and dark eyes. My wife, however, couldn't look more different, a true Scandinavian with blonde hair and blue eyes.

We agreed she would remain Julie Carlson, and I would remain John Cabrelli. Len Bork told me it was a very evolved thing to do. His wife, Martha, said it was just me learning how to dodge bullets. She also pointed out that if we decided to get monogrammed towels, the initials would be the same, so win-win.

Jack Wheeler, our friend across the bay, gave us a wedding gift of two complete fly-fishing setups along with lessons from an expert named Duke. We shared fun and frustration learning how it all worked.

One sunny Saturday, my dear wife and I were flogging the water of Spider Creek when, on a forward cast, she solidly hooked my earlobe with her Muddler Minnow. Julie carefully tried to wiggle the fly from my ear. She also suggested we clip the leader and go to Ron Carver's jewelry store to have him push it through and insert an earring.

But just then my pager fired off, followed by my cell phone. Whether in rural Namekagon County or downtown Madison, crime has a habit of being impatient.

I advised them of my location via radio because cell service was spotty. Dispatch broadcast: "Armed robbery, possible shots fired." A solid yank on Julie's fly dislodged it, and I was on my way.

Dispatch directed me to the Cedar Inn, a comfortable motel on the edge of the city. The parking area was under the city's jurisdiction, and the motel was under the county's. My predecessor had issued deputy sheriff IDs to city officers to give them the ability to cross jurisdictions, and I continued the process. Here in the north country, city and county need to work together whenever possible to avoid jurisdictional issues.

A Musky Falls officer was first on the scene, doing double duty, attending to the victim and scanning the immediate area for an armed subject. She was the one who had advised shots fired and that the victim was wounded. EMS was en route and advised dispatch of their arrival. I rolled in a few minutes behind them.

A motel employee held a double door open and called out, "Down here!"

I followed the EMTs to the scene. Officer Good was using a towel to apply pressure on the leg of a man who was sitting on the floor, his back against the hallway wall. Not wasting any time, the EMTs began cutting away pieces of the man's pants to examine the wound. The Musky Falls officer reassured the victim that additional responding officers were searching the parking area and alleyways, doing everything possible to find the perpetrator.

The victim chimed in. "I don't care about the robber. Just get my briefcase back! I need that case."

"Chances are, if we find the guy who shot you," I said, "We'll find your case. But every minute we waste is him or her being farther away from here."

I left the building to organize our search as units arrived. Officers, deputies, and a canine unit intensified the search as we started to ID and canvas guests at the hotel. Had they seen or heard anything? We knocked on each door but came up empty-handed.

I checked in with EMS to speak with the victim before transport. The wound was clearly painful, but I asked if he could tell me anything that would help our investigation.

"I checked out at the front desk," he said, "gathered up my stuff, and was going to the parking lot. Out of nowhere comes this guy wearing a hooded sweatshirt and mask. He tried to grab the case I was carrying. I held on tight, and that's when he shot me. I fell and released the handle. He grabbed it and took off out the door over there." He pointed to a set of steel service doors. "That's all I can tell you, Sheriff."

I started to ask another question when the EMTs interrupted, stating they were going to transport and that additional questions would have to wait until the attending physician cleared him. The victim identified himself as Dr. Harold Schmutz and was loaded into the ambulance. They took off for the hospital, and Deputy Pave accompanied the ambulance. He would monitor things and try to get more information from the victim if the situation presented itself.

Officers and deputies had taken over canvassing but had made few contacts with no useful information. People casually bumping into someone in a hotel or restaurant rarely remember those people, so I didn't expect much. Witnessing an armed robbery, however, would get just about anybody's attention.

Armed robbery is a strange creature. It seems straightforward: A bad guy points a gun or brandishes a knife and says, "Give me the money." The robber usually doesn't want to shoot anybody; they just want to intimidate. It doesn't take long for the cashier at a "stop and rob" to figure out that fifty bucks in the till is not worth getting killed for.

I've been on calls where an "armed" robber used a toy gun. If he's caught, people look at his toy gun and wonder how the cashier could have been fooled. But when a gun is pointed at you, toy or not, it looks like a forty-four Magnum.

Then there's another class of armed robbers more than willing to use force to take what you have. In this case, our robber shot Dr. Schmutz and had decided beforehand that it might come to that—a decision made final when he brought the gun along. Schmutz put up a fight, and the robber shot him. Lucky for him, it was a painful but not critical wound. The robber, however, had proven himself the dangerous kind, the deadly kind.

In situations like this, law enforcement efforts are quickly prioritized with apprehension and neutralization of the suspect, and treatment of the injured, good guys or bad. Once the scene is secure, information is immediately put out that may lead to the arrest of a suspect: number of perpetrators, physical descriptions, vehicle descriptions, license plates, direction of travel, armed or not armed, and anything else that may be important.

One thing you're never short of is things to do. In some cases there is a lot of information. In this case, there was little.

I was on the radio talking to area cars and, simultaneously, trying to keep track of who was where when a bright red four-door pickup drove into the parking area going too fast. It screeched to a stop, with flashing lights and Namekagon County Fire Department emblazoned on the side.

At that point I got my first indication of how an election for sheriff would go, if indeed there would be one.

I had been working as a special deputy when the governor appointed me to the sheriff's position. My predecessor, Sheriff Jim Rawsom, had been badly injured in a firefight, and Namekagon County sheriff was a good fit for me. Truth be known, I'm not suited for any other kind of employment. In November, should I decide to try to keep this job, there would be an election. The term of the sheriff was four years, with a limitless number of terms.

An election requires at least two people, of course. My campaign committee of Bud Treetall, Tim the Plumber, Doc O'Malley, Ron Carver, and Julie had recently expressed frustration with me. We had filled out the necessary paperwork, but I had not yet filed it. Not sure why. Was I the best man for the job? Did my baggage weigh me down too much?

County Executive Scott Stewart had publicly announced his candidacy for sheriff after speaking at the Lions Club luncheon. He claimed I had brought nothing but trouble to Namekagon County, and my big-city police tactics had almost gotten the previous sheriff killed. Namekagon County wasn't my home, he said. I was an outsider and, sooner or later, would be on my way to somewhere else, leaving a trail of trouble in my wake. The gist of his campaign was not how qualified he was for the job but how unqualified I was.

There was plenty of talk about the potential race. Elected officials in a small community seem to have more impact on the everyday life of its citizens. My law enforcement experience up to this point had been in an urban area with a population that exceeded a million. Namekagon County had just over sixteen thousand. The job of sheriff was a fishbowl for everyone to see. And not by choice—but it's hard to run from the front page. If you're doing your job as a law enforcement officer, inevitably, you will cross wires with someone.

Putting people in jail tends to make them unhappy, especially at the time of the arrest and booking. But once folks are locked up, they usually settle down and wallow in the stupidity that got them there in the first place. That doesn't apply to everyone, but the number of past visits to the clink does have something to do with it.

I laugh to myself at the word *clink*. My old precinct commander told us it was a term that had been around since the 1500s, referring to a prison in Southworth, England. The clink of long ago was a great deal rougher than the clink of today. Sharing accommodations with dog-sized rats gives me the willies. But for some odd reason, I like the name.

It's not just the people who are locked up that's an issue. It can also be the person behind the badge. Any law enforcement officer has a certain amount of authority and power, including being able to deprive someone of their freedom. How they exercise this power is key to their success or failure. A badge-heavy bully? Or a fair-handed servant of the people? I hope every day that I will be remembered as someone who wielded a fair hand.

Scott Stewart was a man who wished to be king. Part of that was demanding the sheriff's department be at his beck and call. He was well known to publicly chastise anyone who dared defy his authority, including me. Stewart had lived in Namekagon County most of his life, coming home after college to take over a family real estate business. He specialized in manipulating zoning laws, allowing him to bulldoze forests, fill wetlands, and build McMansions. According to the locals, after his father passed and he inherited the company, most of his time was spent with the country club set, spending more time raising an elbow than swinging a club. He drove a fancy car and arranged his schedule to spend winters basking in the southern sun.

Stewart got out of the truck wearing an Emergency Management jumpsuit. I noted a holstered pistol on his utility belt. He wasn't a sworn law enforcement officer, but in Wisconsin, open carry of a loaded handgun was permitted by law. While it was off-putting to some people, gun incidents involving law-abiding citizens in Namekagon County are rare.

I exercised one of my best skills and ignored him while I continued with what I was doing. It took extraordinary measures, but he was finally successful in blocking my way.

"What's going on, Sheriff Cabrelli? I heard on my scanner there's a dangerous criminal on the loose."

"Mr. Stewart, I don't have time to waste. We've had an armed robbery. The robbery victim was shot. We are actively looking for the shooter. He or she is considered armed and dangerous. Your presence here puts you at risk. For your own safety, just stay out of the way," I said and walked off. Stewart stayed next to his fire truck.

CHAPTER 2

We searched the area on foot while patrol cars cruised the perimeter. Sometimes it's not the things we find that are important but the things we don't. In this situation we didn't find a shell casing, indicating that the shooter might have used a revolver or a semi-auto that failed to function. It's unlikely the robber knew enough to pick up his shell casing, but it was possible.

Deputy Pave advised me on the victim's condition. A CT scan clearly showed the bullet lodged in his leg, and the wound, while not life-threatening, was serious. An inch or two to the left and it could have been a very different story. The doctor was prepping for surgery to remove the bullet.

Amid all this, a white Ford van pulled up near the motel but out of the scene. The driver called my name, but I didn't hear him. Deputy Plums pointed him out to me, and I walked over to him.

"Sheriff Cabrelli?"

"Yes, how can I help you? Things are kind of busy around here."

"I think I can help you, Sheriff. I'm Jared Price."

"Jared Price? Do I know you?"

"I am your new evidence technician. We've never met, but it

looks like I got here at the right time."

"My new evidence technician?"

"I work with Dr. Liz Masters, assigned to the Namekagon County Sheriff's Office for the next six months. I'm here a few days early to find a place to live and see the sights before I dig in for work."

Then I remembered—we'd been selected to get a crime scene investigation intern.

"What did you say your name is?"

"Jared, Jared Price."

"Well, you can see I've got my hands full right now. How about I catch up with you tomorrow?"

"What about right now? This looks like a crime scene, and I am—for better or worse—your new crime scene technician. I'm ready to go if you are."

"Hmmm..." I wasn't sure about this. A first-day intern at a new crime scene?

"This van is a fully equipped crime scene unit," continued Jared. "Top of the line, paid for by the good citizens of the state of Wisconsin. I can't imagine that they would want either of us to waste a good crime scene."

I wondered if some of that equipment might be just what we needed.

"Okay," I said. "What do you need to get going?"

"I need one of your officers to help me with evidence collection. Hopefully a first responder to help with print elimination, bagging and tagging, and so forth."

"The first one on the scene was Samantha Good from Musky Falls PD. Let me see where she's at."

Officer Good was available, and I introduced her to Jared. Samantha was a fine officer and excited to help process the crime scene.

"Where do you plan to start?" I asked Jared.

"Let's have the motel manager download images from the surveillance cameras."

"One of my deputies is already at it."

We walked across the parking lot to the motel office where Dustin Stevens, the maintenance man, Pat Lorry, the manager, and Officer Plums were talking.

"What have you got?" I asked.

"Nothing we need. The cameras that cover the hallway and parking area where Schmutz was robbed are both out of commission. A couple others on the back side of the building are down too."

"Any video from working cameras of a vehicle leaving the scene?"

"Nothing yet, Sheriff. But I'm going to run them again," Plums replied.

"Wait on that, Plums. This is Jared Price. He's an SI who will be working with us for a while. Arrived at just the right time today. I asked Officer Good to assist him. Maybe you could follow them around and see what they're up to."

"Got it, Sheriff," said Plums.

"Sorry about the cameras, Sheriff," said Stevens. "It's my job to keep them up, but the wires are old and damp. Weather raises heck with them. I checked the video feeds last week after that rainstorm, and several were staticky."

The maintenance man was trying to cover himself for not taking care of the cameras like he should have.

"I patch them as best I can," he continued, "but it's a never-ending job. Truth is, we just don't have much trouble out here. The last time was when someone backed their car into a guest's parked car and took off. Cameras worked fine on that one. I'll patch them again, this time with super caulk. I apologize. Never thought they'd be that important."

"I'll hit the owner up for some extra funds to fix the cables," Lorry added. "I'm sure when he hears about this, he'll want us to do something. Sheriff, can you tell us what happened?"

"Looks like a targeted armed robbery. The perpetrator was waiting for the victim to come out. He might have been hiding in the alcove where the ice and vending machines are. He grabbed the briefcase when he got his chance. Schmutz resisted, and the perp moved it up a notch, pulling a gun. He shot Schmutz, and that was enough incentive for him to give up the fight. He let go, and the perp took off with his briefcase. We're still looking for the guy and will keep looking. In the meantime, our evidence unit is processing the scene."

"I know I speak for Dustin, the owner, and myself that we are thankful no one was killed," said Lorry.

"I'll get on those cables tomorrow," Stevens said.

"If you find anything suspicious, let us know right away."

"Will do, Sheriff," he replied.

I checked in with SI Price, Deputy Plums, and Officer Good. They had recovered several pieces of evidence. The push bar on the left door was covered with everything from unusable smudges to clear full prints. The push bar on the right door had been meticulously wiped clean. Over by the elevators, next to a trash can, was something that looked like a bloodstain. They emptied the trash onto a disposable tarp and found a restaurant-type napkin that appeared to be soaked in blood. They bagged and tagged it and took a scraping of the bloodstain. I didn't know where Liz Masters had found Price, but by the looks of things, he knew his stuff.

Patrol units were searching for suspects and recording the plates of any cars in the immediate area. Deputy Pave was still with the victim at the hospital.

I walked around the corner of the parking lot toward the motel office and ran into Scott Stewart, standing in front of his fire truck. He was talking with a guy I knew was the only reporter from the *Hopper Shopper*, a monthly newspaper stuffed into every mailbox. I hadn't had a lot of interactions with him. The ones I did have left me with a bad taste in my mouth. I could only imagine what Stewart was telling him.

Things were wrapping up at the scene, so I drove over to the hospital and parked in one of two "Police Only" stalls. The hospital receptionist greeted me as I walked in.

"Your deputy and the patient are down the hall, third room on the left," she said.

Pave was sitting in a chair bedside. Schmutz was sound asleep, snoring away in the hospital bed.

"Hey, Sheriff. He's just coming out of anesthesia," Pave said. "Doctor says he's a lucky guy. Must have jerked when the bad guy pulled the trigger. It cut a three-inch channel through the top inch of fat on his leg and stopped there. It was going in the right direction. A little more oomph and… ah… well you know. Bled like heck, that's for sure. I have the bullet fresh from Schmutz's leg in an evidence bag. But I do have a question for you."

"Go ahead, Pave."

"Are we thinking this guy is involved in something and might need to be watched?"

Posting a guard on a patient who isn't a person of interest or under continued threat would be unusual. But the question dealt with one of the realities of law enforcement. Routine calls for service don't stop coming in no matter what's happening elsewhere.

"Not really. I'm just trying to find my way around what was in the briefcase. Did you get anything more on that?"

"That I did, Sheriff. That I did."

"What do you have?"

"Schmutz would rather die than lose that case."

"What's in the case?"

"He won't say. He says it's none of our business, and if we find it, he doesn't give us permission to examine the contents. He wants the briefcase turned over to his lawyer. But is it our business? Or not?" Pave asked.

That put me in a quandary. There are a whole bunch of lawyers spending their careers expounding the law and a whole bunch of judges interpreting those expositions. The first thing that came to mind is we absolutely have the right to inspect the contents of the briefcase. If it's part of the crime and likely the motive for the robbery, the briefcase and its contents are evidence.

My second thought was that the briefcase and its contents may actually constitute a crime. If this guy is willing to get shot fighting over the case, it's probably not full of dirty laundry. Illegal drugs would be a top consideration. Stolen property? Body parts? Who knows? We did know that there was something interesting enough for a thief to take it by physical force and then by deadly force.

The worst part of this whole line of conjecture had to do with cop mentality. Tell a cop not to look at something and they most certainly will find a way to do just that.

When I was a rookie, one of my field training officers (FTO) had been around a long time and had become highly skilled at "creating circumstances" beneficial to crime solving. My first exposure to that came about two in the morning, riding night shift. We found a car cruising alleys in a warehouse area where a high number of thefts were reported in recent weeks. The car was not doing anything illegal that I could see, but my FTO pulled up on the vehicle and hit the lights.

The car stopped in the middle of the alley, engine still running, oily exhaust plumes coming from the tailpipe. We exited our squad. I approached the vehicle from the passenger's side, my field training officer on the driver's side. As he passed the taillight, he stopped for a second, and I heard a *crack*. He got the driver's license while I shined my light around the interior of the car. On the floor in the back was a tool bag, crowbars, lock busters, and two hammers, all in plain view. Construction tools for a couple of hardworking guys? Or tools intended to gain entry into one of the warehouses they were cruising? The driver handed over his ID. A call to data came back with an outstanding warrant for, guess what? Burglary. Also, his driver's license was revoked.

I watched the passenger while my FTO searched and handcuffed the driver. I ran the passenger who, wonder of wonder, also had an outstanding warrant for burglary and aggravated battery. We called for an additional unit to take care of the car, and their vehicle was towed to the impound lot. An inventory search yielded a trunk full of brand-new car batteries.

After central booking, we headed back to the warehouse area to see if there was a business that looked like it had been burgled. I felt a little sheepish for having missed seeing the broken taillight that gave us probable cause for the stop, which led to the arrest of two felons and the recovery of stolen property. After a few minutes, I spoke up and apologized for not paying attention.

My FTO belly laughed and said, "Rookie, sometimes those broken taillights are hard to see unless you get real close."

He reached into a narrow pocket in the thigh of his uniform and pulled out a short club covered with leather. "This here is what's known as a broken taillight detector. Get yourself one, and you'll never miss another broken taillight. Sometimes we have to get creative."

His broken taillight locator was commonly called a sap or

blackjack. I started paying attention and discovered that a lot of guys carried them.

But times have changed since then. Contents of the briefcase were clearly a question for District Attorney Hablitch. Better to run it by him before we overstepped. We had a perpetrator, victim, and briefcase all connected. Up-front advice would be welcome should we find the stolen property.

Schmutz's statements about the briefcase put him in a strange position. All things pointed to the fact that he was the victim of an armed robbery and shot in the process. He was not, however, as cooperative as we hoped he would be.

We needed all the information we could generate to find and arrest the perpetrator: means, motive, and opportunity. Someone wanted the briefcase and presumably the contents. Who would know that Schmutz would be where he was when he was?

This was in no way a case of random opportunity. A bad guy walking by sees someone with a briefcase and decides to steal it, then shoots the victim. According to Deputy Pave, the robber didn't take anything else. Schmutz still had his watch and wallet; only the briefcase was gone.

The crook knew what Schmutz looked like, where he was staying, and when he was leaving. And most importantly, he knew that Schmutz would be carrying the briefcase. It was all about the briefcase. The thief was willing to kill for it, and it seemed like Schmutz was willing to die for it.

Unfortunately, the answer was probably simple. Schmutz didn't look like a drug dealer, but who knows what a drug dealer looks like these days? A regular-sized briefcase could easily carry a hundred thousand dollars of product. Plenty of motive in the illicit drug business.

I was still talking with Deputy Pave when Schmutz seemed to come around. "Dr. Schmutz, I'm Sheriff John Cabrelli. How are you feeling?"

He was a little groggy but still had a noticeable edge to his voice. "I feel like leaving this hospital as soon as possible," he replied. "The nurse told me the doctor will make his rounds soon, and he'll look at my leg. She said he'll most likely send me home in the morning with a prescription, something for infection."

"Before the medical staff descends upon you, we need to talk," I said. Now that you're on the mend, I hope we can get a little more information. It would go a long way toward finding a very dangerous person and maybe getting your briefcase back."

"Sheriff, forget it. What's in that case is my business, and I'm under no obligation to disclose anything about its contents. To that end, I would like to withdraw any complaint. It's likely just a crime of opportunity where some drug-addled kid was trying to steal something he could sell for a few bucks."

I was getting more interested in Schmutz's situation by the minute. "You can drop the complaint," I said, "but I won't. Attempted murder of an uncooperative victim will make my job, and probably your life, harder. But I'm not going to leave a dangerous criminal wandering Namekagon County."

"Leave it alone, Cabrelli," his voice rising. "I mean that. Leave it alone! The minute I'm out of here I'm contacting my lawyer. Do you understand me, Sheriff? I am 100 percent serious. Leave me alone!" he shouted.

The doctor walked into the room. "Is there a problem here, sir?"

"Not really. Sheriff Cabrelli is just an irritating man who has decided to make my personal life his business," Schmutz said.

"Would you like the sheriff to leave while I examine your wound?" the doctor asked.

"He has no business being here in the first place. Yes, I would be thrilled if he left the room."

"My intent was not to upset you," I said. "But I have a job to do, and you have to understand my position."

"And you need to understand mine, Sheriff," he replied.

A few minutes after I left, the doctor walked out of Schmutz's room.

"Doctor, any chance I could get a condition report?"

"Actually, the patient said I could give you a brief on the wound if you agreed to go away."

"I'd like to go away, Doctor, but unfortunately, I have to stick around and figure out who wanted to shoot Dr. Schmutz."

"*Doctor* Schmutz?" the doctor inquired.

"I think a PhD kind of doctor."

"I thought the name sounded familiar. I think he's the professor going to talk at the college. He's combining the lecture with the release of his new book. I've heard he's really good," the doctor said.

"How about the wound, Doc. Anything special?"

"I can tell you this much. It's a close-contact gunshot wound. Some evidence of burning along the edges. Painful but not life-threatening. He'll be on antibiotics for ten days and will need to change the bandage daily. Other than that, not much to report. Now, Sheriff, I have to get to my other patients."

I stepped back into Schmutz's room as soon as the physician left.

"My oh my, Sheriff, what a surprise you've returned," Schmutz said, his voice snarky.

"Dr. Schmutz, I'm not going away. Can't do it. I need to find the person who shot you before he or she shoots someone else. I need some answers and will get them directly from you or will go around you."

"He," Schmutz said.

"He?"

"It was a strong male that robbed me," he said.

"Thanks, I appreciate that. Anything else you recall?"

"I can't describe him because he was wearing a ski mask," Schmutz sighed. "It may not seem like it, but I both appreciate and understand your position. You probably think the case contains some illicit substance. I assure you there's nothing in there that would be of any interest to law enforcement. It's my private property, and only I can make a decision about its value."

"You can understand why we might be a little suspicious," I said.

"I do understand, but that does not change my position."

"Do you have any idea of who the robber might be?"

"No, I don't. If I did, I would give it to you, and we'd both come out ahead. You would get the criminal, and I would recover my property. But I have no clue as to who this guy was."

"Dr. Schmutz, I understand you're going to be giving a presentation at the college in Ashland. Where will you be staying while you're in the area?" I asked.

"Oh well... ah... I don't know yet. I have to check some things." Dr. Schmutz was clearly flustered at the question.

"Is the 2024 Mercedes GLE 53 in the motel parking lot your car? Plate EZ51?"

"Yes, it is."

"If you like, Dr. Schmutz, I can have one of my deputies drop it off here at the hospital. He can give the keys to security."

"I would appreciate that, Sheriff."

"I'll take care of it. If you think of anything else, here is my card with my cell phone number. Day or night, don't hesitate to call."

I left the professor at the hospital and headed back toward the Cedar Inn. On the way, I called Ashland PD and got hold of a detective with whom I had worked a couple of cases. I asked him to check with the university and find out when Schmutz was supposed to be there. He said he'd get back to me.

I headed back to the motel to talk with the Cedar Inn manager.

"Was Dr. Schmutz planning to stay any additional days?"

"No, he checked out before the robbery."

"Since he's checked out, do you mind if I have a look around the room?" With the manager's consent, it was fair game.

"Here's the key card, Sheriff. Drop it at the desk on your way out."

SI Price and Officer Good met me at Schmutz's room and began a meticulous search. In addition, Schmutz had given us keys and permission to enter his car and move it to the hospital. As a result, it was only reasonable to do at least a cursory search and have a canine sniff around.

CHAPTER 3

Sunday morning, I checked in with the hospital. Dr. Schmutz was still there. His vehicle had been delivered as promised and keys left with security.

Rid of his hospital gown, he sat in a chair next to the bed in street clothes. A dignified-looking gentleman wearing a pressed flannel shirt and wading pants with zip-off legs occupied another chair in the room.

"Sheriff Cabrelli, I'd like you to meet my lawyer, Ron Keene."

Keene stood up and shook my hand. "Glad to meet you, Sheriff. We have a friend in common."

"That is?"

"Jack Wheeler. Been close friends since law school."

I stifled a chuckle. Everybody knew Jack Wheeler.

"He told me emphatically you're a man of discretion. That is exactly what my client needs right now. If you wish to call Jack, I would take no offense."

Jack Wheeler, attorney-at-law, was not someone whose name you just threw around. I could see it would be advantageous to hear the two of them out. I might learn something.

"Counselor Keene, I'm happy to hear what you have to say, but that's all I can promise. My main purpose is finding out who shot and robbed Professor Schmutz."

"I'll try to explain to the best of my ability," said Schmutz. "My reluctance to cooperate with you was in no way intended to thwart the law. I'm in a difficult situation and don't know what to do. The only thing I know for sure is that the contents of my briefcase need to remain absolutely confidential. According to Attorney Keene, if my briefcase were to be recovered, it's likely that the contents would be inventoried, especially because the briefcase and its contents would be tied to motive. It has the potential to be public record, a copy of which could be requested. There are only a handful of people in the world who would understand the value in what was stolen from me. As aptly demonstrated, some wouldn't hesitate one whit to shoot me to get what they want. I would prefer that wasn't the outcome. Being shot once is plenty."

"Professor, let's get down to it. What's in the case?"

Keene and Schmutz looked at each other, then the professor slumped his shoulders forward. "A puzzle," he responded.

"Help me a little more with that," I probed.

At that, Dr. Schmutz jumped up and blurted, "Just take me to jail, Cabrelli. I have nothing more for you!" The sudden movement caused his wound to spring a leak. Keene was quick to push the nurse call button. The physician who had treated the professor happened to still be on the floor, and he responded immediately, followed by a nurse.

"Ah, Sheriff Cabrelli. Torturing my patient again," the doctor said. "Everybody out except the nurse."

"Doctor, the sheriff was not acting inappropriately, I assure you," Keene said.

"Out means out! Everyone except my patient!" he ordered again.

We went out into the hall, where Keene and I were immediately subjected to glares from the nurses' station. One nurse, whom I assumed was head nurse, walked up to us and said, "'Out' means out of the building."

Keene and I exited to the parking lot. "Sheriff, I'll call you when I know the next step. Thanks for your patience." Keene walked over to his car.

I left the hospital and started driving—where I didn't know. The great Professor Schmutz had left me hanging. He also had me interested.

I turned my car radio on to catch the *Voice of the North*. Local small-town radio is a jewel of times past, but it's still alive and well in Namekagon County. Most local folks figure if you don't hear it on *Voice of the North*, it probably doesn't matter. At six each morning, every cabin, barn, café, and pickup truck is tuned in to the local news. From seven to eight-thirty, the call-in show hears people's opinions on everything from wolves to walleyes, usually followed by a special guest. Recently, the local ag agent talked about developing suitable habitats for pollinators. After that is the trading post exchange, where people bought and sold anything and everything—a set of four half-ton truck wheels or a trailer load of manure. This is followed by a news recap and a replay of the special guest. The rest of the day is a variety of music, including rock and roll, country, folk, classical, and jazz.

I turned my radio on just in time to catch the special guest show coming back after a commercial for a sale at the Happy Hooker Bait Shop. "I'm here with Scott Stewart, county board chairman and candidate for Namekagon County sheriff. He stopped in to give us an update on his campaign. Our scheduled guest for today cancelled, so let's welcome Scott Stewart. Before we start, in all fairness, we will reach out to Sheriff Cabrelli to give him equal time on the air."

The booming *Voice of the North* host had decades behind the microphone and got the ball rolling. "Chairman Stewart, it's come as a surprise to some that you've decided to run for sheriff. Why did you feel compelled to make that decision?"

"Tom, I've served this community for many years, and we've come to the point where we're facing serious challenges with far more questions than answers. My colleagues on the board urged me to jump in, and after deep consideration, I agreed to step up to the challenge. I've already started tackling issues head-on. No dillydallying around. And I'm proud to say we are well on the road to success, with one glaring exception—the sheriff's department.

"Without exception, ever since John Cabrelli stepped in as sheriff, they've exceeded their budget year after year. In addition, when funds are available, they do a poor job of prioritizing the expenditures they do make. I've worked diligently and closely with the sheriff to try and correct the problem, yet he resists me at every turn."

"Can you give me an example of cost overruns?" asked the host.

"Just look at the staffing budget. Staff overtime is thirty percent over budget. Thirty percent!" shouted Stewart.

"And what's the reason for that? The sheriff must have justified the expenditures."

"The real answer to your question is ugly, and Cabrelli doesn't want to face it. But I'm not afraid to name it."

"Go ahead, Scott. The north country is listening."

"Crime has buried its roots deep into the community. It's eating us alive and costing us a fortune. Sheriff Cabrelli brought his big-city hardcore tactics to the north country, and the result has been terrible. Take the former sheriff, for example. Jim Rawsom, a family man born and raised in Namekagon County, grew up here to be a good, solid citizen. He entered the honorable field of law enforcement, eventually becoming sheriff, and was exemplary in the performance of his duties. How did he deal with the influx of criminals? He ran them out of town before they could get a foothold. At the first sign of trouble, Jim Rawsom was front and center. A brave resourceful man. Now he's struggling, forever bearing his scars for the citizens of this county. And how did this happen? It was John Cabrelli who put him in harm's way! Cabrelli runs from his past with his tail between his legs to Namekagon County, where he can live in the luxury of the north country. Where he can 'find himself.' When will it end? Or does it? Is it already too late?"

"Mr. Stewart, you paint a grim picture of Namekagon County and our sheriff. I'm not sure I agree with you. In any event, can you give me a specific example of something we can improve upon?"

"Absolutely. The communication system, and most recently, the armed robbery at the Cedar Inn. I went to the scene to observe what was going on firsthand and couldn't believe what I was seeing. Patrol units from the Musky Falls PD, Namekagon County sheriff, State Patrol, and DNR driving around like chickens with their heads cut off. No coordination, giving a dangerous suspect the opportunity he needed to escape. Sheriff Cabrelli's lack of command was appalling."

Scott Stewart sang his own praises for the remainder of the interview. I was amazed at how smart he was. I almost gagged when I heard Stewart's last line. "Tom, I challenge Sheriff Cabrelli to a debate right here on *Voice of the North* radio."

"Well, there you have it. Scott Stewart has challenged Sheriff Cabrelli to a live debate on this station. We'll reach out to the sheriff's campaign and see if we can coordinate it."

I turned off the radio as I pulled into the parking lot at Julie's school. She was standing next to a pile of field gear almost as tall as she was and loading it into the truck. For this trip, chest waders and hip boots seemed to be the priority. Preparation like this took place at least once a week for a school field day. Northern Lakes

Academy was a project-based environmental school. Teachers and students worked together with professionals to do everything from prairie, wetland, and shoreline restoration to planting transponders in muskies and fish necropsies. Reading, writing, and arithmetic were blended into hands-on fieldwork. It was a rigorous education, and the kids loved it.

"Can I help you, honey?" I asked.

"Yes, please. Climb on the back ladder to the roof and pack PFDs and wet gear into the cartop carrier."

Julie and I understood the saying, "Many hands make light the work." Gear was stashed in every corner for the morning. We agreed to take a break and head down to Scott and Muffy's Café.

The place had a "sit where you can" protocol, but they always seemed to find a spot for folks no matter how full they were. We grabbed our favorite booth far back in the big dining room, where I could sit comfortably with my back to the wall. Before we settled in, Bud plopped down next to us.

Bud Treetall, Julie's cousin, was a mountain of a man with a gentle disposition who could fix just about anything. He and Julie had been raised together and stood side by side as they navigated the rough road called life. It would be impossible to figure out who was happier when Julie agreed to be my bride—Bud or me. We were a little family with an eclectic group of close friends who shared our joy.

Bud burst out with a laugh. "Julie, John is going to debate Scott Stewart on the radio. I can't wait."

"What?" Julie said.

"He's gonna go on the radio with the Voice and debate Scott Stewart. I heard them say it on the show today," Bud answered.

Julie looked at me with a smile. "Sheriff Cabrelli, politician extraordinaire. I can't wait to hear you debate Stewart. He is such a pompous jerk."

"Well, honey, you'll have a long wait because I'm not going to do it. He can debate himself."

A server came up to us. "Coffee, Sheriff?"

"You bet."

"Mrs. Cabrelli, and for you?"

"Lemonade, please."

"Coming right up."

I picked up the menu and started looking at the specials. "What do you think you're going to have, Mrs. Cabrelli?" I thought the stare she gave me would be a reason to duck.

But it quickly went from stare to laughter. "John, changing the world would be easier than changing you."

I ordered the ribeye sandwich with onion rings, Julie got a chef's salad, and Bud ordered a half-pound cheeseburger with a double order of deep-fried cheese curds.

"Are you really not going to debate Stewart?" Julie asked.

"I already told you I'm not."

"Don't you have to?"

"Nope, and I'm not going to."

"What do you think people will say if you don't?"

"Sheriff Cabrelli didn't have time for the debate. He had too much police work to do," I replied.

"No, seriously, John. You can't just let Stewart run off at the mouth without rebutting what he says."

"That is exactly what I intend to do."

"Sounds like a good strategy to lose an election. What will you do if you do lose?"

"Simple. I will let you support me. Or maybe work part-time in Len Bork's gun shop." After retirement, the former Musky Falls police chief opened a small gun shop a block off Main Street that specialized in classic shotguns—mostly double barrels and antiques. Len was an excellent craftsman, patiently working repair jobs that would "keep these old guns hunting." He loved showing people how these beauties were not just firearms but pieces of art.

"Or I could go work with Bud and help with his building projects. You have plenty of work, don't you, Bud?"

"You can start tomorrow, John," he replied.

Lunch in a northern Wisconsin café is pretty much guaranteed to be good. A café with bad service and a lousy cook opens its doors, but it won't take long before the sign proclaiming the day's special is replaced by a "Closed" sign. Bud and ace mechanic Doc O'Malley made a science of identifying the best places to dine, and Scott and Muffy's was always at the top. The food was great, the portions big, and plates full. After lunch we went our separate ways—Bud to the building he was working on, Julie off to school, and me to Musky Falls.

Chief Mary Delzell called me, and we met at the picnic table behind the sheriff's office.

"Stewart doesn't miss a chance, does he?" she said.

"Nope. I think that's what people running for election do."

"John, can I say something?"

"Sure."

"No one believes a word of what he says. Don't listen to him. This community is thankful to have you. I know it might be hard, but ignore the fool."

"Thanks, Chief, but as Popeye said, 'I yam what I yam, and that's all that I yam.' Stewart can take his best shot, and whether I'm sheriff or not, I'll be fine. Don't worry about me. Tomorrow night there's a county board budget meeting. You should show up. I'll be making a riveting presentation regarding whether we should fix the motor on the big Jon boat or buy a new one. To top that off, the board needs to approve receipt of a grant for an electric four-wheel drive truck."

"An electric truck?" the chief queried. "Where would you plug it in?"

"That's the ten-thousand-dollar question. But it's my job to bring it to their attention. The truck is covered by a grant, but the county would have to put in a charging station. I don't know what it will cost. Anyway, other than that, I'm sure that Stewart will take advantage of having the floor. It could be exciting."

"Well, I should probably go just to keep an eye on him," she said.

"Before you run off, let me tell you I almost had a conversation with Harold Schmutz and his lawyer."

"Did you find out anything else? There's a lot about him online. Schmutz is an award-winning historian specializing in the history of the Great Lakes. Currently he's on tour giving talks at colleges and universities promoting his latest book and his future Nat Geo film. It's interesting. He specializes in recreating the timeline of history involving one or two people. He's scheduled to give a presentation at Ashland in a few weeks about the history and mysteries of northern Wisconsin."

"I hope the bullet wound doesn't slow him down. It may have been part of setting him back a bit."

"Well, I bought a ticket. Julie bought two."

"Julie bought two?"

"She told me she wanted to take you on a date. As soon as I told her I got a ticket, she decided we'd carpool and go out for a fancy dinner."

"Sounds like fun. You know, Mary, I have to tell you something. I'm not the least bit convinced that Schmutz's version of what went down is the whole story. The crime scene team found a bloodstain in the hallway and recovered a blood-soaked napkin from the trash. Our new SI sent them to the lab for DNA testing along with a free-flowing blood sample from Schmutz."

"What's your issue with the blood samples?"

"They were recovered at least fifty feet from where the robbery occurred. The blood-soaked napkin was in the trash, so somebody put it there. The stain on the carpet, well, someone was leaking. It may be completely unrelated to Schmutz, but we need to run it down. He told us he fought with the robber. Maybe he did some damage."

"By the way, John, speaking of our new SI, where has he been all our lives? Not only is *he* meticulous when it comes to evidence, he makes sure everyone else is too. Besides that, Samantha Good reported he was cute. Well, I might see you tomorrow."

I stopped by my office to check in; all was quiet. However, my deputies reported that Scott Stewart had been working overtime in his bid for sheriff. Come election time, he would need to count on my deputies to support him and get other people to follow along. I let my people know that their vote is their vote, whether it's for Stewart or me, no hard feelings on my part either way.

CHAPTER 4

Normal is a good state of affairs in a small northern Wisconsin community. Café theorists had the Schmutz robbery all figured out, and the consensus was that he was a hippie drug dealer or jewel thief. That settled, people moved on to the next important topic: fishing. Early fall fish were active. The dry-erase board at the Happy Hooker had recorded some dandy bass, walleyes, and muskies. Recently the merits and techniques of catching big fish on hookless sucker rigs had been the hot topic. Hot enough that the Hooker had set up another bait tank for extra suckers.

One fish topping fifty inches and ready for a fight came to the boat in Spider Lake. Three somewhat reliable fishermen, Reverend Redberg, Doc O'Malley, and Tim the Plumber, said the fish cleared the water by six feet.

I called Julie and asked her to meet me for a late afternoon fishing excursion.

"John, I can't. I have so much schoolwork to take care of."

"Well, you should come. I'd like to fish the log in front of the cabin and talk with you about the sheriff's election."

"Does four o'clock work?"

"Be there or be square," I replied with a laugh.

Bud Treetall, Sheamus Ruwall, Doc O'Malley, and Len and Martha Bork had gifted us a completely restored fourteen-foot Rhinelander wooden boat. It allowed us to row into quiet places with gentle sweeps of the oars. Sheamus was a master boat builder and restorer and had worked restoring this 1940 boat since Julie and I announced our engagement. Able hands worked the project under the craftsman's watchful eye, and when Sheamus was finished, the boat was a thing of beauty.

I got our gear and slid the boat, officially christened as *Sweetheart,* down the rollers into the lake. The water was calm and cooling off. A splash by the log was followed by a school of minnows swimming for their lives. Spider Lake was truly one of the jewels of Namekagon County.

When I was a boy, unleashed from city life each summer and free to explore, I couldn't wait to dive into the lake and swim along the shore to see how things had changed. I would get out of the car and was greeted by the sounds of Northwoods quiet. Gone were the honking horns, screeching brakes, siren wails, and all the noise I had come to accept as part of life.

Mother Nature quickly wrapped her arms around me. My hikes took me down deer trails and fire lanes. City sidewalks had no place in the backcountry. Time was well spent, swimming in the cool water and catching bluegills off the dock. But mostly furthering my education under the tutelage of Uncle Nick and Aunt Rose. They taught me things I would never learn confined to a desk. I learned from a different perspective, mostly in three dimensions.

If Uncle Nick and Aunt Rose had an agenda for a somewhat wayward boy, it was with the best intentions. They wanted to teach me to think, to be smart, self-reliant, and most of all, to be kind. As a result, I was first in line to help Aunt Rose when she activated the church ladies for a worthy cause. It wasn't until I was quite a bit older that I figured out that Uncle Nick's constant scheduling conflicts with those charitable events may have been more by planning than happenstance. He warned me that church ladies like nothing more than to find a man with his hands in his pockets.

Uncle Nick truly loved the land and was a dedicated student in its ways. He and I went to a public zoning meeting for a house planned to be built a couple of miles from us on Spider Creek. We listened while people gave their opinions, often raising their voices. On the way home I asked him what all the yelling and arguing was about. He explained that the best use of land was different from one person to another. A developer may see vacant land as the next best place to build a subdivision, employing local plumbers, carpenters, and other tradesmen who go on to support the rest of the local economy and provide places for people to live. The farmer could look at the land and estimate the bushels per acre or how many cows he could pasture there. Someone else might see the proposed building site as a natural treasure that should be left as it is. It might become the classroom for generations of hunters as they passed down their traditions. Hikers would hike; foragers would find mushroom delights. "The answer," he would say, "is finding a balance in all things big and small."

I understood what he said, at least somewhat. It wasn't always easy to see. He explained that everything has a place; nothing exists by itself. A clear flowing stream has its place quietly running through the forest. The bed of the stream is covered in water-worn rocks. Pines tower over the stream. Each rock, each tree has its place. Follow the trail they leave, and it's inevitable that you will come to something else in its place. Everything is part of a jigsaw puzzle with countless pieces, and most of those pieces can't speak for themselves. Sometimes humans have to speak for them.

One time Uncle Nick was faced with a situation where he had to speak for a log—my musky log, the log where Julie and I were going to be fishing. That log had been in the water next to the shore for a long, long time. Big muskies were known to patrol the shallows, providing endless hope for me. The log was huge, and it was more in the water than on the shore.

Uncle Nick and I were painting flower boxes for Aunt Rose one sunny afternoon, having a grand time, when a sleek fiberglass boat—ten feet too long for Spider Lake—came racing into the bay. The operator realized too late how small the area was and cranked the wheel hard to avoid hitting the shore. He missed land by a few feet but ran hard into the log. Two people appeared to be thrown down on the deck.

The speedboat sat in the water, engine howling, trying to spin in a circle before the operator got up and shut it down. My uncle and I jumped into the shallow water and went to the rescue. The passenger had a pretty good lump on her head, but the operator was okay. We helped the disabled boat over to our dock.

Examination of the damage immediately showed there was only one blade left on a three-blade prop. Likely the result of the log's spatial companion, a big boulder that nature had set exactly at prop height, known to the locals. The log, too, had taken its toll, putting a crack in the fiberglass hull.

Once the operator saw the damage, he let loose with a vicious stream of profanity aimed primarily at the log, boulder, boat, and lake. Uncle Nick asked him if he had a spare prop and suggested it might be in stowage areas in the boat. He found one and then began to curse about the fact that he had no idea how to install it.

Aunt Rose had had enough and walked out on the dock. "Mister, if you want, I'm sure my husband and nephew would be glad to fix your boat. However, there is a condition. If you can't control your mouth, you will be paddling that boat back to your dock."

That calmed things down, and Uncle Nick and I started on the prop. Aunt Rose gave the girl an ice cube wrapped in a dishcloth to hold on the growing lump on her head.

Prop installed, we pushed the boat out into a little deeper water. The operator turned over the engine, and it started without a problem. The couple idled the boat out of our bay and headed north. We were glad to see them go.

A few days later, a Namekagon County truck trailering a work boat with a hoist pulled into the yard. A young guy and an older man got out and introduced themselves. Uncle Nick knew them as part of the county conservation crew whose job it was to keep things going, whether replacing a road culvert or trapping beavers back flooding a stream. It was a good job if you didn't mind hard outside work.

"What can I help you guys with?" Uncle Nick asked.

Pointing to our log, the younger one said, "It's been determined to be a hazard to navigation."

They explained the complaint. Uncle Nick stopped them before they got very far. "Johnny and I were here for the whole thing. We even helped the guy change out his prop. He blasted into this little bay at top end. Truth is, he's lucky he didn't kill someone."

"That's not what he said," replied the younger man. "Anyway, we have orders to remove the log, and that's what we are going to do." I remember thinking he was talking like a smart aleck.

"You guys think things will be better here if you remove the log?" Nick asked.

The older of the two answered. "I don't think *better* is the word, but it's in the nav channel. Bottom line is the boss has ordered us to remove it."

"Not much of a navigational channel here. Young Johnny and I can barely get our canoe in the water on the way to Spider Creek. It's mostly just a backwater bay where the lake runs into Spider Creek. I don't know how long that log has been there, but it's been a long time since anything that big was cut and floated down to the mill. It's too shallow for a boat of any size, unless they idled in and out with the motor tilted up. Add to that plenty of lilies and pickerel weed, and it's easy to see why someone could have problems. To hit that log, you'd have to be pretty much looking for trouble."

"Kind of what I was thinking," said the more seasoned county man.

"Well, we got the word from the office, and they've determined it's a hazard, so I'm sorry. It's just got to go," repeated the younger man.

"I'm not trying to be personal," said Uncle Nick, "but how old are you?"

Red faced, he answered in an agitated voice, "What does that have to do with anything?"

"Just humor an old man," my uncle replied.

"I'm twenty-four," he said.

"You'd probably agree with me that that log ended up here long before you were a sparkle in your daddy's eye." The young man grumbled no real answer. "So, before you decide to chop it up and haul it out, let me speak my piece."

He walked over to the shop building and came out carrying a metal contraption with a point on the end and a large hook on the bottom.

"Gentlemen, my wonderful wife, Rose, and I have lived here for over forty years. That log was there when we moved in. Anyway, a few years ago I was wading along the shore out to a spot on the log that held my Mepps Number Five. The treble hook was buried deep in the wood. Deeper than just a snag. I contributed to my own problem because when I snagged the log, I mistook it for a musky strike. I set the hook hard once and then again."

Max, the older man, smiled a knowing "been there, done that" smile.

"I couldn't wiggle it loose, so I waded out to get it, and my foot came in contact with something. I reached down alongside the log and couldn't quite grab it. Finally, I bent over and put my head under. Several pulls with a firm grasp, and it broke free. This is what I recovered. It's called a *peavy*, and in its working days it would have had an eight-foot-long wooden handle. I've since learned that it was invented by a Maine blacksmith named Joseph Peavy in the 1850s. My guess is it belonged to one of those tougher-than-boot-leather loggers putting logs in position to float them on the spring flood. Water was impounded behind a log dam, and his peavy handle must've broke, and the head disappeared between jammed-up logs. This very log might've caused the jam, and if so, he would've been giving it his all. When they finally sent the timber downstream, the river took most but left a handful of logs behind, including this one.

"Since then this old log has become sort of the town square for this little bay. Structure for the fish, basking spot for turtles, and the way it lays it protects the shoreline from waves. Now I know you're concerned about shoreline protection and habitat, just like I am, so rather than haul this log out, let's give thanks to the lumberjack who put it there for us and saved us all this work. You two can get on with the stuff you have to do, and I promise to keep an eye on that log. Any problems I will let you know immediately."

The older man looked at Uncle Nick and smiled. "You know, to be honest, the more I look at that log the more I wonder if one end is above the ordinary high-water mark. I don't think we have the authority to make that determination. We'll probably have to leave the log until the engineers take a look."

"What do you mean?" said the younger man. "No way!"

"Maybe not, but we really should measure that just to make sure." The older worker turned back to my uncle. "If you don't mind, Mr. Cabrelli, I think we will leave the log be. If your offer still stands, we would sure appreciate it if you'd keep an eye on it. Any problems, don't hesitate to call."

They walked back to their truck and drove off, thereby providing me with endless opportunities to cast for fish and get snagged.

I heard Julie's truck pull in and headed up to meet her. "I'm going in to change clothes, okay?"

"Put on your new fishing vest. You look so cute wearing it."

We were set. I used a wide-blade boat oar to gently paddle two sweethearts out toward the end of the log. Our heavy spinning rods were loaded—today was not the day for light fly gear. I couldn't hide my smile. Everything was here: the lake, my traditions, and the love of my life.

She couldn't wait. "Are you going to tell me about the sheriff's race or not?"

"I told you I'd fill you in, honey. I've made a decision and hope you will support it. I'm—"

Julie jerked her rod and stopped me mid-sentence. She jerked it again, a perfect double set. The water exploded, and the war was on. *Sweetheart* had a shallow draft, and during two of the runs the fish actually pulled the boat. We had gotten only a brief look, but it was acting like a big one.

Julie kept her rod tip up and reeled with steady pressure. I readied the net to ease the fish in. That big boy had other ideas, however, and wasn't done by a long shot. One glimpse of Julie and the net, and it ran hard for the log, stripping line. It wasn't just any musky; it was the kind that lasts forever in anglers' dreams.

Finally, it came to the boat. Once in the net, we could see its powerful back slowly swishing a broad tail. Julie pulled her phone from her vest pocket and took countless photos. I unhooked the lure and dropped the net away. I lowered the behemoth back into the water, gently held the tail, and moved the fish back and forth. The fish was worn out, and we both were concerned that the fight may have been too much. Then, in the blink of an eye and a swish of the tail, it was gone.

We sat on the wooden boat seats staring at each other, and at the same minute both burst into laughter.

"John, can you believe the size of that fish? It was huge. It was giant. I can't wait to tell Bud! Have you ever caught one that big? I mean, it's not just my imagination. It really was as big as I think it was. How big was it? You took a measure, right? How long?"

After a minute or two, my wife recovered from her first case of musky fever. I paddled the boat back to the dock and put *Sweetheart* on the hoist. Julie was on the phone to Bud and, in the retelling, suffered another bout of fever. We sat down at the picnic table and caught our breath.

She remembered. "So, John, you were going to tell me something before we were so wonderfully interrupted."

"Well, I need to ask what you would think if I put in my nomination papers?"

"Is that what you've decided to do?"

"No, I haven't. You and I are making the decision now. We make decisions together, and this is a big one. I need to hear what you have to say about the whole thing."

"Well, I've given this a lot of thought. Together we've faced the realities of being a law enforcement family. We don't need to go over all that; we already know the answers to those questions. You could go to work with Bud or Len and would probably enjoy it, but Sheriff John Cabrelli, you were born to wear that badge. I think we should go down to the courthouse and file your papers together, number one. And number two, send Stewart packing."

"We'll put in my papers, but I'm not playing Stewart's game. If people want to talk about real issues, I'm glad to listen, but I have no intention of being part of a circus sideshow. The bottom line is, Julie, I am who I am—the good, the bad, and the ugly—and winning or losing the election won't change that. Now, how about we go inside and celebrate your fish?"

CHAPTER 5

On Monday, Julie insisted on attending the county budget meeting that evening despite my strong suggestion she forgo it. "It's just a budget meeting with no other issues other than where we'll spend money. I'll be making an exciting presentation on an electric truck a local dealership wants to give us and what to do with a ten-year-old outboard motor. You should take advantage of the alone time and do some reading."

"I'll admit it sounds boring, but I'm going with you. Consider me your personal bodyguard. If Scott Stewart wants to get to you, he'll have to go through me first." Five feet four inches and 125 pounds may not seem like much, but couple that with an indomitable spirit, and she could be someone to reckon with.

Budget meetings tend to be poorly attended unless there's a hot-button issue. We pulled up to the county building, and I immediately noticed this was not a typical meeting. The "Law Enforcement Only" sign was the only thing that saved us from a hike across town.

Ron Carver and Jack Wheeler, members of the Law Enforcement Advisory Committee, and Chief Delzell were already seated at the long table. Scott Stewart was holding court with a small cohort, partially blocking the doorway. He shook as many hands as he could while running on with his pronouncements. I made my way in, keeping extended conversations at a minimum. I sat next to Ron. Julie sat behind us.

"Should be a hot time in the old town tonight. I heard you filed your papers," Ron said. "Now we'll see what happens."

Scott Stewart walked up to the podium, smiles and handshakes all the way. Then he called the meeting to order. The county board finance committee was listening to the budget proposals.

The public works director went first. Heavy, wet snow last year made for a tough winter. The equipment was not abused but it had been used hard. County service techs spent warmer months working on the trucks, making sure they were ready for the inevitable. If the coming winter was another tough one, some of the older pieces of equipment might not be up to the job. He planned to put two of the newer trucks with better plows on the main roads, and the older trucks would be used on the secondary roads. He also brought up the inevitable potholes. The north country is not kind to blacktop roads, and patching crews were working overtime filling tire-eating menaces. The price of hot mix blacktop had almost doubled, and public works didn't have enough money to cover the extra cost without shorting something else. The committee agreed that the public works director should submit an estimate of cost but, in the meantime, keep filling potholes.

Next was law enforcement. Ron Carver, chair of the Law Enforcement Advisory Committee, came to the podium. Before he started to speak, Scott Stewart stood. "As the county executive, I am invoking Rule 2305, Sec. 1a, dealing with emergency allocations of funds. I want to table any agenda items that are not covered under 2305, Sec. 1a. Does anyone wish to be heard on any budget items that meet the criteria?" No hands raised. "Again, let me ask does anyone wish to be heard on a Rule 2305, Sec. 1a issue? Hearing none, I will ask the finance committee to formerly table any further budget issues to the next meeting and yield the floor to the county executive."

The finance committee looked confused. Jack Wheeler whispered in my ear, "This can't be good.

Ron Carver said in a louder voice, "I wonder what that horse's hind end is going to pull now."

Stewart waited until everyone had eyes on him. "The other night, as I am sure you are aware, there was an armed robbery and shooting at the Cedar Inn. A nationally renowned author and historian was the victim. When I heard about the robbery on the scanner, I felt it was my responsibility, no, my *duty* to go to the scene of the crime and take an objective view of the events. There were several law enforcement officers and emergency medical technicians all trying to do what they were trained to do. The robbery became a manhunt for a vicious criminal who shot an innocent victim in the commission of the crime. The perpetrator then fled and remains at large.

"It was clear to me, and I'm sure to emergency personnel that their lives were in danger, unable to communicate with one another because of an outdated communication system. I had implored Sheriff Cabrelli to come up with a proposal to update this vital equipment. How can we keep this community safe if our emergency services are not afforded basic technology to communicate with one another? There is no thinking person in this room who doesn't agree with me—that is, except maybe Sheriff Cabrelli."

The pin dropping was loud and clear.

"Sheriff, what budget items did you bring tonight to put before the finance committee?" Stewart asked.

I didn't answer.

"Cat got your tongue, Sheriff?" he said in a louder, demanding voice.

"Stewart, knock off the crap," Ron Carver said. "John, don't bother wasting your time with this."

"That's okay, Sheriff. I have your proposal right here in front of me. Let's see here. Repair to an old outboard motor on a boat we hardly use. That's the first one. The next one, though, is a real winner, an electric pickup truck valued at eighty thousand dollars. Where in the world will you plug in an electric vehicle in Namekagon County? These are your priorities? Even though you know the communication system is an issue, you would rather see yourself driving the back roads in the silent comfort of an electric truck. By the way, Sheriff, I couldn't help but notice that you arrived with your wife. Did she ride with you in your police car?"

I didn't answer.

"Never mind, Sheriff, it's not important. It's just interesting to note that you drive your wife around on the county's fuel while citizens pay for the gas."

Julie started to come off her chair but was encouraged to stay put by Jack Wheeler.

"He knows John is on call twenty-four seven, and this issue was hashed out when Jim Rawson was sheriff," Julie said.

"Julie, don't engage him. That's just what he wants. Let it be," said Jack.

A member of the finance committee raised his hand to speak. Stewart ignored him. "So let me get to the point of all this. I have a document to hand out. Lois, if you'll help me.

The paper was entitled "Namekagon County Emergency Services Budget Request." It explained the need to allocate funds to purchase new communications equipment. A detailed equipment list and costs took up multiple pages. I recognized it immediately; it was the same document I had developed and submitted twice to the county board, only to have it shot down by none other than Scott Stewart. That was enough for ol' Ron.

"Stewart, the Law Enforcement Advisory Committee spent weeks putting together this proposal..."

Stewart interrupted, "You mean you wasted weeks, and we still have outdated equipment putting our emergency responders in danger every day. I'm putting a stop to that right now. I've retained outside counsel to prepare the emergency expenditure request you have before you and will bring it to a full vote of the council next week. When it's approved, and it will be approved, the communications contractor will begin work with some initial updates that will patch the system together until it's fully operational. I just have one thing to say before I'm done. You have my word. If I am elected as your new sheriff, I will give these critical items top priority.

"I'm done for the moment," Stewart continued, "but before we adjourn, I haven't heard much from you, Sheriff Cabrelli. Do you have anything to say?"

I didn't respond immediately but knew I had to. "I guess I would like to say something."

"Please go ahead. You've got the floor. Also, I'm sorry about your new electric truck, but priorities are priorities," Stewart smirked.

"I would like to thank you, Mr. Stewart, for leadership on this issue. You are absolutely right. We are in desperate need of an updated communications system. This will be a real benefit to the community."

With his smile replaced by a grimace, Stewart adjourned the meeting, and people moved out the door quickly as if they were in critical need of fresh air.

I didn't quite make it. Stewart stepped in front of me. He put out his hand to shake mine. "John, I'm in this race to win. You've taken us through some tough times, but now it's time for a change."

I walked past him and out the door. The cool air felt good. North country air is different than any other place. It's cleaner, clearer. Sounds resonate more.

Julie and I got to my squad, and she opened the passenger's door. I stopped her.

"I'm sorry, Julie, you're going to have to walk." She found no humor in that or anything else I said on our way home.

Inside the cabin she had her say. "John, you just stood there and let Stewart take credit for your hard work. I remember very well how much time you and the committee spent preparing estimates and getting the required funding together for a new radio communication system. Why would you let Stewart take all the credit?"

She was starting to steam, so I waited.

"Can I speak?"

"Please do, and while you're at it, explain why you let Stewart turn the budget meeting into campaign buffoonery."

I waited while she decompressed.

"He wanted me to argue with him in front of the audience and budget committee. He would twist my words when I was speaking and never let me say anything. He wanted a platform, and I didn't give it to him. I don't plan to give it to him in the future. For now, my dear, I'm going to bed. I am worn out, and who knows what tomorrow will bring?"

I gave Julie a kiss and moved in the direction of the bedroom when my cell phone rang. The life of a sheriff. It was the chief reporter of the *Namekagon County News*.

"Hey, Sheriff, sorry to bother but I'm plugging in the last pieces for this issue. You know how it is—deadlines, deadlines." Bill Presser was a good man. He was the kind of reporter that spent his time reporting on real news not making up stories to sell shampoo.

He and I had a lot of history.

"Anything specific, Bill?"

"I guess so."

"What's up?"

"First, word on the street is that you filed paperwork to run for sheriff, and unless someone else jumps in, it will be you against Scott Stewart. Have I got that right?"

"As far as I know, Bill."

"Second is the budget committee hearing. I have a quote from Scott Stewart regarding the meeting. He said, and I quote, 'I could see that Sheriff Cabrelli was totally unprepared for my progressive approach regarding the future of the Namekagon County Sheriff's Department. My proposals at the budget committee meeting were only the beginning,' end quote. Any comment, Sheriff?"

"To be honest, I'm excited to hear what his additional proposals are. I welcome citizen input and will pay attention to anything that might benefit the community."

"I have a copy of the most recent budget and proposal sent over by Stewart. I compared it with your previous proposal, and other than Stewart having his name all over it, they are identical. He resubmitted the same proposal he vetoed last year."

"I knew it sounded familiar."

Presser was quick on the uptake. "I get it, John. Stewart removes his veto by making the proposal his own, and the sheriff's department gets its new radio setup. All you had to do was stand there like a deer in the headlights. Have you got a quote for me, John?"

"Make something up. I'm tired, and I need to hit the sack."

"Goodnight, Sheriff. Let me know if anything else happens." ❖

CHAPTER 6

Tuesday morning Julie was off to school earlier than usual. We agreed to dinner *à la leftovers*. My wife was now a dyed-in-the-wool musky angler who suggested if we got done early, we take *Sweetheart* out for a little fishing foray.

I phoned into dispatch to see what was going on. One of the senior communicators took my call.

"Nothing, Sheriff. A moving family fight that circulated between three different houses. A disturbance at the Quick Stop. No one went to jail."

"Good. Quiet's good. I am coming into the office to do some follow-up."

"Sheriff, one more thing. Everybody in the department heard about the meeting last night." The drumbeats of the other law enforcement communication system were apparently still working fine.

"When you put together the plan to update our comm system, we all weighed in. Not much of a jump, and Stewart pulls the old switcharoo and copied all your work and submitted it as his own. I had a similar plan myself going on in sixth grade. Anywho, if we had to use two cans and a string it would be better than having Scott Stewart as the sheriff. We've got your back."

"Thanks, Mack."

In my office I found the reports regarding the Harold Schmutz armed robbery. I sat back in my chair and carefully read each word. I wanted to fill in any holes I could. I wrote up a priority list.

The next file I got was of the vehicles in the lot and close proximity to the Cedar Inn. I looked over the list, not very many cars. Other than Schmutz's Mercedes, nothing else stood out. Solving crimes often requires coming up with plausible theories regarding what had happened. One theory I had was that Schmutz was selling something in his briefcase, possibly to a party he'd never met. Once they got together, the bad guy tried to take Schmutz's case, and they struggled. The perp had a gun in his pocket or wherever and shot Dr. Schmutz. The shot ends the historian's resistance, and the bad guy runs off or jumps into a car. Schmutz is in shock after being shot, sees the blood on the floor, and notices it's coming from his leg. He has a restaurant napkin in his pocket and uses it to stop the bleeding, but it doesn't work. He throws the napkin in the trash and heads for the lobby door. The more he walks, the more he bleeds, so he sits down and waits.

It took the Ashland officer a bit, but he got back to me with the information I needed. Schmutz's house had been ready for him for over a week, and he hadn't used it yet. Inconsistency number one: Dr. Harold Schmutz, author and renowned historian, had a cozy house waiting for him on Chequamegon Bay but decided to stay at the Cedar Inn instead to take care of personal business. That personal business and the Cedar Inn where the robber was waiting are more than coincidental. Schmutz may not have known the person he was meeting, but he sure knew the people that had connected them. He wanted his case back but not bad enough to lead us to the perpetrator. They already shot him once, usually enough for most people.

I had seen this mentality before. Gangs did it all the time. Some guy gets shot. If he lives, he goes to the hospital. The hospital calls the police. The cops ask who shot him, and the victim has no idea, although in reality he knows exactly who it was. There is a perverted code of conduct in these tight-knit groups. Most of what they do is below the radar. To join them, the price of admission is usually steep.

I could call my former partner, now the commander of the Organized Crime Task Force, and ask if he had come across a street gang of PhDs.

There is another way of looking at this that has been adopted, particularly in areas with high levels of gang activity. "Help those who help themselves is the rule." A guy gets shot, and he cooperates with the police. Tells them who the shooter is. The police capture the shooter and lock him up.

The opposite side of that coin is if you don't want to help the police ID who shot you. Then maybe the police don't look too hard. FNU (first name unknown) or LNU (last name unknown) and no description, that has a gun, sadly describes a bunch of people.

My cell phone rang. It was Dr. Schmutz.

"Hello."

"Sheriff Cabrelli, I am ensconced in my cozy abode on the bay. My lawyer has gone back to his passion of fly-fishing. He said to call if I needed him. I don't think I do. I am sorry to have ended our meeting at the hospital so abruptly. My antics managed to open the wound again. Sheriff Cabrelli, when it's convenient we need to talk. I know you're busy so whenever it works with you will be fine with me."

"How about now, Dr. Schmutz?"

"Perfect. Do you know where I am?"

"I do. I'll see you in an hour or so."

It's about sixty miles from Musky Falls to Chequamegon Bay. It was a nice enough day, so I took the scenic route along Gichigami. I needed some thinking time, the one thing I couldn't buy enough of right now.

I have always tried to do what's right. I am not always successful, but it's the driving force behind what I do. Scott Stewart's obvious attempts to push me to react foolishly hadn't worked as well as he might have hoped. There were a couple of reasons. Stewart had been a pain in my neck pretty much since I came to Musky Falls. I got over an overwhelming urge to punch his lights out some time ago.

The other reason that was really bothering me was that while I had filed my papers, I still had some doubts about continuing to be sheriff. It wasn't just a passing thought either. I had been seriously thinking about it for quite a while.

Even though Julie was behind me all the way, I had to reconcile things in my own mind. She and I were wife and husband, and maybe someday, just maybe, mother and father. The possibility was more than I ever dreamed of. I saw it in kids' faces whenever I watched them pour out of the school bus. Big smiles. Lives full of possibilities. As sheriff, I put myself in harm's way every day. My family would always hold in the back of their minds the possibility of a knock on the door. I knew all about a law enforcement career and a personal life. I couldn't, wouldn't put Julie in that situation. The easy way out was to lose the election to Scott Stewart, and I was certainly headed in that direction with my lack of engagement with him.

For the moment, however, I was still Sheriff Cabrelli, and I had a job to do. Once I hit Ashland, I took a right turn on Highway 2, which took me to Schmutz's townhouse. The place was familiar.

Last winter, Julie, Bud, and I participated in "Book Across the Bay," a 10k trek across the frozen surface of Chequamegon Bay. Over four thousand people participated and raised money for local kids. A woman on snowshoes faltered in the crowd at the finish line. Big Bud was right behind her, and the momentum generated by a man that size was hard to stop. It looked like he was going to run her down for sure, but that's not what happened. He took a step to the right, swooped down with one huge arm, lifted her into the air, crossed the finish line, and deposited her safely on the other side. Once the crowd figured out what happened, they burst out in cheers. I smiled at the memory.

I didn't have to look very hard for the house where Dr. Schmutz was staying. He was sitting on the retaining wall out front, staring at the bay. He didn't acknowledge me when I pulled up and parked.

As I approached him, he turned his head and looked at me.

"Hello, Sheriff Cabrelli. Did you have a nice drive?"

"Actually, it was peaceful."

"If you don't mind, I am still a little sore, so I arranged transportation for us. I think better when I am moving, looking."

He limped over to a golf cart and asked if I would mind driving.

I asked where we were going, and he said, "Anywhere will do as long as we can see the lake."

We began a leisurely trip down a blacktop bike path along the bay. He pointed to a wide point in the trail shoulder, and we pulled over. The view was beautiful, and we sat silently in our own thoughts for a few minutes.

"You know, Sheriff, these inland seas have carried people for thousands of years. Indigenous people followed weather, animal herds, as well as the bird and fish migrations. In 1654, Pierre Radisson and Medard des Groseilliers camped right about where we are now. They set sail in *Nonsuch*, a square cloth two-masted schooner fifty feet long armed with eight guns. These people were bold adventurers and soon learned the lessons of the lakes. These seas could conjure up violent storms at a moment's notice, dashing the biggest ships upon rocky shores, and have sent over ten thousand people to watery graves.

"It is estimated that there are over five hundred fifty shipwrecks in Lake Superior and another six hundred or so in Lake Michigan. There are many more that have not yet been discovered or accounted for. Explorers encountered and traded with native people who plied the waters of the Great Lakes in canoes and carried with them significant information about navigation.

"It has always been my dream to be one of them. To be the first to see what lay ahead. The best I could do was travel with these people through my research. I have come to know them by their first names. How many children they had. Where they are buried. Each story amazing in its own right. Each a treasure waiting to be uncovered. I am fiercely proud of our work. My team and I have brought history to everyone's library and television set.

"Then things changed. I was sitting on the screened porch of my house one early evening. A spring peeper chorus provided sweet music, with occasional accompaniment of a short musical trill of a gray tree frog. I was reviewing a research project done by some colleagues of mine. It was well done and thoughtful. Unfortunately, it was deeply ensconced within the constraints of civil academia. Concepts to be mostly thought about not acted upon.

"As strange as this sounds, I stared at my feet and noticed that I was wearing rubber slip-on sandals. I went inside, dug through the back of my closet, and, low and behold, found just what I needed: my boots. They were worn but still serviceable. I slipped them on over a pair of my favorite socks and knew I had made the right choice. It's hard to explain, Sheriff, but it was the only choice. I needed to walk the trails and paddle the rivers of history. I needed to walk with them. Shoulder to shoulder, feet wet, mud on my boots.

"I realized then and there that I may never paddle a birch bark canoe or hike the trail of the Anishinaabe. Or stand where the history makers stood and sleep on the ground and wake with frost on my nose. Or fight logs with a peavy as they crashed down the river like a herd of wild horses. So, I went to my sponsors and told them I planned to take a sabbatical. Another book, another show were not immediately forthcoming. It was not well received. I had not signed a new contract. Then they played hardball. Through the grapevine I heard my job had been offered to someone else.

"The bosses demanded a meeting. It was held at a 'jet in' hotel office suite. I was definitely outnumbered. The chairman of the network saw my actions as an attempt to increase my compensation. He delivered veiled threats, telling me that the television market was saturated with top shows waiting in the wings. He explained, as my friend, of course, that we could talk about other options, but now was not the time to take a break.

"It was not money I wanted. It was something else—something completely different. He gave me a copy of a new contract and told me he would need it by eight the next morning; email would be fine. Without it, our professional relationship would end. By eight, I had been on the road for four hours heading north. That was just over three years ago."

His pause signaled me. "Professor, I'm guessing they relented and hired you back. I mean a new book, speaking tour. Looks like things are going well."

"No, actually, I am self-funded with the help of an anonymous donor, and things are going well. My presentation in Ashland is the debut. I haven't been this excited in years. I am going to tell a story like I have never told before. Sheriff Cabrelli, I believe I am almost home. Not there yet but almost. So let us talk about my briefcase. As my lawyer said in our meeting, you are a man of discretion. I believe that to be true. I self-servingly think you may be the best chance of retrieving the case.

"Sheriff, inside the stolen briefcase is the culmination of my life's work. While mostly done in the last three years, it is rich in history never before recorded. The story is of a legend. Two incredible people who are largely unknown; maybe 'undiscovered' is a better term. That's not to say I didn't know about them. They popped up now and again, providing only a snippet of their lives, always in the distance, always on the edge. I never really tried to pin them down. Now, through an almost impossible circumstance I have found them. We have traveled together for over a thousand miles from Savannah, Georgia, to this place you know so well."

"So, how did you first contact the seller? How did the seller contact you?"

"Let me explain something, Sheriff. Buying historical artifacts is a strange and sometimes very mysterious business. Most things that are offered for sale are fake, some very good fakes but fakes all the same. Then there are those items that are real, some passed down through generations, others purchased at a farm auction. Some people want to donate these items to museums. Others want to sell them. If they are to be purchased, they have to be appraised to establish value. Sometimes people with real artifacts want to remain anonymous. There are various reasons. Mostly they have something they think may be stolen or worried the government will come after them.

"In my case the seller called me on the phone and told me what he had. I asked him a couple of questions that would not easily be answered. He answered the questions quickly and accurately. He asked if I was interested in seeing what he had. I said yes. Then he gave me my instructions. He told me to go to the outdoor patio at the Cedar Inn and sit there until a phone rang. When the phone rang, I was to answer it. I did as instructed, and he told me exactly what I needed to do.

"When I was leaving the Cedar Inn, I had a thought and decided to go back and retrieve the phone he called me on. No more than five minutes had passed, and the phone was already gone. He had me hooked. I am so close, and few people could answer those questions. The robber would have known that I would bring something I had for comparison. So, I was at the Cedar Inn at the correct time and place and proceeded to get myself robbed. I had a wad of cash and a Rolex watch; all he took was the case."

"What do you think he was after?" I asked.

"There were several journals, diaries, and ships' logs that are attributed to the same family. I am almost positive it was one of the handwritten journals. Sheriff Cabrelli, there are just not very many people who would know what I had or what to do with it. I am just about certain that if you catch the person, it will be someone I know."

"If I came across the case, what would I expect to find inside?" I asked.

"Only old paper to you: maps, diaries, journals, and letters, as well as some notes. I am sure now they have gone through the papers in great detail. They had to have discovered that they didn't have everything; two big pieces are missing. One is me, and the other is a coded journal. I have come to believe that there are two separate journals. One without the other may be impossible to decipher. Without all the pieces of the puzzle this becomes unbelievably complicated. Others who have tried to follow this circuitous trail have found dead ends at every turn."

"The person who robbed you was willing to kill you for your briefcase. If there are only a handful of people who may be interested in what you have, then that's where we start," I said.

"I'll think about who might be on that list." His response was noncommittal.

"What is the value?"

"Sheriff, value, especially when it comes to history, is judged by the beholder. The bullet tied to the death of a famous old west outlaw may be worth thousands of dollars. Without that provenance it would be a hunk of lead worth a dollar or two. There are only a handful of people in the world who can begin to understand how history and historical objects fit in, where they go, and where they lead. When I announced my sabbatical, there was quite a buzz. Everybody and their brother in my business were trying to guess what I was up to. Theories went from me having cancer to having been fired by the network. Or sailing the world on a three-masted schooner with a chocolate heiress. Which, by the way, I found very intriguing. I even made some of the grocery store tabloids.

"I was and am on a journey of my own, which I will follow to its natural end. It is no different than you building a criminal case. Every piece of the puzzle needs to be put in place. I was absolutely distraught after the theft, as you may recall. Now I realize they cannot find or open the right door without me. If you have a few more minutes, Sheriff, I would like to show you something of importance I have back at the townhouse. I think you will appreciate it, maybe not, but I think so."

The townhouse was designed to welcome the lake to come in. The furniture was a perfect cross between comfortable and a sea captain's quarters.

Dr. Schmutz went to another room, and I looked around. Papers covered many of the surfaces. An ink drawing of a stunning woman with long black hair and deep brown eyes caught my attention. She wore a dress open at the collar, revealing a tattoo on the upper portion of her left breast. Unlike the rest of the drawing, her tattoo was in color. It was an intricate, blazing sun. Bright red in the center with a yellow ring around it. From the yellow ring were what appeared to be waving tentacles of some mythical beast. Cutting across the tattoo was the placard, the likes of which would be most often found bearing the name of a ship at sea. This banner simply said, "Maria." A black and white photo of a man from perhaps the 1800s lay next to it.

"Ah, I see you have met Samuel and Maria Benson. They came to Namekagon County after the Civil War. Historical accounts say Benson just appeared one day with two Navy Colts tucked in a sash around his waist and began to buy large tracts of forested land. But here, this is what I wanted to show you."

Schmutz laid a wooden case with brass hinges and latch on the counter, opened the latch, and almost reverently removed a sword. He handed it to me. It was rough, with a crude CS casting on the cross guard and a star on the pommel. Although I had little or no experience with swords, there was no mistaking this was a battle weapon.

"Sheriff, this is a Confederate twenty-four-inch CS & Star Foot Artillery Short Sword. Also referred to as Roman Sword. This sword is extremely rare. Its manufacture predates the Civil War, but it saw action in the war between the states, often in close combat situations. I have one more thing to show you, Sheriff." He handed me a velvet pouch. "Take a look."

I retrieved a gold coin from the bag. It was almost mystical.

"Ah, I can see it captures you. It is a Napoleon III 1862 one-hundred-franc gold coin. Many details show up on coins like this: proof marks, mint marks, and so on. If you were simply a collector, you would hire an expert to prove their authenticity. I have no interest in doing that. I am absolutely positive that these items are authentic."

"Professor, these items are fascinating. They must be valuable."

"The sword and the coin are worth thousands of dollars. We could sell them online before lunch. In this case, the real value is where they were found."

"Where was that, Dr. Schmutz?"

"In your backyard, Sheriff. The coin is from the Namekagon River, one of very few that have been found. The short sword is from a roadside antique shop on Highway 13 in Port Wing. How they got to where they were found is of critical importance to my research. What was taken from me is part of this mystery."

Dr. Schmutz and I parted ways. I had a new appreciation for what he was doing. I also learned a fair bit about who the armed robber might be. On my drive back to Musky Falls, my mind was buzzing on one side with thoughts of swords, coins, and Dr. Schmutz. On the other side, the election.

CHAPTER 7

I turned off to stop at a boatyard on the way back to town. A small canoe hung from a placard that said, "Wooden Boats for Sale and Repair ~ Sheamus Ruwall, Proprietor."

Sheamus was a good man, always willing to lend a hand to help someone. He started his wooden boat restoration as a hobby after retirement and found out he had a real knack for it. Before he and his wife Janet knew it, his passion to "keep old boats floating" was a going business.

I pulled up to his shop where he was toiling away with a sanding block on the hull of a wooden boat resting on sawhorses, with wedges and rollers holding it in place. He looked up and smiled when I got out.

"Sheriff Cabrelli, have you come to take me in? I will go without a struggle. Janet can finish sanding this hull."

I laughed. "Nope I was going by and, as part of our community policing program, wanted to check with our local businesses."

"Well, welcome. You are just in time to help me roll this boat over. You take the stern; I'll take the bow. Let the rollers do the work. Too much muscle and we'll send this fine craft out into the yard."

The rollover took five minutes and went flawlessly.

"Can't have a boat wiggling around while you're working it," said Sheamus. "John, it seems to me you've got something on your mind."

"I don't know, Sheamus. I was just thinking about... Julie. Julie and I went out in *Sweetheart*. I was using that long paddle and quietly moving us around our bay. It was calm, until it wasn't. A muskie clobbered her lure, and war was on. It was a beautiful fish, and she was overjoyed."

"Good for her. Have her send me a picture. Now, nothing else on your mind? Like maybe Scott Stewart digging his heels into you?"

I didn't respond but began to wish I hadn't stopped.

"Well, since you opted not to speak, let me go ahead with my two cents. Scott Stewart is a self-important, conceited pain in the stern. He has plenty of people fooled, but not as many as he thinks. His recent personal appearances at every little café in the county are as phony as he is. Just the other day I stopped for breakfast at the Spider Lake Café. Stewart was running his mouth to a table full of seasoned citizen voters. The minute he left, the guys summed up the feeling around here. They laughed about Stewart as sheriff and unanimously supported you before they dug into breakfast. I agree with them—you're the right man for the job, and you've proven it. You don't need to run your mouth to us. You got the right stuff. Whether you want the job or not is up to you. Just a little piece of advice, though: If you're going to run for election, you'd better get to it. Filing your papers is not enough. People are counting on you. If you don't really want the job they'll understand. If you do, they'll back you, but don't leave them in limbo."

I drove out of the boatyard weighed down now with a feeling of guilt. I needed to give the election my best efforts. Otherwise, I was letting these people down who have become my friends and neighbors.

Much to my happiness, my squad radio provided a ready distraction. The Wisconsin State Patrol requested backup for a suspected drunk driver who was being uncooperative. I was a stone's throw from the location of the stop.

I pulled up and saw that things were consistent with my life's experience dealing with drunks. The trooper was a cool head that had been around for a long time. The driver was in the car with both hands locked on the steering wheel at the ten and two position. He wasn't fighting, but he also wasn't moving.

"Hey, Denny," I said to the trooper. "What do you have here?"

"John, this fellow here took out a dozen or so traffic cones at the road construction site at River Road. County highway called it in, and I picked him up on the way to town. Someplace about fifty to sixty yards from where he stopped, he pitched a bottle of some sort out the window. He hasn't been violent, just unresponsive and stubborn. The registration comes back to Hans Johnson. You know him?"

"We have definitely met. Let me try and talk to him for a minute, okay?"

"Be my guest, Sheriff."

"Say there, Hans, how are you doing? I need to ask you a couple of things before we get started here. These are questions you really should answer. Let's start with the condition of your heart. Are you a heart-healthy guy?"

That got Hans' attention. With a booze-slurred voice, he answered, "Why do you want to know?"

Now the trooper was smiling.

"Well, Hans, we can't leave you in the car. We have to take you out. Now we could call a couple more squad cars and have a donnybrook right here in the road. The result will be you're arrested, maybe injured, and charged with resisting arrest. Your own stubbornness will make your situation worse. Nobody wants to go that way. So, we have an alternative. The wonder of electricity."

"What...'lectricity?" he slurred.

"This," I said as I pointed to my taser. "It was made just for situations like this. Big stubborn guy doesn't want to comply. We don't have any choice. You've got to go with us one way or the other. The easiest thing is that I shoot you with this taser. If things go right, it'll knock you on your can, giving us time to handcuff you. In very rare situations, the electric shock could affect your heart. Probably won't but could. Recently, I heard about a case where a guy got hit with a taser, and from then on, he couldn't control his bladder. Likely nothing like that will happen with you. Just thought I'd bring it up."

I pulled my taser and pointed it at him. "So, Hans, what's it going to be?"

"Alright, I'm comin'. I got high cholesterol, and I don't need no more heart problems. Them pills is expensive."

Hans should have factored into his budget the fact that a ticket for drunk driving usually costs the violator about ten grand. Hans refused a breath test, and the trooper hauled him off to jail. While I waited for the wrecker from Bill and Jack's Garage and Guide Service to tow the car, I walked back along the shoulder and recovered a pint bottle of Early Times with about an inch left in the bottom. I bagged it and tagged it and would turn it over to Denny later.

Doc O'Malley showed up and backed his flatbed into position. He was his normal cheery self. He recognized the car and its distinctive partial camouflage paint job. "Musta got one of the Johnson boys, huh?"

"Hans," I replied.

"When those guys are sober, they are great workers. When they are out on a bender, they are great drinkers. Hans give you any trouble?"

"Not really."

"He's not much of a troublemaker. His brother Ole is another thing altogether. Any release orders on the car?"

"Somebody shows up sober and has proof of ownership and insurance. Send them to our office, and we'll do the paperwork."

"Okay, Sheriff. You got it."

"Thanks, Doc."

One thing that is nice about being the boss is that I don't have to respond to routine calls for service. Not that I mind most of the time. I don't see myself much different than the rest of our department. If a call comes in and I'm close, I'll take it. Someone needs backup, I am on it. If all's quiet in Namekagon County, I'll take the back roads, stop, say hello to anyone I meet up with. It seems that people across the north country are, for the most part, nice folks. There is always a cup of coffee to be had. I thought of them as my people. In my short tenure, we had shared tragedy and joy. But most importantly, Namekagon County was my home; it was where I lived with my wife. It was where, God willing, we'd spend the rest of our life together.

The *Voice of the North* host Tom Stockten called shortly after I'd arrived home. "Sheriff, any thoughts on the debate with Scott Stewart on my show?"

"Tom, I've thought a lot about it. At first, I wasn't going to participate. After Stewart's performance at the finance committee meeting, it's clear that bending the truth is in his repertoire of strategies. I don't want to spend all my time rebutting what he says. If I do that, I will never be able to talk about important issues."

"I would have some control over that, but I recognize Stewart will try to control the show."

"When do you need to know by, Tom?"

"The sooner you let me know, the better. I would like to get the word out. So, if you let me know next week, that should work," Tom said.

"I have one request."

"What is it, Sheriff?"

"Instead of having it on your radio program, let's have a live debate in front of an audience in the county building. You will be the moderator."

Tom gave a low chuckle and said, "It works for me. Are you going to do it then?"

"You're on. I'll let Ron Carver know."

I hung up and turned to find Julie. The expression on her face told me she had heard at least one side of the conversation. Shock slowly changed to a smile from ear to ear. At least one of us was ready.

CHAPTER 8

First thing Wednesday morning I was on the way to the Musky Falls PD for a video meeting with some other police and sheriff's departments, and I stopped at Karin's Coffee trailer and picked up a couple of cups of arguably the best coffee in Namekagon County. Coffee was an interesting point of discussion in my life. My dear, sweet wife maintained that I drank too much of it, and too much of anything was bad for you. I explained how I handled it. I intentionally never read any articles that said coffee was bad for me. On the other hand, I read everything that came my way that said coffee was good for me. So, my answer to the query was, "I don't know about you, but I personally don't recall ever reading a single article that says coffee is bad for me."

Chief Delzell and I sat in the conference room with the big screen in front of us, along with a deputy from Sande County and an officer from the Town of Frost PD. We had these meetings with our neighboring law enforcement agencies every so often. Agencies big or small really benefitted from this.

I didn't care much for virtual meetings. In-person events allowed us to really spend time with one another, and a lot of things got hashed out over lunch at a local café. But times had changed. There was no formal announcement of these meetings, but they were posted at each department, and anyone was welcome to come.

During the last meeting, the owner of a local marina stopped by. He had three dozen boats stored against his back fence. They were boats that didn't get frequent usage. He went to put one of them in the water for the owner and saw that all the motors against the fence had their props removed. He reported the theft and thought they were long gone. However, just that morning on the local radio program, he heard a guy call in with some used props to sell. The marina owner called and made arrangements to buy a couple. The fire number was out in the county. He stopped and looked over a couple dozen boat props along with a bunch of other marine equipment. The props were definitely his. He bought two of his own back and brought them to the meeting. The prop salesman got himself charged with felony theft and burglary.

Today the Douglas County sheriff was first on the agenda. Superior was plagued with theft of catalytic converters. After dark a car would pull up lights off next to another car parked on a residential street. The passenger door would open, a person would climb out, and skinny under the car with a battery-powered reciprocating saw. Two quick cuts and the catalytic converter dropped free. The saw man crawled back out, jumped in the car with his saw and converter, and off they went. Total time? Just shy of two minutes. There had been twenty-five reported thefts in the last week. He went on to tell us that they suspected a junkyard south of the county was buying the converters for cash.

At that point the door opened, and Scott Stewart walked in. "Mind if I join you, folks?"

The detective running the meeting asked, "Who may you be?"

"I am Scott Stewart, county executive from Namekagon County.

I'm running for sheriff. Based on the current crime wave, I think it is my duty to learn as much as I can about law enforcement and our community."

No one objected, and Stewart grabbed a chair.

The next was a detective from Superior PD, Sharon Subinski. Just about everyone knew Sharon or knew of her. "I've got something to pass on to you. We think we have a couple of different gangs giving us some real fits. They're smash and grabbers. They started out at a jewelry store in the mall. Four of them in hoodies, masks, and gloves hit the showroom hard. No one saw a gun, but one of the punks had a hand in his pocket, maybe a finger maybe not. Anyway, he was the lookout. Three others smashed through the glass in the showcases and scooped up piles of watches, rings, and bracelets. According to the surveillance video, they were in and out the door in five minutes. We have physical descriptions based on the video footage.

"The next hit was three days later. There was a coin and jewelry show at the convention center. Collectors get together to buy, trade, and sell items. This event had some jewelry but was focused mostly on coins. They must have scoped the place out. There was armed security present twenty-four seven to watch the display area. One of the high-end collectors closed his booth every night and took his goods with him. He and his wife left the center and were going to their car Saturday night. Four masked bad guys came out of the bushes along the parking lot and grabbed the cases they had. The coin dealer is an older fellow and drew a pistol. One of the bandits took it away from him, and they ran off. We have some video footage of a black late-model SUV with fancy wheels leaving the area minutes after the robbery. We got a plate number, but it wasn't much good. Turned out the plates were stolen from a vehicle in Minnesota.

"We have no real leads on these guys. One or two things do

come to mind, though. The stuff they are grabbing is mostly high end, and at this point they are already into quantity. Unless they are recreational thieves, they have to fence what they got somewhere to make this all work for them. Most of what they grabbed was not serial numbered, except for some expensive watches. The rest of the items are distinctive—rings, bracelets—and would be identifiable by the victim. Some will have maker's marks, engraving, or endearments. The victim has meticulous records on each piece.

"The dealer said that coins are different. Gold and silver coins can be melted down and sold over the counter to anyone who advertises they buy gold and silver. Coins can be sold easily. Most coins are similar to others and don't have special identifying marks. But not always. In some cases, a tiny mark can make all the difference. The victim explained he had several twenty-dollar Liberty Double Eagle gold coins in inventory, averaging in price between two and three thousand dollars, depending on condition. Well over a million of these coins were minted, all pretty much the same. Two he has in secure storage that were not with him when he was robbed, thankfully. They are worth between ninety and one hundred thousand dollars each. The difference between a three-thousand-dollar coin and a one-hundred-thousand-dollar coin is a small letter on the back. He said there are some unscrupulous collectors who would love to have one, no matter where it came from. Thieves wouldn't know the difference.

"Selling the stuff around here is possible, but more likely in Chicago or the Twin Cities. Our current theory follows along that line. We think they are probably out-of-towners who swing in, find a target, and then when things look right, they make the hit. Eight hours to Chicago or two hours to Minneapolis. If they have someone waiting to do business, they can get paid, turn around, and head right home."

Stewart interrupted, "Could I ask a question?"

"Of course, that's what we're here for: information exchange. So go ahead," answered Subinski.

"This is for Sheriff Cabrelli. Is this the first you have heard of these kinds of robberies?"

"No. Variations of this theme have been going on for a long time. The only thing I have noticed is that they seem to be getting more violent. Guns are showing up more often," I answered.

"So, you see them as being dangerous?"

"Yes, Mr. Stewart. Strong-armed and armed robberies are dangerous."

"Well, I was just thinking how many stores in Namekagon have glass display cabinets. It seems to be a pretty common form of display. Wouldn't you say?"

"Yes, I would."

"So, we agree on that, Sheriff?"

"We agree," I replied, just waiting to see where this was going.

"So, Sheriff, what have you done to protect our businesses and their customers from these vicious criminals?"

"Everything we can," I replied.

"Like what?" Stewart pressed.

"I can't say, Mr. Stewart."

"Most likely because you haven't done anything."

"Not the case, but I can't say. We don't want the whole world to know what security measures are in place."

Chief Delzell and I had recently updated a silent security system that was developed by Ron Carver and my Uncle Nick a few years before. Totally silent, it went right to dispatch. We had a good laugh when we were changing out components at Ron's jewelry store. It was pretty much general consensus that anybody who tried robbing his store would find they had made a foolish choice.

"What's going on in Superior might find its way to Namekagon

County and vice versa. Information exchange is critical to successful law enforcement. Keeping those channels constantly open takes staff time, and it turns out as time well spent. The smash-and-grab robber of today might be the fleeing murderer tomorrow," I replied.

"I am not disputing that information exchange is important, but it is a fiscal issue. So, let me ask Sheriff Cabrelli, how much does this information exchange cost us? If you even know."

I needed to take a breath before I spoke. "Scott, I know exactly what it cost us."

"Would you mind sharing with me?"

"It costs us nothing. Our time is paid for by a grant sponsored by Superior PD. They invited us to join their group. The detective felt that since there is so much rural area between us and the Cities that we could learn something from each other. It has worked well."

Stewart stayed until the end of the meeting. No one was sorry to see him go.

I patrolled the back roads. There were some vacant cabins along the north shore of Spider Lake, and one had been broken into sometime during the preceding week. No real damage other than a busted front door lock. The remaining evidence consisted of two empty bottles of generic brand whiskey and a barely consumed bottle of vodka. There was a large circle of what looked like partially digested sausage pizza and a trail of the same headed to the bathroom.

I cruised this area and others like it often. People left all sorts of things locked up in their cabins, including alcohol. The miscreants that were involved were mostly younger kids. Seeing a squad car was often enough to send them back the way they came.

I came upon a car pulled off on the side of the road. Bikes were on the top of the car. I hit my lights and pulled up behind. As I got out of the car, a couple dressed for a day of riding approached me while continuing to engage in the most dignified argument I could ever remember on a road shoulder.

"Hi, folks, what's up?" I asked.

"Nothing, Sheriff. Just preparing to change a flat tire," the man said.

"Although it would seem unlikely that the job will be completed anytime soon due to the well-meaning but incompetent efforts of my friend here."

"Glenda, it is most difficult for me to complete any task here due to your nonstop questionable advice bestowed upon you by a great-great-grandfather or uncle some years ago."

"Again, your lack of mechanical abilities put us in a dilemma," Glenda said.

All the time Glenda and Peter never raised their voices.

"Well, we have plenty of road shoulder here. Why don't I give Peter a hand?"

They had already removed colorful packs and camping gear from the luggage area. I pulled up a storage space cover that revealed the spare, jack, and tire wrench.

"Peter, would you help me get the spare out?"

He went right to the task, unscrewed a large wing nut, and everything was free. Peter and I set the jack, took off the flat, and replaced the tire in no more than fifteen minutes. Peter stored the defective tire and tools and started to reload their packs and gear, but Glenda stopped him.

"Excuse me, Sheriff."

She took over, removing two packs and a nylon bag that Peter had put in. She replaced the items almost exactly where Peter had placed them. Once done, she pushed the electronic switch that closed the hatchback.

She turned to me and said, "Thank you, Sheriff. The male of the species often finds itself in desperate need of a woman to get things done."

As they drove off, windows down, I could hear snippets of the civil argument continuing.

Unfortunately, domestic disputes were often much more difficult than polite tire changers. Every cop on the beat has faced a family fight raging out of control. Alcohol and drugs were the catalysts that lit the fuse. From there, it was anyone's guess how things would go. Families are hard to figure out.

It brought to mind a call I took with another officer we called "Crime Dog" for his tenacious attitude toward criminals.

The husband, a big strong guy, met us in the driveway. The guy was drunk and loudly cursing. We kept our distance and took positions that allowed us to both see him but only allowed him to watch one of us at a time. The drunk ramped things up. He pulled a big knife out of his belt and held it by the blade as if in the position to throw it.

He said, "Faster than a man can draw a gun." A line from an old western movie. He raised his arm. I drew my gun. With every step closer, the danger increased for each of us.

We had trained for this situation. It was a famous drill called the Tueller Drill. Sergeant Dennis Tueller on the Salt Lake City Police Department wondered how quickly an attacker with a knife could cover twenty-two feet. He timed volunteers as they raced to stab the target. He found out it took 1.5 seconds.

A police officer with a weapon has a dilemma. If he shoots too early, he risks being accused of murder. If he waits until the attacker is clearly in the striking range and there is no question about motive, he risks injury and possible death.

Thankfully, something got through to the guy's alcohol-sodden brain, and he dropped the knife and saved his life. Crime Dog and I cuffed him. At that moment the drunk's wife, brandishing fresh cuts and soon-to-be bruises inflicted by her husband, leaped on Crime Dog's back and began to pummel him. Both spent the night in accommodations paid for by the county and cursed us all the way to jail.

The next morning, several residents of Musky Falls, including Scott Stewart's brother, started their cars to go to work and were surprised by loud exhaust systems, a direct result of some midnight saw work.

First order of business when I got to the sheriff's office was to sit everybody down and go over the Schmutz robbery. I filled them all in with what Dr. Schmutz had told me. Even if there was nothing new, it all bore repeating. I wanted to make sure it was still on everybody's radar. I'd learned long ago things get away from you unless you pay attention. SI Price was off chasing a thread and let me know he might be a bit late.

We had just gotten started when SI Price came in. He was clearly excited about something. I didn't get a chance to ask.

"Sheriff, I just came from the Cedar Inn. I stopped to go over things again with the maintenance man, Dustin Stevens. He showed me the location of the malfunctioning camera. I asked to see where he had located the defective portion. He pointed to a removable ceiling panel. The cable was already repaired, reconnected, tested, and put back in place. Stevens was concerned about his boss' unhappiness and wanted to get things squared away as soon as possible. I asked what he had done with the damaged cable parts. He told me he threw them away. When I asked where, he turned to look at a green dumpster with a bear chain around it. He said, 'It was just a couple of pieces of cable. I pitched them in the dumpster. Or maybe in the trash can next to the door. I just threw them out.' Stevens was clearly getting agitated. So I thanked him for his help and backed off for the moment. He asked me if he could go and said he needed to get on the road for some parts. I thanked him again, and he got in his truck and left.

"When he was out of sight, I went to the manager's office and got the key for the bear chain. I unlocked it and looked inside. There was trash, but it wasn't too bad, so I jumped in. I guessed the cable pieces would not be inside a bag. It took a while before I found anything. Three items that I think are interesting."

Jared held up an evidence bag. "First, in this bag are two pieces of cable. I looked at them under a magnifying glass, and it looks like they were cut with some kind of serrated blade." Then he held up the next bag. "A utility knife with a serrated blade. In the same dumpster."

Price continued, "I wanted to have another look at where the bad connections were without Stevens. I retrieved the step ladder Stevens conveniently stored in a corner to climb up and push the ceiling panel aside. On the next panel to the right was what I have in the third bag here: another piece of cable. It was cut through with some type of cable cutter. Stevens blamed the failure on corrosion, but the cable was not corroded at all."

Just getting his feet wet or not, Price had done what good cops do and kept turning over stones. He continued. "Someone took a ladder, climbed up, and pushed the ceiling panel out of the way. They knew right where the cable was, and it probably didn't take a minute. The perp was going to want to move quickly so they weren't discovered... unless he didn't have to. Someone who can crawl around in a ceiling without raising an alarm. Someone who could climb up, cut a cable, climb down, put his ladder away, and head to another part of the motel complex. Even if he were seen, he wouldn't be noticed. The maintenance man, Dustin Stevens,"

SI Price said.

"Any idea where he is now?" I asked.

"He said he was going to Eau Claire to get some hot tub parts."

"That's about an hour and a half each way. We need to get on this. Let's set up before he gets back."

I called Chief Delzell and let her know what we had and that we were going to have a talk with Stevens. She agreed to cover one driveway in an unmarked car, and Deputy Pave would cover the other. Inconspicuous enough unless you were looking for it. Officer Good and SI Price set up in the crime scene van within sight of the motel. It may be nothing, but we needed to be ready if he tried to take off.

I scanned the area and realized he could make a run at the rear driveway. I started to get one car to move, but it was too late. The Cedar Inn pickup pulled in before I was ready for him. Stevens got out and took a box out of the bed. He looked right at my squad. I did the only thing I could do. I put down my window, smiled and waved, and drove up and parked in a spot next to the office.

"Hey, Dustin. You got a second?"

"I have to repair the whirlpool before I take off for the day. That's going to take a least a couple of hours. So I gotta get to it."

"I just need a minute, then you can get to work."

"Alright, let's go in the office so I can put down this pump. It's heavy."

The manager, Pat Lorry, said hello and then asked Dustin about the whirlpool part. "Did they have the right one this time?"

"Yup, they gave me a credit and the new pump. Mr. Lorry, the sheriff wants to talk to me. Can we use the back office?"

"Sure," Lorry said.

We went to the office, and Stevens went to close the door. Then he said, "Sorry to ask you, Sheriff, before we get going, I really gotta use the head. Do you mind?"

Stevens stepped inside the bathroom, slid the bolt, and smashed his way out the back window. I saw him head toward the motel truck while I was running out of the office to catch him. He was quicker and jumped into the driver's seat. I reached for the door handle, and he swerved toward me, knocking me off. The tires on the pickup squealed when Stevens jumped a curb and headed for the highway.

Delzell saw that the rear driveway wasn't completely blocked. She tried to move forward to block the truck just as it raced by her. She put her foot through the floorboard and was in hot pursuit. Dispatch activated the repeater, alerting all listening units.

A high-speed chase is one of the most dangerous situations law enforcement officers and perpetrators face. Speeds will often exceed a hundred miles an hour. The violator runs red lights, goes down one-way streets, and does everything they can to shake the cops. Of course, each of their many maneuvers puts every other car on the road in grave danger. The mom and dad with kids in the car just leaving the grocery store never dreamed that there was a four-thousand-pound bomb racing down the road toward them. The officer, or more likely the officer in charge, will make the call whether to break off the chase or not. The first step is to employ things that will stop the offender's car. Road spikes work well but are not perfect.

Currently, nationwide there is an ongoing discussion regarding high-speed chases. They are dangerous. The sequence of events usually presents some options. Every one of them is likely to be wrong. It starts when a law enforcement officer activates their emergency lights to pull over an offender. As the officer approaches the car, the violator sees their opportunity and takes off. The officer gives chase. The violator's only means of escape is to outrun the pursuing officer as well as any other officers.

Some argue the seriousness of the offense should dictate the extent of the pursuit. Are you chasing a teenager with no driver's license or a wanted fugitive? The argument all boils down to this: People are often injured or killed in high-speed chases. It is against the law to flee an officer. The person doing the fleeing is causing this whole event by breaking the law. Sometimes you know why the person is running, and sometimes you don't.

Recently, a high-speed chase made the headlines when three people committed an armed robbery and stole a vehicle. The police tried to stop them, including deploying road spikes. They avoided the spikes but not the oak tree. All three were killed. A suit has been filed against the police for reckless endangerment.

So what's the right call? Bad people do bad things, and innocent people are victims of their behavior.

Deputy Pave came on the radio. "10-33, 10-33. County highway is working on the bridge on 63 with a full crew." Dispatch advised the Namekagon County highway crew to clear the road repeatedly, with no response.

Delzell reported. "We are at approximately eighty miles per hour. Oh no!" Delzell yelled. "Subject just drove into the oncoming lane. An oncoming car took the ditch hard. Send EMS. Accident is at the River Road intersection."

Two minutes behind Delzell, I broke off to check the vehicle in the ditch.

"We are coming up on the bridge, dispatch. Please advise." The tension in the chief's voice was felt, not heard, across the radio. "I am gaining on the truck. I am going to take it out. Standby."

Delzell accelerated as the highway workers ran for the ditch. She came up alongside the pickup and cranked the wheel hard, hitting it in the driver's door. Stevens slammed on his brakes. They locked up, and he skidded sideways, his truck fighting the pressure from the chief's car. The truck stopped, hanging halfway across the missing bridge. Stevens was scrambling, trying to get out of the driver's side window. Delzell stumbled as she ran toward him.

The county highway foreman ran up to the truck, grabbed Stevens, and dragged him out by the neck. Then he bounced him hard on a bridge piling. Any steam he had left was gone. With the help of a crowd of highway workers, the chief cuffed Stevens. Other than some highway department-issued scrapes and bumps, Stevens was uninjured.

Officer Good and SI Price got a good look at what a high-speed chase looked like. The wheel turned the wrong way. A zig when you needed a zag could change the outcome in a second. Everyone knew it, but no one needed to say anything. Chief Mary Delzell's driving was amazing. The county highway crew would be counting their blessings tonight.

Price and Good drove the van over to where I was with the family of three who had been in the car Stevens put in the ditch. The father was unscathed but the mother and daughter sustained minor injuries that needed medical attention.

The State Patrol arrived to begin checking the accident scene. EMS was right behind them. Doc O'Malley was able to slowly winch the Cedar Inn truck back onto a remaining piece of pavement. From there, he was able to get it loaded onto the flatbed. The truck was hauled to the impound lot we shared with the DNR. The local warden advised that, other than two poached deer in the freezer, there should be plenty of room in the fenced-in portion.

Our seemingly slow-moving investigation just hit a hundred miles an hour. We needed to catch our breath for a minute and get organized. I talked with DA Hablitch. He wanted to make sure that we had done what needed to be done. Delzell had exercised deadly force. As a result, he suggested that we ask the Wisconsin State Patrol and the Wisconsin Department of Criminal Investigation to conduct the incident investigation. Nothing was going to happen until the next morning.

I strongly suggested anyone involved complete their reports. The DA would determine the charges based on those. In this case, I hoped the proverbial book would be a thick one.

The chief's car was crinkled but drivable once Doc O'Malley used a slam hammer and bar to open up some room for the right front tire. The headlight, directional fender, and hood were going to need some real attention. The squad, though, would go to the impound area pending results of the investigation.

The chief rode with me to our respective offices so we could make official requests for investigations by outside agencies. No matter how little involvement, being the subject of an internal investigation makes a person nervous. I found my request to have somebody investigate me in this situation strangely calming.

The chief was quiet.

"Are you okay, Mary?" I asked.

"I don't know what I am. At least I think I'm alive," she replied.

"I hope you know how much worse that situation could have been had you not done what you did.

Where did you learn to drive like that?" I asked.

"To be honest with you, John, I have no idea. Once he turned onto 63, I could only think about him running over all those highway workers."

"I know, but you squeezed right to the edge so he didn't go over into the river. That took skill."

"Oh that. No, actually, that was the one thing that didn't work out. I wanted to push him over the edge. I was hoping he'd drown. I guess you can't do everything perfectly."

Chief Mary Delzell was one of a kind. ❖

CHAPTER 9

I headed over to the Cedar Inn early Friday morning to get more information about Dustin Stevens. I didn't know what to expect from the motel manager. Broken window, people racing through his parking lot, and locking up his maintenance man. Turned out he was apologetic about all the trouble. He offered to tell me anything that he could.

"When I placed an ad for a maintenance man, he applied. He could do just about anything—handy guy, that's for sure. He was honest about his financial trouble. He had lost a bunch of money in building two four-unit condos. He worked with a guy from the Cities who owned the development company. According to Stevens, he had just about finished construction when the developer disappeared. Within a week or two, bill collectors were all over Stevens. I got to tell you, Sheriff, I wouldn't pick him to be a crook, but I guess you never know. I do know one thing. I should be looking for a new maintenance man."

"I don't know what the outcome will be, but he has certainly got some trouble coming his way. Did you ever see anybody suspicious hanging around here? Maybe not a guest, just someone visiting?"

"Really, Sheriff, we have plenty to do keeping this place up, not much time for visiting. Dustin and I compared a to-do list every Monday morning. He got right on it, and I got on with my stuff."

"Did Dustin ever mention the video feed failing because of corrosion?" I asked.

"Yes, it was involving this incident. Under normal circumstances he wouldn't have mentioned it. He would've just gone on and fixed it. The only things we really discussed were guest safety issues and things that needed an outside contractor or were going to be expensive to repair." A flash of recollection gave the manager pause. "Wait one second, Sheriff, I do remember one guy who showed up here a couple of times looking for Dustin. I figured he was a bill collector. Big guy, kind of rugged looking. Both times I sent him on his way. He left without a problem."

"Well, if you think of anything else, let me know."

"Sure will, Sheriff."

While the investigation of the chase and capture of Stevens was ramping up, I still had an armed robbery to investigate. I had identified two involved parties: Dr. Schmutz and Dustin Stevens. I needed to ask Stevens some questions, figure out why he ran. Did he respond to the robbery, or did he instigate it? He certainly had the opportunity to mug Dr. Schmutz. As the maintenance man, he could easily cut a video feed.

I stopped at the jail but shouldn't have wasted my time. Stevens wasn't interested in talking. That wasn't too surprising. DA Hablitch told me he was demanding a lawyer. Hablitch and I met in my office.

"What do you think you have?" Hablitch asked.

"I was hoping you'd tell me."

"At least eluding, endangering, several counts. Both solid felonies. Party to crime armed robbery? We aren't there yet."

"I don't know. Should I give him another chance to talk?"

"Forget it for now, John. Everything goes through his lawyer unless someone changes their mind."

Dustin Stevens went in front of Judge Kritzer. The judge does not take it kindly when the citizens of his community are endangered, and he refused to set bail. He reckoned from the bench that Stevens had a propensity to flee.

I followed up with Dr. Schmutz and any connection he may have had with Stevens. He maintained that he had no idea who Dustin Stevens was.

This case had lots of different parts and pieces. I didn't know what, but there was something going on. Or maybe not. Maybe I was just reading too many Northern Lakes Mysteries.

I did what I always did when I was confused on a case; I called my old partner, JJ Malone, the commander of the Organized Crime Task Force, which had become a useful tool for law enforcement. Working in conjunction with the Feds on Racketeer Influenced and Corrupt Organizations, better known as RICO, they specialized in accumulating information regarding criminals and criminal enterprises. When the manure hit the fan, there was nobody better to have on your side. Malone had helped Namekagon County in the past; it was likely he would in the future. Actually, I was counting on it.

I placed the call, knowing full well he would grumble, groan, and growl at the request. The growl was why he was affectionately called *Bear*.

I was not disappointed when he growled, "Malone."

"Bear, how the heck are you? Don't really want much, just kind of checking in. How's Tanya?"

"Oh no, not my old buddy John Cabrelli. He never wants anything. At least it starts out that way. Then just when you least expect it..."

"Bear, Bear, I just need some information, or just to see if you had anything. If you do, you do. If you don't, no problem. No crime in asking."

"Good, then let me ask you this. Are you really running for election? I can't believe it. You're a good choice for the job but a poor choice for a political candidate." When we rode together, we were in complete agreement on our thoughts about running for public office—we would run when Hades froze over. Yet here I was running for public office.

"Gee, thanks, Bear. At least I got it half right."

"Alright, tell me why you're bothering me so I can get on to my real job."

"Harold Schmutz PhD, Dustin Stevens. I need to know if you can find anything out about those two names. I sent you DOBs, etcetera, but I don't have much else. We have some charges pending against Stevens. Nothing on Schmutz other than he was the victim of an armed robbery and got himself shot in the process. Not a bad wound."

"You mean Harold Schmutz, the author? He got shot in Namekagon County?"

I was not surprised that Bear knew of him; he was an avid reader.

"That's the one," I replied.

"It just so happens that Tanya and I have been reading his book about the Great Lakes. It is really interesting." Bear would have made a great pirate captain. It was safe to bet his ship would be equipped with a short plank for long walks. I could just hear him bellowing commands. "You know something, Cabrelli? Schmutz estimates there have been over six thousand shipwrecks and thirty thousand lives lost on those lakes. If I could convince Tanya, we'd get scuba certified and go treasure hunting. A conservative estimate of treasure lying on the bottom is hundreds of millions to billions. Heck, I don't need half that to retire in style," he laughed.

"Well, Bear, sounds like something you and Tanya should check out. Schmutz is giving a talk here in a few weeks."

"I'd love to, Cabrelli, but I can't. I have got budget meetings nonstop. As a matter of fact, I should be looking over the mutual aid budget right now. You're familiar with that. That's what funds the mutual aid you always request."

"Will you check anyway, Bear?"

"Fine. I'll check. Just remember, you owe Tanya and me a guided musky fishing trip. Or did you forget?"

"Nope, Bear, I will get that booked." A retired county sheriff's deputy was a well-known musky guide. "Anderson's the name. I'll get a hold of him."

Bear hung up. A bit on the difficult side, but no better man to have your back.

Other than the normal operations of the department and a nagging feeling about Stevens and Schmutz, I also had agreed to debate Scott Stewart.

We would face each other in the county meeting room. I recently noticed signs posted around the county: "Truth and Justice ~ Scott Stewart for Sheriff." A local politico told me that he thought Stewart was trying to get me into a sign war.

If so, I'd have to concede in that war, seeing how, as far as I knew, there were only three "Cabrelli for Sheriff" signs in existence. They were four-by-eight sheets of plywood painted on both sides. One was in the bed of Bud's pickup, another was on Tim the Plumber's truck, and the last was on the back of Doc O'Malley's wrecker.

Julie called me to check in and, more likely, to see if I was planning to skip the debate.

"Well, are you ready for tonight?" she asked

"Julie, honey, I am as ready as I'll ever be. What time are we going?"

"Jack said to be there at six."

"Do you want me to pick you up?"

"Normally, yes, but I don't want to have my mode of transportation a campaign issue."

"Okay, I'll see you at the courthouse at six. Unless I get called out. You never know." I could only hope for a call out to leave Scott Stewart on the stage debating himself.

By five-thirty, the parking lot at the county building was full. I felt a little queasy. It was a lot of people for a political race that, in the past, only drew a handful of folks. Well, if the people of Namekagon County voted me out and Stewart in, then it was as it should be. I stood outside, looking up at the county building. I checked my watch and considered whether half an hour was enough time to check on the jail and our handful of prisoners.

Ron Carver grabbed me by the arm. "Hey, Sheriff, in case things don't work out, I could use someone to fill in at the store." Offers for employment if I lost the election just kept coming in.

"I'll keep it in mind, Ron." Next, a face much more to my liking walked up.

"John, we need to get inside," said Julie.

The conference room was packed. The custodian and volunteers were rolling in carts of folding chairs. Stewart was already standing on the first step up to the stage, smiling his idiotic grin and shaking hands.

Jack Wheeler pulled me off to the side. "Let me hook up your mic."

"Jack, I know this is an important job, but why such a big crowd? I mean, Stewart has really gone all out on this. Signs, radio interviews, door-to-door. I can't see why this job is so important to him."

"It's not about the job, John. Stewart doesn't care about that.

It's all about winning. He needs to win. He'd probably be a lousy sheriff, but that won't be an issue, as long as he wins."

"But the crowd? Why such a big crowd?"

"I personally think they're all here to watch you kick Stewart's butt. The Voice is ready for you. Better get up there."

The moderator boomed, "Good evening, ladies and gentlemen. Please find a chair so we can get going here. There are some folding chairs on the right side of the room."

When everyone was seated and quiet, I sat on one side of the front table facing the crowd and Stewart on the other. Doc O'Malley, Tim the Plumber, Julie, Bud, Ron, and Jack sat in the front row on my side. I noticed retired Police Chief Len Bork and current Chief Delzell were conspicuously absent.

Stewart was wearing a suit and tie. I was in my uniform. One of the good things about a uniformed law enforcement job is picking what to wear.

The Voice stood and came to the podium. "Ladies and Gentlemen, welcome. Scott Stewart has challenged incumbent Sheriff John Cabrelli to a public debate. Both have agreed to participate tonight, live in front of the voters. Questions have been prepared for the candidates. Each will be given three minutes to answer. We will alternate who answers first. For the first question, the winner of the coin toss will choose to go first or second."

The coin was tossed, and Stewart called "tails" which was only appropriate. He won the toss and decided to go first.

"The first question of the night. Drug abuse, sales of illicit drugs, and, unfortunately, drug-related deaths have plagued our community and the communities around us. How will you handle the drug problem?"

Stewart began, "I believe I speak for our community at large. It is time to get tough on drugs. We must relentlessly pursue these criminals and get them off the streets. We need to put every last one of them behind bars. The first step is to identify the perpetrators and watch for them. Every chance we get, stop their cars and haul them off to jail. We know what they look like and how they dress."

I was shocked when he didn't use his full three minutes.

"Sheriff Cabrelli, same question," the moderator said.

"I believe our first line of defense is law enforcement backed by the community. Illegal drugs, and all the things that come with it, are a community issue, and we need to work together. If you see something, say something. We will arrest those who violate the law, and we will continue to make cases that stick. We can't lose cases because of poor policing. I have already made a mutual aid request to the state Department of Narcotics Enforcement and asked them to put some resources in our area. We have a hotline in place that is staffed twenty-four seven, 365 days a year. The hotline is confidential unless the caller agrees to further contact. Even then, we will keep their names strictly confidential. Let me say it again: If you see something, say something. That's how we are going to get bad people off the street.

"Next, and more importantly, is how do we keep them from being involved in the first place? The truth is that all our measures deal with some part of the problem. But in my opinion, the real solution is through education. Our teachers are on the front lines, working with parents and law enforcement for the common good. To that end, I have asked Becky Chali, our local counselor, to work closely with community members. I am asking this group to tell me whether we have the resources we need to address the problem. If we do, let's put them to use. If we don't, let's get what we need.

"As to arresting people based on how they dress, well... it may sound like a good idea to you, Mr. Stewart, as long as you don't mind the potential consequences of harassing innocent people."

"Any rebuttal, Mr. Stewart?" asked the Voice.

"Maybe Sheriff Cabrelli is not up to the challenge of rooting out the bad ones." Then Stewart lowered his voice and, with a concerned tone, said, "I would be the first in line to thank the sheriff for his service. He has certainly been through a lot. Maybe it's time for him to step down."

"Sheriff, any response?" asked the Voice.

"No."

Several questions later, I had kept my cool, and Stewart had explained how he was the answer to all the world's problems. He gave his closing statement first and confirmed my suspicion that he didn't have some deep-down redeeming feature.

"First, let me thank you all for coming tonight. It will be up to you when you step into the voting booth. I am your friend and your neighbor. You need to listen to me when I tell you what I have to tell you: John Cabrelli is a menace to our community. His big-city police tactics have gotten us into the situation we are in now. He is only wearing that sheriff's uniform because the good man who wore it before him was almost killed in an unnecessary shootout involving a violent criminal, a murderer. The criminal fled and terrorized the citizens of Namekagon County. It was only because retired Chief of Police Len Bork, showing calm and professionalism, stepped up to end the threat. John Cabrelli has a long history of violence that follows him wherever he goes. He has no place as part of Namekagon County's future."

The room was silent. The Voice even took a moment to recover. "Do you wish to say anything, Sheriff Cabrelli?"

"No, I don't."

Uncle Nick taught me that if you're looking for a fight, you can always find one, but it should be the last resort. Try to be the voice of reason and get people to see your side. Good advice has served me well as a law enforcement officer, at least most of the time. Nick also told me that I would inevitably encounter the fight. When that happens, the only thing you can do is give it your best shot. In that situation, there is no such thing as play fighting, no fancy moves that will flip your adversary into the air. Fight like your life depended on it, because it probably does.

The double doors in the back of the room swung open, breaking the silence. Everyone turned to see Jim Rawsom walk in, flanked by Chief Delzell and retired Chief Len Bork. Jim looked around the room. Then, staring at Scott Stewart, he said, "I have something to say." Rawsom walked with a cane through the crowd and up to the podium.

"This is inappropriate!" Stewart shouted. "Sheriff Rawsom must not be allowed to speak. Tell him to step down. I demand it!" He was so mad his neck vein was pulsing. The Voice said nothing.

"For those of you in the room who don't know me, I'm Jim Rawsom. I was the sheriff here. I loved my job. When they pinned that star on me, I was so proud I thought I would bust. I raised my left hand with my right one on the Bible, and I was sworn in. My friends and family clapped, and my wife and kids ran over and hugged me tight. We knew the job had its risks, but I had given my solemn word to protect and serve my community. To stand in the face of danger.

"Then one day the devil came to Namekagon County. He was a known killer and a danger to every man, woman, and child in our community. We did not ask this threat to come here; he came of his own accord. It was my job to take him off the street. As dangerous as it was, John Cabrelli, Chief Bork, Chief Delzell, and others stood with me that day. We faced a withering attack, but we did not back down, and we prevailed.

"John Cabrelli is a good man. He's your sheriff, and you can count on him to stand fast for this community. Times are changing. Namekagon County is too. We can pray every night, but I am afraid that a time will come when we must again face danger. Who will face it on our behalf? John Cabrelli or Scott Stewart? Who will risk their life to save yours? John Cabrelli or Scott Stewart?" Rawsom turned to me but spoke loud enough for the crowd to hear. "John, I am certain that you would prefer to remain silent on the whole issue, so I figured somebody should speak on your behalf."

A few silent moments passed before a buzz began in the crowd, quickly intensifying. The Voice of the North did the only thing he could do—he thanked everyone for coming.

It should have been over, but it was not. Scott Stewart was furious. A small group of supporters gathered around to calm him down but to no avail. He exploded out of the group and charged across the room at me, stopping a foot from my face, raising a fist in my direction. Chief Delzell started to move in, but I stopped her.

"Scott, if you have decided that the only way to solve this is a physical fight, then so be it. You will lose, and you will be sorry you were ever foolish enough to have lowered yourself to that point. I am not afraid of you or people like you. You bully your way into positions of power. Since I arrived here, you have seen me as a threat to you, always behind the scenes, pulling strings. Throwing your weight around. Please listen carefully to what I'm going to tell you. You just raised your fist to me. Don't ever, ever do it again. Do you understand what I'm telling you?"

Sweat began to bead up around Stewart's face. My old training officer used to say, "He's the one that called the music; you get to pick the dance."

"Scott, seems like you might have reconsidered. I hope so," I said. "Just let me ask you one question. If you get elected sheriff, what will you do when you can't reconsider? Are you ready to stand between the devil and your community? Are you willing to do whatever needs to be done? You better already know the answer to this question because, sure as you're standing there, it's going to happen."

Scott Stewart wilted, turned away, and walked quickly out the door.

Mary walked up to me and laughed. "Can you imagine the headlines? 'Two Sheriff's Candidates Brawl at a Debate.' Absolutely above the fold."

At home, Julie and I sat by the fireplace. I was lost in my thoughts.

"John, you seem kind of sad. Are you okay?"

"It's this whole thing with Stewart," I said.

"He's digging himself a big hole. I don't think you have to worry about him anymore."

"That's not it. I never worried about him. I don't like or trust him, but I was never worried about him. Would slugging it out have made me the better man? Absolutely not. When I faced him down like I did, it made me no better than the bully he was. To top it off, the sheriff of this county was ready and willing to be part of a brawl that was no different than what we break up every Friday and Saturday night. Julie, I am not perfect, and I made a mistake. I used poor judgment. Unfortunately, that's not the worst part of this."

"What else, John? Tell me." She implored me with her sympathetic blue eyes.

"I really wish he'd have taken a swing at me. I would have loved to knock him right on his self-righteous butt."

Julie chuckled. "My husband, still waters run deep. It's a good thing none of the bad guys know how sweet you really are."

CHAPTER 10

Saturday morning we both got up early. The local paper was three days from being out, but Stewart and I were already the talk of the town. He spun it as best he could, but some of the steam was gone from his campaign.

Julie started coffee, and I got working on Italian eggs and sausage. We took advantage of the good weather and cruised the backroads to the Superior shore, the coldest and deepest of the Great Lakes. Its history was the source of many tales. Three-masted clippers and two-masted schooners had long ago sailed its treacherous waters. Today the cold water slapped hard against the shore. We stopped at little stores along the lake. Prices were reduced as the shops wound down from the peak of the tourist season. An old-fashioned-looking place caught Julie's eye, and she found her way inside. It was much different than the modern tourist traps. Shelves were full of interesting things, and items hung on dozens of hooks. Everything was a step above what you'd usually see.

I was perusing the books when Julie called out from a back corner of the store.

"John, look at this. Isn't it incredible?"

She held a two-by-three-foot wooden topographical map of Lake Superior with the depths carved in detail. It was beautifully hand-painted, capturing the subtle hues of Lake Superior. We'd never seen anything like it before and asked the older woman behind the counter if it was for sale.

"If you buy that, I will truly be sorry to see it go. I am sure you've heard that from other shopkeepers trying to make a sale. In this case it's true. As a matter of fact, until recently it hung in my little house on the lake. It was handmade by a local craftsman. He worked for the U.S. Geological Survey mapping the depths and exploring the lakes for many years. The board used to make it is an old piece of ship's planking, probably from a three-masted clipper. He collected bits and pieces of wrecks that came ashore during storms. Most of the boards and timbers that wash up become fuel for beach party bonfires, so he was always quick to be out as soon as the weather cleared. He felt these pieces should be used in some way, part of a shared legend. That is one of only a handful I know he made. It has a patch on the back nailed together with square nails and retains some of the marks of an adze.

"His name was Hugh Olson. We were close. He was a scientist, and I an artist. Two kindred spirits captured by the beauty of the lake. In October and November, when Superior pitches its fit, we would sit on the porch of my store and watch the drama. Cool evenings, sipping tea, coffee, or even a little brandy. A couple of winters ago he was out on the ice drilling a hole to drop a line, just off the shore from my shop at a secret fishing spot. I closed up and drove over to the little general store down the way to pick up a few things. When I returned, he was lying on the ice. I ran to him, breaking through the crusty snow all the way. He had passed on. Hugh looked peaceful, smiling. No place he'd rather be when his time came." She looked out at the lake wistfully and dabbed at the corner of her eye.

"We were both widows, and as far as I knew, he didn't have any next of kin. I knew Hugh's lawyer, who showed me the paperwork he'd drawn up. Hugh was not a poor man, and he had left most of his money to fund college scholarships for students to study the Great Lakes…" The woman trailed off.

"I am sorry, I do rattle on sometimes. Probably the product of being an old woman keeping pretty much to herself. I am sure you young folks have got things to do and places to see," she said.

"If it's for sale, my husband and I would like to buy it," said Julie.

"I wasn't ready to figure that out today. It's the only thing I have left of Hugh other than memories. But I sense it's not just the map. Is it special to you too?"

"It's a good day for stories. Here is ours," Julie began. "Before we married, we were walking along the shore in front of your store. I spied an ancient beauty, a Lake Superior agate. We took it home, where I polished it. The rings revealed the inner beauty of the stone. A friend of ours is a master goldsmith, and he mounted a section of our stone in each of our wedding rings." Julie held out her hand to show the woman her beautiful ring.

"That ring is stunning. Can I ask who the goldsmith is that made them?"

"Ron Carver. He has a store in Musky Falls."

She laughed like a whispering wind. "Ron Carver has been a friend of ours for a long, long time. I live down along the Namekagon River. Ron and I spread Hugh's ashes up here on the waves of Lake Superior." Then, suddenly, as if startled, she said, "Oh my gosh, I know who you are! I mean, we've never met, but I know who you are. Sheriff Cabrelli, the hero, and Julie Carlson, the wonderful teacher at Northern Lakes Academy. I'm not mistaken, am I?"

"Well, only with one part. I'm no hero, but my wife here

certainly is."

"Ron thinks the world of you two. I have always wanted to meet you. Where are my manners? My name is Marie Bennet, and I know we just met, but would you do me a favor?"

We are asked this question often, and I was about to answer my standard, "If I can," but Julie was quicker on the draw. "Of course. What can we do?"

"Let me take you out for dinner, my treat. There is a place down the shore that we loved to visit." Then she blushed. "I am so sorry. You two are probably already booked solid. I am sorry for putting the pressure on. We can make it another time," she said.

"Now works just fine for us," Julie answered.

Marie's stories were enchanting. She had found the store she owned by accident. "One summer day I was driving along the shore to a gallery showing of my work. The artist I shared the space with had the honor of being one of the most pretentious people I'd ever met, and certain he was God's gift to women. He was forever courting a punch in the nose due to his relentless carnal pursuit of me. He was over an hour and a half late for the showing. Then, for dramatic effect, he spun into the room with a cape around his shoulders. There was a large blank canvas on an easel. Underneath it was a drop cloth covered with multicolored splotches of dried paint. People in the crowd were made aware that artistic greatness was in the offing and began to move toward his exhibit. I couldn't help but notice several of the best-known art critics were gathered to watch the show. The artist sat silently on a stool, gazing down in front of the crowd. Finally, when he had everyone's attention, he abruptly looked up.

"He told the crowd how, over the months, he'd studied the reality of the abstract expressionist style and its impact on the observer. How it was the boldest form of painting, each canvas telling its own story, while at the same time telling the story of the observer.

People appeared to be impressed. He asked that the spotlights above him be shined directly on the canvas. All the other lights were dimmed. The crowd was silent. The artist reached into a bag on a small table next to him. His hand came out holding a small, open can of paint. Once everyone was watching, he threw the paint hard at the canvas. The first one followed by another and another and another, each a different color. The artist stopped when he appeared exhausted. The audience carefully, quietly examined the paint-splattered canvas. One of the art critics I knew well finished his critical review of this art. He said to his peers: 'Awful, I could have done better in the paint department of my local hardware store. It's insulting.' Then the senior critic spoke, 'It's genius.' People flocked to buy his work.

"I love my art. I agonize over each detail. Perspective, depth, engagement. I wanted anyone who saw my paintings to see something different each time they looked at them. I would never, could never throw cans of paint at blank canvases and call it art. I became even more painfully aware that beauty and art are in the eyes of the beholder. I was not completely forgotten. Some of my works were sold, but not what I thought were my best. Then a dignified man approached me. He pointed to one of my personal favorite paintings and asked, 'Superior shore looking north?' Surprised, I replied, 'It is, but how did you know?' He said, 'Superior owns each of its views, and those of us who have seen her in all her glory never forget that.' He bought the painting. And I bought the store."

After a delightful dinner, we dropped her off at the shop. She asked us to wait a minute while she went inside and came out with the carved Lake Superior.

"I would like you two to have this as a gift from me and Hugh," she said.

"We can't do that. I would be glad to pay for it," I said.

"It is a gift. Please take it with you."

The evening went too quickly, and we were soon on our way home. Julie put her head on my shoulder, and I fell in love all over again.

Julie, Bud, and I were on board to volunteer all day Sunday at the Clear Lake landing. Students from Northern Lakes Academy and another nearby school, Eagles Academy, were deep into a field research project, working alongside Professor Newlin and DNR fishery biologists, tagging and tracking muskies and catching and removing invasive northern pike from the chain of lakes.

The students, wearing bright tie-dyed t-shirts with a stylized musky on the front with *Esox masquinongy* below the picture, spent weeks preparing for this weekend's event, working with volunteer anglers. The shirts, designed by Julie's student Chris, said "Fisheries Research Team" on the back. The anglers would bring northern pike to the students at a designated boat landing, where the smaller fish would be used to feed birds at the raptor recovery center, while the larger ones would be filleted and turned into fresh fish cakes for the local nursing home and food pantry.

We were in charge of bringing coffee, orange juice, and donuts. It is amazing how many donuts high school students can go through. It was equally amazing how many Bud can go through.

Bud was looking forward to working with the kids and took the day off from restoring an old saloon in town. It had turned out to be a lot more work than he figured. The building was built with timbers, some of which were huge. While there were cracks and sags, they were, for the most part, sturdy. Some just needed to be put back in place. A few needed to be replaced. That was the real challenge. Bud was having difficulty finding the right replacement timbers, especially the ridge pole. As a result, he was working from dawn to dusk. When this saloon was built, white pine logs were readily available. When the residents at the time determined the town needed a saloon, come spring when lumberjacks arrived, they were glad to lend a hand to help build what they called the "Meeting House." Rough-sawn lumber and white pine timbers built it strong enough to last over a hundred years.

DA Hablitch and I met at his office on Monday afternoon to discuss Dustin Stevens. Usually, I would have gotten us a couple of chairs in the back corner of a small coffee shop, but the election heightened interest in the sheriff's doings, which made it difficult to have a confidential meeting in a public place.

"Gee, John, I am sorry I missed the debate the other night. I am even sorrier that I face reelection about eighteen months from now. As DAs and sheriffs, we are periodically required to stand trial in front of our constituents. I haven't decided if I am going to run again, but I am glad you're going first. So, what do you think about Dustin Stevens?"

"Well, I am going to hold him as tight as I can. He is a critical link to finding out who robbed Schmutz. According to his court record, he is dead broke and facing bankruptcy. His motive is most likely money. For the most part, he's an honest guy. No record except for his recent run from the law. I'm hoping we can find something that will tie him to the armed robbery. Maybe that would encourage him to cooperate with us, whittle down the charges in trade for testimony. He's got a public defender now, so maybe we can work with him."

"It would be interesting to know if there might be something on the table. He doesn't seem to be the kind of guy who wants to do time. Any luck with relatives or acquaintances?" asked Hablitch.

"So far nothing, but my people are on it."

Law enforcement is zero to a hundred miles an hour in seconds. I answered my cell phone. It was one of the staff from Ron Carver's jewelry store.

"Sheriff," she said, "a guy just walked in with a gold coin. He says he found it and wants to sell it. It could be one from the smash and grabs in Superior. You'd better come over."

"Excuse me, Steve. I've got to go to the jewelry store right now."

Hablitch waved his hand, used to how it all works.

I could have parked in front of Ron's store, but it would have been a poor choice. I ended up parking in the back alley and knocking on the locked security door. I advised a Musky Falls unit of what was going on, and they took a position down the block with a full view of the store. One of the sales consultants let me in. She was clearly glad to see me. I tried to keep a cool demeanor when I walked out into the showroom area.

I spotted a tan, lean guy wearing a wide-brimmed hat, jeans, and cloth field vest with pockets containing pens, pencils, and small notebooks, including a waterproof one like mine. A gold coin lay on the glass display case. It took just a moment for the man to notice me and speak up.

"Sheriff, I am guessing you aren't here as part of the welcoming committee. Somebody missing a gold coin?" he asked.

"That's the gist of it. Gold coins were stolen in a robbery not too far north of here. We are on the lookout for anyone trying to sell something like that."

"I can see why you might find me a little suspicious."

"Would you mind showing me some ID?" I asked.

"Not at all." The man pulled out his wallet and produced a driver's license, which identified him as Ken Hetland.

"Mr. Hetland, can I ask where you got this coin?"

"I found it," he answered.

"When was that?"

"About a month ago."

"Can you tell me where?" I asked, pushing a tiny bit harder.

"Well, Sheriff, this is where things might get a little complicated."

"Why is that?"

"I don't want to tell you."

"Okay, why?"

"I don't know for sure, but a guy's got to wonder if there might be more where I found this one. I am an optimist by nature. I figured that when I was done with the survey I'm doing I might hike back and see what else I can find. Who knows?"

"Mr. Hetland, what did you say you do for work?"

"Well, Sheriff, I do for work whatever work I find that needs doing. I'm a registered land surveyor, and I'm doing a survey on a piece of property that was purchased for the public by the state stewardship fund. Actually, what I will be doing next is why I'm here. When I'm done with the survey, I plan on hooking up with a buddy of mine and spending the next eight or so months camping out, working on a backcountry lodge."

"How does that get you here?" I asked.

"Well, Sheriff, the project I'm talking about is at least a two-man job, and you currently have one of the two locked up."

"Dustin Stevens?"

"That would be him. I've got his dog out in my truck."

I took a step back and a breath. Hetland and Stevens were connected as parties known to each other. Stevens looked like a first-class suspect in the Schmutz robbery. Hetland walks in off the street with a gold coin and wants to sell it. Schmutz, Stevens, and Hetland tied together. I needed some time to think and figure out how.

"Mr. Hetland, you've got to excuse me, but the connection here is pretty remarkable. Maybe you could help me clear things up," I said.

"Whoa there, Sheriff, slow your horses down. Before you jump to any conclusions, I can see how you may think this looks suspicious. I had nothing to do with any of his troubles. He called me from the jail after all this went down. Truth is, he was worried about his dog. A retired guy down the road had agreed to watch her for a while, and he was wondering when I may be getting back to take over."

"Would you mind just answering a couple of questions?" I asked.

"I wouldn't mind depending on what they are, but let me tell you this. I can absolutely account for where I was for the last month. I was about two hundred miles away from here for three weeks getting certified on a new piece of surveying equipment. I had perfect attendance. I spent another week doing a surveying job for an engineering firm in Columbia County, surveying a wildlife area along the Wisconsin River. Dustin's been a friend of mine for a long time. My only involvement now is trying to raise his bail. That hasn't exactly worked, seeing how they haven't set bail yet, and according to the lady at the courthouse, when they do, it's going to be sky-high. Neither of us is rolling in the dough, so I figured I could sell the coin and help him out."

One of Ron's staff members handed me a piece of paper. I took a couple of minutes to read it over. "Gentlemen, I have something here that might clarify some issues. There is an email and cell number for the head of the Numismatic Association. That is who to contact regarding items that were taken in the robbery. If you guys are good with it, let's give him a call and see if your coin matches one of the stolen ones. What do you think?"

"Mr. Hetland?"

"I don't want anything to do with stolen property or illegal activities of any kind, so I say give him a call."

I called the number on the bulletin.

A pleasant voice answered, "Joel Bolin's office. How may I direct the call?"

"This is Sheriff John Cabrelli from Namekagon County for Joel Bolin."

"I'll put you through to Mr. Bolin."

I explained the reason for the call. Bolin's response was immediate. "I can be on the road in half an hour. What is the address of the store?"

Hetland seemed relaxed and asked to use an open, small room to transcribe some of his survey notes, using the waiting time wisely. Based on the circumstances, I needed to stick around. It was almost exactly an hour and a half when Bolin pulled up in front of the store.

Bolin walked in the front door just as Ron Carver came in the back, returning from an errand. Ron was clearly surprised. To avoid spooking any more of his customers, he guided Hetland, Bolin, and me into a viewing room attached to the showroom.

Then Ron asked, "What's going on here, Sheriff?"

"This gentleman, Ken Hetland, brought a coin in to sell. One of your staff was paying attention to the most recent bulletin regarding the smash-and-grab robbers and wondered if Mr. Hetland might be involved, so she called me. Mr. Hetland agreed to have this coin looked at by Mr. Bolin to see if it matched what was stolen."

Ron extended his hand to Bolin. "We've never met before, but I am aware of your credentials."

We sat down around the viewing room table. Bolin laid out a blue cloth, a small tool kit, a laptop, and a camera on a very short tripod. Hetland handed the coin over, and Joel Bolin froze for a moment when he saw it. Slowly, Bolin deftly examined every part of the coin. He searched for things on his laptop and took dozens of photographs. After nearly an hour, he sat back, exhausted. We gathered around, ready for his findings.

"I have several things to tell you about this coin, but more research should be done. Here is what I can say with some certainty. This coin is not one that was taken in the theft. That does not mean it wasn't at some time stolen; it almost certainly was. If I had to put a date on that robbery, I would say somewhere around 1863. I would go as far as to speculate that the robbers either wore gray or blue uniforms, flying the Stars and Bars of the Confederacy or the Stars and Stripes of the Union. That is not for sure, but many experts would agree with me. I have only seen one coin like this before. It was almost a twin to this one. What you see here is a Napoleon III gold one-hundred-franc coin minted in 1862."

Bolin showed us the obverse side of the coin with an image of a man with a wreath around his head and pointed out the words "Napoleon III Empereur" and "Barre" for the engraver Albert Désiré Barre. He flipped the coin and pointed out an eagle on a beam surrounded by the collar of the Legion of Honor with the lettering "Empire Francais," "100 Franc," and "BB1862." He said the "A" mint marks are from Monnaie de Paris.

"The coins are rare and valuable. Prices vary wildly on condition. The current gold spot price today is upwards of $3,000 per ounce. The weight of this coin is 32 grams, just over an ounce. It contains .9330, just a little under an ounce of pure gold. The coin passed both the intense magnet test and chemical testing. I believe it is real gold and authentic."

Hetland was grinning.

"Having given you my two cents, I think we need to go further," Bolin continued. "There is a remote chance that this coin could be tied to a significant historic event. Real Napoleon gold coins have volumes of lore attached to them. I do not speculate on the veracity of these tales. Some, however, thrive on them."

"Mr. Bolin, if I wanted to sell this coin, what would be the best way to do that?" asked Hetland.

"That's an interesting question. If the coin is authenticated, in its condition, I would think it should bring top dollar at a well-advertised auction."

"What if I wanted to sell it right now? To be honest, I really need the money. Mr. Bolin, would you buy it?"

"It would be within the services my company provides. However, there is a circumstance that comes up from time to time. If we list and market the coin for you, it potentially becomes something we would be interested in buying. I would ask you for a last bid right of refusal. If we wanted to buy the coin, we would not be able to bid. At the end of the bidding, we would be able to top the highest bidder and forego any commissions. In my business, there can be no suggestion of impropriety. If there was, we would drop out."

"You've got a much better chance of selling this coin than I would," said Hetland.

"There are several high-end collectors in Wisconsin and across the country who seek out coins like this. For them, condition and authenticity are the only thing that really matters. They often buy and sell rare items for high-end collectors. I would suggest that you engage them, Mr. Hetland. They aren't cheap, but they usually make up for it by being pretentious and obnoxious."

"Will you handle this for me, Mr. Bolin? I'm a land surveyor, not a coin dealer."

"Mr. Hetland, before we go any further, I think you should think about this. Maybe for now, it would be in your best interest to keep quiet about the coin. I need to be perfectly candid here. I told you I don't trade in tall tales about hidden treasure and so on, but in this case, the discovery of this French coin may be very significant. This is not the only coin like this that has been found around here.

"A few years ago, a coin just like this one turned up in Namekagon County. Circumstances over that find got a little bit strange, much more involved than just the sale of a coin. We handled the sale. Since then, several highly credible researchers have been poring over the known documents about one of several lost gold shipments. The interest has peaked this last year. The rumor is that previously unknown documents have been discovered and are providing clues to a possible location of a lost treasure. I would say, Mr. Hetland, you are now in possession of an important clue. A great deal depends on where you found this coin and the circumstances. Even the smallest bit of information now becomes important."

Hetland picked up his coin, put it in his pocket, and said, "I'll get back to you."

CHAPTER 11

I got a call from Steve Hablitch on Tuesday morning. Judge Kritzer had announced that the leaves were quickly falling, making for perfect grouse hunting conditions. The judge had chased some early birds around, but now peak conditions were approaching. To compound the issue, Judge Kritzer had a new pup to try out, and Len Bork reported that his Fox twenty-gauge double was tuned up, cleaned up, and ready to go.

He let everyone know that he was anxious to clear his calendar and expected our help. My inclination was to try and hold on to Stevens. Also, just because we were going to have a hearing didn't mean he was going to make bail.

The chief and I sat behind DA Hablitch. Sitting with the accused was none other than my close friend and neighbor, Jack Wheeler. The judge asked why the public defender assigned to Stevens wasn't here.

"Well, Judge, the bail hearing was kind of short notice. Our public defender had another obligation, and I am second on the list, so here I am. If that doesn't work for the court, we can postpone the hearing. I would ask for an extension to give the defendant time to raise the bail."

"Does anybody object, or can we get to doing what we already know we're going to do?"

No objections. The judge picked up a paper in front of him and scowled as he reviewed it. "Mr. Stevens, you certainly have caused a ruckus. Shirley, read the charges for the record."

"Knowingly Fleeing an Officer 346.04, two counts."

"Mr. Stevens, how do you plead?"

"Not guilty, Your Honor," replied Stevens.

Shirley read the next charge. "Endangering Safety by Conduct regardless of Life 941.20, eight counts."

"Mr. Stevens, how do you plead?" asked the judge.

"Not guilty, Your Honor." Stevens hung his head, eyes on the floor.

"DA Hablitch, what are your bond recommendations?"

"We propose twenty-five thousand dollars cash bail."

Jack Wheeler stood. "We object, Your Honor, and have a bail proposal. The defendant has no previous criminal record. He is gainfully employed at the Cedar Inn as a maintenance man. To that end, the manager there has been unable to find a replacement for Mr. Stevens and would be glad to take him back. Stevens owns a house on Hatchery Road, showing he is clearly invested in staying in the community. Other than his one-time foray, he is no flight risk."

"Objection, Your Honor," Hablitch said. "Stevens is a person of interest in the investigation of an armed robbery."

"Let me see what you have on that. I assume that you brought it up because you are prepared to charge him."

"Not at this time, Your Honor."

"Bail is set at twenty-five thousand dollars. Ten percent cash. In addition, the defendant will notify the court within twenty-four hours of posting bond in writing that he has secured employment with the Cedar Inn."

Ken Hetland posted cash bail for Dustin Stevens the next morning. He was back working as the maintenance man at the Cedar Inn by noon. Hetland, on the other hand, made himself scarce.

I made it a point to check up on Dustin that afternoon. To be honest, I was sure he would make a run for it the first chance he got. According to the manager, he was a model worker. Stevens even let the manager know where he was going if he had to leave. I was doing a Cedar Inn drive-by, and Stevens was out front on a ladder fixing a yard light. He saw me and waved me over. I got out and walked over to him.

"What's up?" I asked.

"Sheriff, I was going to call. But if you've got a minute now, I'd rather talk in person."

"What about?" I asked.

"Not here. I don't think that would be smart. As it is, just you being here this long makes me nervous. I'd like to meet someplace private. I don't want anyone to see us together. You know the old canoe landing off the road on OO?"

"I know it," I said.

"What about meeting there when I get off work?"

"Sounds good, but it's not going to happen. I've been a cop too long to set myself up like that."

"Sheriff, this is really important. No funny stuff on my end. You have my word on it."

"I tell you what, Dustin. I'll meet you there, but I'll bring Chief Delzell with me. We'll come in plain clothes, drive her Jeep. It's the best I can do, and I'm not even sure I should do this."

He thought for a minute. "Six o'clock?"

"Works for me. I'll check with the chief. If you don't hear from me, we'll be there."

I called the chief. "Mary, Dustin Stevens wants to meet with us at six o'clock at the old canoe landing on OO. I volunteered you to come with me. I also volunteered to use your Jeep."

"My almost new Jeep?"

"Plainclothes operation."

"What does he want?"

"I guess we'll know when he tells us."

Mary picked me up. We pulled in at almost the same time as Stevens and exited our respective vehicles. This landing was rarely used because it was prone to disappearing during heavy prolonged rainstorms. Under normal circumstances it pitched and rolled for seventy-five yards before it smoothed out.

"What can we do for you, Dustin?" I asked.

"I want to make a deal with you guys and get you to drop all the charges against me. I have been offered a good job as a carpenter, but I need a clean record, which I had until now. I figure this is my chance to get straightened out."

"It's not that easy. The charges against you are serious. Felonies don't just fly away."

"What if I knew something that you wanted to know? Isn't that the way it can work? I give you information, and you drop the charges against me. I know for sure you'll be interested in what I know."

"It can work that way, but that's not up to me. That's up to the DA and Judge Kritzer. I can tell you this: There's no deal unless we know what you're putting on the table."

"What if I tell you, and you use the information and leave me hangin'?"

"Trust plays a big role in how all this shakes out. Depending on what you know, you may have to testify."

"If I can get out of this mess, I will be glad to testify."

"Can you give me a hint?" I asked.

"It's about the robbery. I'm not saying anything more." A head popped up in the window of Dustin's beater truck. It was his Labrador. I walked over to give her a pet. She wiggled from her nose to the tip of her tail.

"Your buddy bring her back to you before he pulled out?"

"Yeah, he did."

"Nice looking dog, Dustin," I said.

"I just got her from the Retriever Rescue. Someone had spoken for her and never came back. I figured I could use the company."

"What's her name?"

"Sadie."

"Well, hello, Sadie. It's nice to meet you," I said.

"Dustin, the best I can do is this. The chief and I will talk it over. I will call the DA on our way back and set up a meeting for tomorrow morning. I'll run it by him and see what he says. Just so you know, Dustin, I am all about second chances. If you get one, make the most out of it."

"Sheriff, I will. My life of crime is over."

DA Hablitch answered on the first ring. I explained Stevens' offer. Our DA had been around the block many times and heard just about every one in the book. The cases where a deal is made require everybody to do what they agreed to do. Hablitch agreed to try to contact Stevens' lawyer in the morning but made no promises.

I took my time driving home. The radio was quiet. I really hoped that the deal with Stevens could work out. Julie was knee-deep in student papers when I walked in. While some teachers would find reading through these creative efforts drudgery, Julie loved it.

I hung my gun belt and gear in the closet, and she wrapped things up for the night. We discussed the election for a few minutes, and I realized that I hadn't really given it a thought for the last twenty-four hours. I was pretty sure that Scott Stewart was thinking about it.

Bear called early Thursday with good news. There was enough money in a federal grant to make our crime scene intern position full-time.

"What do you think about that, John?" he asked.

I jumped at the chance. "Tell me what we need to do."

"First, you should ask Price if he's interested. This is a sworn position. He'll be wearing brown and assigned to your department. However, the position will be shared by Musky Falls PD. If he's interested, then Price, you, me, Liz, and Chief Delzell need to sit down and figure this out."

"Bear, what if Jared says no? Is the position specifically for him?"

"According to Liz, it must be an extension of an existing position. There are two others just like it, one in Appleton and one in Iowa County. They are bound by the same conditions."

"I'll get on it right now, Bear."

"Good boy, John. By the way, make it easy on me. My shoulder still hurts from one of our past adventures. The other day, Tanya heard me on the phone with you. When we hung up, she reminded me that we were closing in on retirement. She's not going to be happy if you get me killed."

"Okay, Bear, tell her not to worry." Truth be known, Bear was a far bigger threat to criminals than they were to him.

I was on the phone with Price and the chief and asked them to come by my office posthaste, asking Mary to arrive fifteen minutes early.

Before they arrived, I called DA Hablitch. The meeting with Stevens was set for the following morning. Everybody was on board. I was anxious to hear what Dustin had to say. In a case like this one, with a lack of supporting information and evidence, even the littlest thing could be significant.

Chief Delzell was early and brought me one of Tommye's homemade cinnamon rolls.

"Chief, I've got two things for you. Are you ready?"

"As I will ever be. Go ahead, John."

"Stevens, Jack Wheeler, and the DA are going to meet in the morning and go over the particulars. I let Hablitch know we're not going to make any deals with anyone until we talk it over."

"What does he have?"

"I don't know, but we'll find out tomorrow morning."

"Keep me posted. What's next?" the chief asked.

"Liz Masters and Commander Malone have come up with enough grant money to fund Jared in a joint position between your department and mine. Full-time permanent."

That brought a big smile to the chief's face. "That is great news. Really great news." With a small staff we were always under the gun, trying to wear as many hats as would fit on our heads. Price had already proven himself to be a real asset. Keeping up with forensic science and evidence collection was a huge job in and of itself. For two rural departments with limited capabilities, there was always lingering doubt not about the evidence we collected but about what was missed.

My door was open, and Jared walked in.

"Chief, Sheriff, what's up?"

"Sit down. Let's talk."

"Okay. Is there a problem?" he asked.

"No, no problem. Jared, have you thought about your future? I mean careerwise," I asked.

"Not really. I like what I'm doing here, and I am learning a lot. My internship will run out before I know it, so I'm trying to pack in as much as I can."

"What if your internship didn't run out? What if you can stay on in a permanent position? Would that work for you?" asked the chief.

"What position?" he asked.

"A sworn officer evidence technician?" I replied.

"How does that work?" Jared said.

"When I started in law enforcement, we had a couple of squad cars called equipment cars. They had a trunk full of gear used for processing the scene and collecting evidence. A sworn officer manned the car, and their first responsibility was to respond to requests from other officers to process crime scenes and collect evidence before a scene gets contaminated. It worked well, and as soon as the rest of the troops began to understand how to protect a scene, those cars and the officers made a lot of cases. I was thinking along those lines."

"When I wasn't processing a scene, would I be on patrol taking calls?" he asked.

"Yes, you would. You know firsthand that we are short-staffed. We can't afford to put a car on the street that doesn't cover lots of bases when needed. I wish it wasn't that way, but it is, and I don't see it changing anytime soon."

"I've got to say this is an attractive offer, but I need to think it through if that works for you."

"Jared, you do that and let us know."

"I will. Now, if it's okay, I am going to meet Deputy Pave down at the impound to double-check our inventory."

"Go ahead, I'm going to head out myself. Chief, before you take off, I just remembered something. I ran into Warden Asmundson. He's trying to catch up with you about setting a barrel trap in the alley off First Street."

"Right, the night shift officers said a bear tore the dumpster apart. I tried to reach Asmundson a day ago, but he was back in an area without cell service."

"He's going to be in his office later this morning," I said.

"Thanks, John. I'll make sure to catch up with him."

I spent the rest of the day and into the night thinking about things. Something was going on that I couldn't quite put my finger on, but I needed to. Professor Schmutz's stolen briefcase and Stevens' shenanigans were all part of it. I strongly encouraged the DA to agree to go along with Stevens' deal. I have never been a big fan of making deals with criminals. I knew some pretty good cops who never made a deal and just worked things out using good police work. But the truth is, the minute the rats start leaving the ship, someone's reaching out to make a deal. ❖

CHAPTER 12

Julie had been up late burning the midnight oil. Before I hit the not-so-mean streets of Namekagon County, I had to wake her so she wouldn't be late for school. I checked with dispatch who immediately advised that the Wisconsin State Patrol was requesting assistance at the scene of a motor vehicle vs. pedestrian accident at Highway 77 and Hatchery Road. Deputy Plums and EMS were already en route.

"I'm 10–76 to that location," I replied.

I rolled up on the scene, and Plums came right behind me, adding to the abundance of warning lights. Law enforcement officers know all too well how an accident scene can trigger another accident. I exited my vehicle and walked toward the WSP squad car and was met halfway by Sergeant Denny Kruger.

He wasted no time bringing me up to speed. "It looks like a hit and run, called in about six this morning. EMS is on the way, but the victim is clearly deceased. The accident was reported by a school bus driver. He said it looked like the vehicle was chasing someone. He found the victim several feet up in the branches of a large white pine. The vehicle took off down the highway—no skid marks up to what looks like point of impact. A rough field estimate though looks like the victim was thrown a good sixty feet."

"Do you have an ID on the victim?"

"Yes, we do. Tentative at the moment but probably solid. He had one of those IDs on a lanyard around his neck. The name on it is Dustin Stevens," said the sergeant.

My reaction immediately got his attention.

"What about it, Sheriff?" he asked.

"Dustin Stevens is part of an ongoing criminal investigation."

"What investigation?" asked Kruger

"The armed robbery at the Cedar Inn."

"Do you think the robbery is connected to this?"

"Could be a coincidence," I said. "But we've got to treat it like it isn't."

"Well, as far as it goes now, we're treating it like the homicide it is. Intentional is what you're thinking?"

"I think we need to look at this as premeditated until we know different," I said.

"I agree. Everything bagged, tagged, measured, and photographed."

EMS arrived and went to the location of the victim. I paged out the ME requesting him at the scene and called in SI Price to help with evidence collection.

Some automotive body parts were recovered in the ditch along Highway 77. The pieces, which included most of a headlight assembly, were bagged and tagged. Close examination showed what appeared to be brown hair stuck to the headlight.

Tire impressions had been protected, photographed, and cast. The tires left a travel pattern that continued past the scene of the accident. The soft road shoulder showed bits of tire impressions where the vehicle left the shoulder completely, got back on the highway blacktop, and went east. The WSP sent another trooper from an adjacent county to assist. There would be impressions on the scene from the first responders, so they made sure to eliminate those by comparison.

There were also footwear impressions that came up the soft shoulder of Hatchery Road, where they continued onto the shoulder of Highway 77 in a westerly direction. The stride attached to the impressions increased significantly when the individual came onto the shoulder of Highway 77. He was running. The victim's lug sole boots were consistent with those impressions. The victim and scene were photographed, and the location of recovered evidence was triangulated.

Dr. Chali arrived and did a cursory evaluation photographing the body from every angle. Dustin Stevens was pronounced dead. He was carefully removed from the tree and put in a body bag. The ambulance transported Stevens to the morgue.

I asked Plums if he had a current address.

"Dispatch ran down the most current: 2244 Hatchery Road, Musky Falls."

I called Sergeant Kruger over.

"Denny, with what you have and the connection to an ongoing investigation, I would like to call the DA and see if we can get a search warrant for the house. I know you've got your hands full. I'll leave SI Price with you. Deputy Pave is on the way to help with the search."

"That's good with me. Just keep us advised," Kruger said.

The team redoubled their efforts to cross every t and dot every i. Kruger requested assistance from WSP's Traffic Reconstruction Unit.

Dispatch sent Pave to the Stevens residence. I was waiting for him at a two-track turnoff. He was an old hand, as good a cop as there was.

The high-tech map in my squad showed four houses, including

the one with Stevens' fire number. The gravel driveway meandered back and forth. Pulling off to the side to hide my squad was just asking to get stuck. I could not see the house from where we were and stopped in the middle of the road, blocking it in case someone tried to make a run for it.

We geared up and took off on foot through the woods to establish a vantage point where we could have cover. Deputy Pave carefully approached, looked in the windows, and saw no one in the residence. As we moved in to take a position for entry, I saw a fresh blood trail heading toward the house. We continued our approach, knowing that two people to sweep a house is not enough. In the big city an emergency response team would be on their way. In the Northwoods of Wisconsin, "on their way" might be a long while.

The blood trail led to the front porch, allowing a search under the auspices of exigent circumstances. Entry without a valid warrant puts the investigating officers at risk of having evidence thrown out at the request of a canny defense lawyer. But a law enforcement officer's first mandate is to protect life. Fresh blood leading to the house was most likely deposited by someone alive.

A series of three nods put us in the front door. We swept the house, gun muzzles leading the way. Entering and searching as if executing an arrest warrant on a hardened and dangerous felon. There was no one home.

Furnishings were sparse, but what was there was made by the hands of a real craftsman. A large tarp was spread out on the wood living room floor with a half-finished bench in the center. Hand tools were littered about. Next to the stone fireplace was a dog bed and chew toys. Desk drawers had been pulled out and emptied. Any other area that might conceal something received the same treatment. A hand axe was buried in a structural stud, where it appeared to have been used to chop through a wall. Clothing from a closet was strewn around.

Blood on the front door's antique knob, bloody fingerprints on two of the three glass door panels, and blood spray on the walls gave me the impression that someone was being chased, trying to escape from someone wielding a weapon.

Before going any further, we called the DA on duty and advised him of our situation. The preliminary search had been done based on exigent circumstances. No one was found in the house, and the initial blood trail stopped on the front porch. We requested a search warrant. For the next few minutes, I dictated to him why a search warrant was necessary. He advised us that Judge Kritzer was in chambers and would walk the warrant over for his signature. Meanwhile, we should continue to locate the source of the blood.

A whimpering coming from under the front of the house struck my heart. The porch was set on cement blocks, creating a space about two and a half feet high underneath, with a dirt floor. Slivers of light coming through the spaces between the old boards barely cut through the darkness. Lying down on my stomach, I half crawled, half shimmied across the dirt. I was almost all the way in when I heard another whimper. I pulled myself forward and reached out toward the noise.

I was rewarded with a painful bite to my outstretched hand. I pulled it back, recognizing there were now two bleeders underneath the porch. Pave handed me his mini-mag, and I held it in my mouth, keeping my hands free. The light revealed the victim: a chocolate Lab cowering in the corner with a profusely bleeding shoulder and wearing a blaze orange collar still attached to a blue webbed leash.

When injured, one of a dog's first lines of defense is to fall back on its most formidable weapon: teeth. Eons of canines have used four teeth of the same name for ripping, tearing, and holding their meat. A lab's two hundred and thirty pounds of bite pressure gets your attention. Usually not a jaw-locking bite, but more like a hard nip that says, "Back off unless you want more." I learned long ago that dogs react to the way you speak to them. Harsh and mean may just get you something you don't want. Soft and gentle, especially for a Labrador, is most often a safe bet.

I carefully reached for and grabbed the end of the leash. I didn't move any closer but started to talk to the pup in my most soothing voice. "Hi, you good pup. You're a good pup, aren't you? Yes, you're a good pup. I'm not here to hurt you. I want to get you out of here so we can help you. Good pup, you good pup."

The next round of "good pups" got me a little wag of the tail. Progress. Then I remembered what breed of dog I was dealing with. Pave went inside, raided the refrigerator, and came back with a chunk of roast beef and tossed it to me. I broke off a small piece and gently threw it to her. Pain or no pain, food was food, and slowly but surely, the dog came closer. I took up the leash inch by inch. She came out from under the porch but didn't know what to think of us. I wrapped the leash loop around her muzzle to prevent another bite. I recognized her as Sadie, confirmed by the tag on her collar. Her foreleg hung at an ugly angle; her shoulder showed a deep cut. She needed a vet right away.

Pave looked at the pup and then my hand. Me pulling one way and Sadie pulling the other resulted in a nasty bite that left a flap of my skin dangling. He suggested I take the dog over to Kouper's and then go to urgent care to get my hand looked at. He brought over his first responder kit and wrapped my wound. A sheriff dripping blood all over the crime scene was no good.

Dr. Pederson Kouper, a specialist in large predatory animals, was working part-time for a semi-retired equine vet, Jim Coners. Kouper recently relocated to the area after a cougar moved into Namekagon County and alarmed people when it started acting like what it was. It's all part of living in a place defined by four w's: water, wilderness, weather, and wildlife. Spending time outdoors requires that one gives it the respect it has earned over millions of years. Disrespect any one of these things, and the result could be serious, sometimes fatal.

Officer Good pulled in and walked up the driveway, search warrant in hand. "The DA sent me with this, said you needed it immediately. The chief said I should stay and help you."

I looked over the search warrant. DA Hablitch had been thorough. He covered all the possibilities and probabilities. At my request, he had listed Dr. Schmutz's briefcase and its contents.

It was now murder, and a murderer was running loose. The worst criminals have been quoted as saying, "The first murder is the tough one. After that, they're all free."

I reminded Officer Good and Deputy Pave of what they already knew by heart. They finally dismissed me when I told them, for the second time, to leave a copy of the warrant on the kitchen table.

Pave lifted Sadie into my car and set her comfortably on the back seat. He did another wrap of my hand to keep the squad clean.

Dr. Pederson Kouper answered his phone when I called to alert him that we were on the way. We pulled into the vet clinic, and Pederson came out to meet us.

"Who does this beautiful pup belong to?"

"Her owner was the victim of a hit and run this morning."

He carefully crawled into the back seat and did an initial examination. Sadie showed herself to be quite the trooper while he examined her. The shoulder was cut to the scapula. The right foreleg was fractured. Kouper decided to administer a tranquilizer while she was in the back seat.

Once she was out, we slid her onto a stretcher and carried her into the clinic. The vet closely assessed the injured dog on the exam table with gentle, knowing hands. Pederson proceeded to clean and repair the wounds. First, he laid the flap of skin down, treating it with an antibiotic. Then he stapled it in place along with a small drain tube.

Repairing the broken leg took more time. X-rays showed the fracture would need to be immobilized with splints. Gauze and cloth were used to wrap the leg so it would be protected and remain stable. As I helped Kouper wrap the leg fracture with a plaster and cloth mix over the top to dry in place, I banged my bitten hand against the stainless steel examination table and yelped.

Pederson wrapped an additional bandage around the uninjured shoulder so it would be hard for her to chew on. For right now she needed a safe place to wake up. A big soft pillow in a recovery kennel was just the ticket.

"The dog's wounds are serious. Restricted activity is a good idea until things start to heal. I suppose the county receiving the vet bill will just add more fuel to Stewart's fire. Now, Sheriff, what happened to your hand? Is that from Sadie?"

I nodded.

"Rabies is always concern with dog bites. I noticed a rabies tag on the Sadie's collar from my clinic. I'll check her vaccination status. Let me see your wound," Kouper insisted. He prodded and poked. "Sheriff, you're going to need to get that sewn up."

"I kind of figured, but I don't have time to wait at urgent care."

"Why don't I sew it up? This isn't something I'd normally do, but in an emergency situation, it's allowed."

"But you're an animal vet," I said.

"And you are mammalian, in many regards not so different from your canine companion. Do you want a little shot to numb the cut before I get started? Or do you want to tough it out?"

"Painkiller, please."

After three or four shots of lidocaine at specific locations, Kouper was sewing away. It seems that Sadie got a better bite than I figured, taking a chunk of meat with her. Probably swallowed it along with the roast beef.

Pederson Kouper was an artist with a needle and thread and was able to neatly close the gap. He gave me some white pills in a bottle.

"Give her one of these a day and take two a day yourself. It will protect you two against getting an infection."

Then it dawned on me. I had a dog that needed a place to stay.

"Dr. Kouper, the owner of this dog is no longer with us. Can you keep her here until I can make other arrangements?"

"Under normal circumstances I would say of course. But Professor Newlin and I are going to be tracking a cougar in Bayfield County. Probably a young male, as usual, he is inquisitive and courting danger when he shows up in someone's backyard or a farmer's field. This one's got a cougar sense of humor. A guy out on Highway J was sitting in a lawn chair, reading the *Outdoor News*, when he looked up and saw the cougar licking out his dog's food bowl. We'll be gone for at least a couple of weeks."

"I'll call the Northwoods Humane Society. They're good folks. They can probably take her," I said.

"Actually, Sheriff, the dog needs rest and someone to change bandages. They have their hands full just caring for the huge number of strays they take in."

Sadie started to wiggle and moan a little. Her hind legs moved like they were running in pursuit of a dream rabbit. I left her with Dr. Kouper and promised to pick her up before he and Professor Newlin were supposed to leave.

I drove back to the Stevens residence and went in. SI Price and Deputy Plums had finished up at the accident scene and were methodically going through things, noting anything that may be even remotely involved. They wore paper booties and gloves. Price was scanning the room with a camera, and Plums was collecting anything of interest.

"Have you found anything that's going to help us?" I asked.

Price chuckled; so did I. We had both been trained by or worked with Dr. Liz Masters, who would have responded immediately with, "How do you know what's going to help until you find everything you need to find?" She was known in law enforcement circles as one of the best and had been instrumental in Namekagon County, helping us clear cases and get solid convictions.

"Well, Mr. Stevens lived a pretty bare-bones life," said Price. "We did find a couple of firearms, an LC Smith sixteen-gauge shotgun and a Colt Police Positive, chambered in thirty-two Colt, both well used but looked well cared for. The Colt was lying on the floor near the door; it held six rounds. Two of the six loaded in the gun had been fired. The shotgun was hanging on a wall rack made of deer legs. The rack also had a place for the pistol. We partially disassembled the shotgun and packed it up too. We unloaded both. I'd guess people around here don't have much use for an unloaded gun," said Price. "Sheriff, we also found something of interest in what must be the main bedroom if you want to take a look."

We went into the room.

"We waited for you before we pulled this apart," said Pave.

It was a security box meant to withstand a fire, but it couldn't survive somebody going at it with an axe. The small, heavy door was closed, but the lock was destroyed.

"Go ahead. Let's see what we've got," I said.

Between the chunks of safe material, we found Dustin's treasures: letters and pictures from those in his life he loved. A photo of two adults and young Dustin holding a beautiful musky. A handwritten letter dated a few years before from his former wife, telling him that she was leaving. The paper was dotted with watermarks, maybe teardrops that fell as he read. A lone grouse feather and an antique pocketknife. The vault and most contents would be dumped in the trash if taken to a pawn shop in one piece.

Some of the contents had spilled out. Mixed bills strewn across the floor, toward the door. Several of the bills were still caught in an oversized rubber band. The perp probably grabbed some cash on his way out. Was Stevens' money stash hard earned and hidden from creditors or a payoff to cut a wire? Depending on how this played out, I couldn't help but be suspicious of the fact that the perpetrator here had left cash. In the Schmutz robbery, the perp didn't take his watch or wallet. Maybe the same bad guy was looking for the same thing.

"We also searched two outbuildings. One held a canoe on sawhorses and lumber that was stickered just right to dry along the airy wall," said Pave. "The other building was in the process of being structurally reinforced. He was using peeled eight-inch red pine logs. They were neatly fitted into joints that would make them doubly strong."

There was nothing to indicate that Dustin Stevens was prone to any kind of misbehavior until most recently. But somehow he got involved up to his neck, and my guess was that his involvement in the robbery at the Cedar Inn is why he died.

The house was secured. Price and Pave transported the guns and a few other things to the evidence storage locker at the sheriff's office. SI Price indicated on his list the things that would be tested for DNA. They would stay there until needed. Signing them in and out would keep the chain of evidence intact. During our search, we specifically looked for Schmutz's stolen case. It was nowhere to be found. Maybe that's what the previous searcher was looking for too. No way of knowing if he found it.

A couple of people, mostly Stevens' neighbors, had come to

the scene to ask what was going on. They were politely asked to return home and that an officer would contact them. Most of them saw no reason to stick their nose where it didn't belong. Folks up north tend to be friendly but somewhat on the private side. Deputy Plums and one of the troopers followed up with them, and I asked for the reports before they clocked out. No problem. They understood crimes like this are most often solved in the first forty-eight hours. No one drags their feet. Complainers will find themselves on the night shift patrolling between Seeley and Cable when it's forty below.

Darkness was moving in, and we were done for the day. Everyone had done a good job. If we missed something, we hadn't missed much.

I arrived back at the vet clinic as Dr. Kouper and Professor Newlin were finishing packing up for their trip.

"How's the pup?" I asked.

"She is doing good, but her shoulder is sore. I loaded up a box of bandages and antibiotic and anesthetic cream. She needs to take it easy. No running, swimming, or chasing balls. If that drain comes loose, or there are any other issues, call Jim Coner."

"When Charlie and I get back, I'll check on her. Here is a big pillow for her to lie on in your back seat. Once you get home, bring the pillow inside and put it where you want her to sleep. You'll be surprised how quickly she will adjust to it."

On my way from the vet clinic, I called Julie.

"Honey, I'm on my way home, and I am bringing a house guest with me."

"John, a house guest? You should have let me know. I have schoolwork covering every flat surface in the living room. I need some time to clean up. How long before you're here?"

"An hour enough time?"

"I'll see you then. I'll put new sheets on the guest bed."

"Julie, I wouldn't worry about that. She'll be sleeping on the floor."

"She will? SHE!"

"Bye, honey. See you soon," and I hung up.

We headed for the cabin, and I was glad. I had a lot to digest.

I pulled up in front, and Sadie gingerly got out of my squad. Julie opened the door a moment later, ready to greet our house guest. Sadie didn't bat an eye. She walked right past Julie into the cabin, took two turns, and curled up on a braided rug in front of the fireplace. Sadie looked up with those Labrador eyes that have sold millions of puppies and went to sleep. It had been a hard day for all of us.

Julie brought me a bottle of Angry Minnow beer, two Tylenol, and a cup of tea for herself, and we sat in our respective chairs to share our day.

She smiled at me and said, "So where did you get this young lady?"

"My first call this morning turned out to be a fatality hit-and-run."

"Who was killed?" she asked.

"Dustin Stevens. Do you know him?"

"I know who he is; I don't know him well. Isn't he the guy who crashed into Mary's squad car?

"That's him."

"He never seemed like a troublemaker to me."

"Everybody we've talked to says about the same thing. Nice guy, hard worker, ran into bad luck after he invested in a development. Working his way back up."

"Now, tell me about our house guest."

"The dog belongs to… or belonged to Dustin Stevens. The hit-and-run happened right at Hatchery Road and Highway 77."

"Is that what happened to her leg and shoulder?"

"Most likely."

"What about your uniform? Were you rolling in the mud?"

"The pooch was crouched under the porch of an old cabin. I had to wiggle underneath to get her out. That's actually how I got wounded."

"That was my next question. What happened to your hand?"

"I tried to grab her to pull her out, and she bit me."

"Is it bad?"

"I took Sadie, that's her name by the way, over to see Dr. Kouper. He fixed her up and said he'd sew me up too while I was there."

"You know, John Cabrelli, I'm not the least bit surprised. I'm more surprised you didn't use the superglue you keep in the car."

"Kouper did a nice job. Julie, I was wondering if we could keep Sadie here until we find her a home?"

"She looks like a nice dog, but I don't think we should keep her locked in the house for twelve hours a day while we're at work."

"You're probably right. I've got a feeling this Dustin Stevens thing is only going to ramp up."

At about the same time, we both said, "What about Bud?" He would be a total sucker for a homeless pup.

"I'll give him a call tomorrow," said Julie.

We were quiet during our dinner of venison backstraps from the freezer, wild rice, and mushrooms. Afterward, we settled in on the couch and each picked up where we'd left off in what we were reading. Julie was reading student papers; I was starting Dr. Schmutz's new book. She and I were married to each other but also devoted to our jobs. Each of us felt that there was good in the world that needed doing.

My wife spent her professional life teaching those who wanted or needed something different. Students who get labeled as "at-risk" or are nonconventional learners are often swept off to the side, while mainstream students get the attention. By providing "hands-on, feet-wet" education, as she called it, students learned that success was based less on opportunity and more on the willingness of the individual. They learned that in order to get, they had to give. Mostly she gave them her heart. Julie will never forget being a little girl in Barbie pajamas who was saved on a cold, rainy night. A small cabin Nick had built behind ours had two extra beds, so when someone needed a place to stay, we welcomed them. No questions asked.

I believed strongly in her methods, not just because she was my wife and I loved her, but because I had seen it work. I had watched the transformation. I also believed that education was the cure to many of society's ills. Together we were a good team, getting better and stronger all the time. Julie was my hero.

Our relative silence was briefly interrupted when our house guest limped carefully over to the front door, wagged her tail, and barked once. Julie went over and opened the door, and Sadie went out to take care of business. When she was finished, she walked right back in the open door, but instead of returning to her adopted rug, she went out to the kitchen and began sniffing along the counter, stopping at our dinner plates.

"She's hungry, John."

We didn't have much in the way of dog food, but we did have a big piece of venison left. I cut it up into small pieces, put it in a bowl, and added warm water to make some gravy. She enjoyed every bite of what would have been my next day's lunch. When she was done, she curled back up on her rug.

The day had worn me out. I can go full speed for a long time, but once I stop, it is tough to get going again. We crawled into bed, quickly fell asleep, and pretty much stayed that way all night... at least Julie did. ❖

CHAPTER 13

Saturday morning we turned the sheriff's office into a command post, and all the principal investigators were front and center by eight, ready to go. Dedicated professionals, each with their own skills, their own viewpoint, all trying to get to the same place. Turning over every rock and following every thread.

My dog bite was twice as sore as it was when it happened. It was unavoidable that I would bang my injured hand on any hard object close to me. When Chief Delzell heard the story of how Dr. Kouper had stitched me up, she suggested we go back to him and fashion a protective plastic cone to keep me from licking. There was no shortage of laughter at my expense.

Sergeant Kruger, Chief Delzell, SI Price, along with Deputies Pave and Plums, each told their story. Deputy Plums and a young trooper provided a verbal report of the neighborhood canvassing effort. Everyone knew Dustin Stevens. He was a good carpenter and helped the neighbors out when they needed it. His next-door neighbor told us about something he was involved in.

An elderly man a half mile down Hatchery Road from the Stevens' place needed his porch roof repaired. He was a guy who spent his whole life doing things for himself and was proud of it. Dustin was driving by his place and saw the guy climbing a wooden ladder onto the porch roof. He slammed on the brakes, backed up, shut the truck off, and got out. Dustin asked the old timer if he could help. He told Dustin he had everything under control. That was when the wooden rung he was standing on broke. Dustin caught him on the way down. Nobody really got hurt, but the old guy was pretty shaken up. Stevens offered to come back over the weekend and help him with the porch roof. The old guy said he couldn't because he was leaving town over the weekend to see his great-granddaughter play softball. He'd call when he got back. He returned from his great-granddaughter's softball tournament the next Monday to a house with a new porch roof. Dustin Stevens denied knowing anything about how that had happened.

No one recalled Stevens having any notable visitors. Maybe a pickup would pull into his place now and again. No one recalled hearing anything that might have been noise related to an accident.

Plums and the trooper pushed the rest of the neighbors as hard as they could without creating memories. The bottom line was that Dustin Stevens was, by all accounts, a good guy. He had chosen to become involved in a robbery when he cut the cable at the Cedar Inn. He had to have known the location where the robbery was going to take place.

Price stood up to a large whiteboard flanked by poster sheets on the wall. He was excited to examine the random list of items seized as potential evidence that, with any luck, would be woven into a tale that would tell us what happened.

Large poster sheets are a great tool, but writing something down gives that idea the illusion of permanence. Sorting things out in my mind works for me. I can put things in different places in the blink of an eye and, dumb or not, don't have to justify my idea.

I use this kind of processing fairly often. I have found, without a doubt, the best environment for cultivating productive thought comes when I'm swimming across Spider Lake, walking the ancient hunter's trail, or mindlessly casting to unknown fish.

In this case, it seemed that inconsistencies were the only things that were consistent. I took the lead and started. Anyone who had something could jump in.

"So, here's what we know. A famous historian and author, Harold Schmutz, is in northern Wisconsin for a presentation and the release of his newest book. The college provided him with VIP accommodations on Chequamegon Bay. But the night of the robbery he was staying at the Cedar Inn, a nice place but a clear step down from the place on the bay. Stevens was the maintenance man at the motel. We can put Stevens and Schmutz at or close to the robbery scene. When confronted, Stevens flees. After posting bail, he's the victim of a hit-and-run."

We agreed to take separate tasks and begin putting the pieces of the puzzle together. In the margin we wrote names or skills that we might need to help us with the case.

A call came to my phone. I recognized Dr. Chali's number. "Sheriff, I know you're up to your elbows, but I'd like you, SI Price, Sergeant Kruger, and Chief Delzell to come to my office. I have some questions, and I think it would be more expeditious if we met and I put my theories out on the table. Then we can discuss them. It will impact some of what happened on Hatchery Road."

"We'll be on the way," I said and quickly notified everyone else.

The difficulty of a small law enforcement community becomes readily apparent when the bear poop hits the fan. Everybody needed to know as much as they could. Following the victim through the stages both pre- and post-mortem. Establishing a foundation for the investigation. The next step was meeting with the ME. It may not be conclusive, but it would, without a doubt, be informative.

Deputies Pave and Plums, along with a city officer, would handle calls within the county and city. Chief Delzell, Sergeant Kruger, SI Price and I would attend the meeting with the ME.

The Namekagon County medical examiner escorted the three of us into the lab office. Dr. Chali looked tired—the kind of tiredness that comes with the territory.

"Well I don't know whose department is going to catch this case, but you all should pay attention. The vehicle that struck the victim was traveling at a very high rate of speed. The organ, tissue, and bone fractures were catastrophic. During a high-resolution search of the clothing and body, we recovered some tiny flakes of gray metallic paint. That has been packaged and, based on your directions, will go to the state crime lab. They have an extensive collection of paint samples. It's impossible to find a match in our lab here."

Dr. Chali pulled up an image. We stared silently.

"The victim died from the injuries sustained when the vehicle hit him. It was massive trauma. His spine was broken. His rib cage was crushed, puncturing both lungs. He also sustained cardiac damage. I have prepared a list of his injuries and the extent of damage. In my opinion, Dustin Stevens was struck from behind by a vehicle traveling at a high rate of speed. The height of the impact appears to be approximately forty inches, which is consistent with the bumper height of an average vehicle. He sustained spinal fractures at the fourth, fifth, and sixth thoracic vertebrae. In other words, Dustin Stevens was running away when he was hit and propelled a significant distance from the impact. He was trying to get away from someone. That's not all. Before being hit by the vehicle, Stevens sustained other injuries, almost certainly inflicted by another party. He was shot once in the right cubitus or elbow joint, and the bullet lodged there. The wound would not have been fatal, and we were able to retrieve the bullet. All my findings will be available in detail by the end of today. Any questions?"

Dr. Chali was a top ME and could find a job anywhere. He believed strongly that one of his responsibilities was to speak for those who cannot speak for themselves—namely the dead. I had watched as he had grown into his role in rural Wisconsin. He laid out the details in the autopsy with minimal technical jargon. There would be plenty of that in the final report. What he had given us in common language, not jumping to any conclusions, outlined the physical facts.

"So, Dr. Chali and crew, if you don't mind, let me run with this," I said. Everybody silently nodded in agreement. "Stevens comes home from working the night shift at the Cedar Inn, and someone is tearing his house apart looking for something. He wants it bad enough to commit a burglary. Stevens, who is a relatively non-confrontational guy, asks him what he's doing. The guy says, 'I want what you got. Give it to me, or I'll shoot you,' then does just that and pulls out a gun or takes Stevens' Colt revolver off the gun rack. Stevens is not so keen to comply. The burglar lets him know he's serious and, to reinforce that, shoots him in the elbow where it definitely hurts but will still allow him to talk.

"Stevens figures this guy is going to kill him and must have seen a tiny little window of opportunity and takes it, bolting out the front door. He runs down Hatchery Road toward Highway 77, and his dog follows him. The perp still needs to get something from Stevens and goes after him. At some point, the bad guy realizes that if Stevens gets away there are lots of possible outcomes, none of them good for the robber. It's a pretty good guess he's going to run for the police, call 911 on his cell, and get the troops on the way. Maybe one is just around the corner. Flashing lights and sirens are not what the perp needs. Stevens likely knows him, and he may be one of the guys Stevens is about to burn. The perp probably heard something in the wind that a deal was going down with the DA.

From whom exactly is a big question.

"Regardless, the bad guy can't take any more chances. He didn't get what he wanted, and now Stevens is getting away. He jumps in his car, buries the gas pedal, and flies off down after the already wounded Stevens. The perp hits him and his dog at seventy miles per hour. One thing is for sure: Stevens had something this guy was willing to kill for. He blew his chance. Running Stevens down was second best. At least it kept him quiet. We're certain this whole thing is tied up with the robbery at the Cedar Inn. I think we need to do a better job of figuring this out. Me especially."

"What about the bullet? Any particular kind of gun?" asked Delzell.

Dr. Chali brought up the picture of the bullet recovered from Stevens and a picture of the Colt pistol recovered at Stevens' house during the execution of the warrant.

"The bullet you see is solid lead and weighs 71.29 grains. We were able to extract several different fragments to bring the weight up to just over 74 grains. The bullet is soft lead, which is the type often used in target ammunition or ammunition for antique guns. It appears to be a thirty-two-caliber bullet consistent with something fired by semi-auto pistols as well as revolvers. The crime lab lists many, many guns chambered in some form of thirty-two caliber. They range from high quality and well-made to pot metal junk. According to the crime lab, almost all thirty-two-caliber ammunition is commonly available. I will send the bullet and recovered fragments, as well as the firearm, to the crime lab as soon as we're done here."

I asked Denny about the headlight assembly found at the scene.

"John, a couple weeks ago there was another accident sustaining minor injuries but significant vehicle damage. The headlight assembly we found was actually from that vehicle. Two adults with two kids in the back seat hit a deer that ran out onto Highway 77 from Hatchery Road. The car had to be towed, and the driver and occupants caught a ride with the wrecker driver and the squad car. The first exam by the lab indicated that the hair around the headlight assembly was from a whitetail. We will still run it down and put it with the car."

"So a dead end for me," I said. "Well, I guess we need to see if we can come up with a cell phone. I'm betting we don't. It was probably smashed into a million pieces or thrown into one of our fifteen thousand lakes. Jared, see if anything turns up. We are going to work with the State Patrol in the search of the murder weapon—the vehicle. The height of impact, the distance the body was thrown, and tire impressions indicate some sort of truck or SUV. Brush guards on the front of pickups are common and would explain the lack of broken vehicle parts, particularly plastic, which replaced steel a long time ago."

The only way I could think to handle this involved using all of our available resources. We would come up with a list of questions and go where each answer took us. As suspects or people of interest appeared, we would need to know how hard to push them. Murder is big stakes.

Bear checked in.

"Bear, I've got one body, and I am afraid there are more to come unless we get on top of this. We find the perp, maybe we save someone's life. The victim we have is dead—run over and shot. The guy was a maintenance man, and I suspect he cut the wire on a surveillance camera so that there wouldn't be a recording of an armed robbery. It appears he was a guy up to his ears in debt trying to make some cash. Looks like he was a small part of this thing. He was out on bail and reached out to me. He wanted to trade his charges for information on the armed robbery. Before he could give us anything, he was killed. Whoever killed him was looking for something that he thought Stevens had. Something bigger is happening here than what it first appears. We have players who are associated in strange ways."

"Get Price on the tech side of this, technology over boot leather. Let me know if he needs something," Bear said, then hung up.

I needed more help to understand all I could about what was going on here. I had to start somewhere, connect with someone who was in the circle of information but not a person of interest in the criminal investigation. My first call was to Joel Bolin, the coin expert. He agreed to meet with me at my office.

I led him into the biggest of the interview rooms. He turned down my offer of coffee or water. He looked nervous. We sat down at the table.

"How can I help you, Sheriff?" he asked.

"Well, Joel, I need some help understanding things. One of the suspects in the Schmutz robbery has been killed. We have determined that this was a premeditated murder. The victim was the maintenance man at the Cedar Inn."

"Oh, my, Sheriff. That is horrible. I'm afraid that I have nothing to offer you. I would help in any way I could, but honestly, I don't know anything about a murder."

"That's not what I want from you. Of course, anything you come up with that you think might be helpful about the robbery or murder, please don't hesitate to let me know. What I am interested in is the artifact community and how it functions. I know it involves a fair amount of money. Now, an internationally renowned historian is robbed just before he is about to publicly release his latest sure-to-be bestseller book. You were obviously very excited when you saw the 1862 French coin found by the land surveyor."

"Well, Sheriff, the robbery has certainly started an undercurrent of discussion. People in my world love a good mystery. Right now the biggest one is right here in Namekagon County. Where would you like me to start?

"Wherever you want," I replied.

"Are you going to Dr. Schmutz's talk?"

"Yes, my wife and I are."

"It should be exciting. Although they might not look it, you'll be rubbing elbows with the treasure-hunting elite. People who have spent fortunes hunting for lost treasure. In my opinion, Schmutz has got something that will take him where he wants to go. He is largely self-funded now, and the timing of his book release may help him raise the money for the continued search. Sheriff, I would say that he thinks he's close."

"Any idea what treasure he's looking for?"

"Only about a hundred guesses, all probably wrong. My favorite is the story of the Dancing Ladies Wanigan. Next would have to be Chequamegon Ell Pingers Hidden Loot. Then again, it's not every day that someone brings me a Civil War vintage one-hundred franc Napoleonic gold coin found in Namekagon County. It's exciting. I think it might fall into the category of a new clue to an old mystery."

"I'm sure he's got some competitors. Who might they be?"

"When it comes to lost treasure, everybody is competition. From the farmer who finds a silver dollar digging in a fence post to national network television shows. Treasure or rumors about treasure are everywhere. Northern Wisconsin is no exception. In the real world, Harold Schmutz has competitors, but he is, without a doubt, at the top. His meticulous and far-reaching research is second to none. Most of his competitors respect him—with some exceptions.

"It's not been much of a well-kept secret that Schmutz and company have been seriously pursuing some leads in the area. I don't think he'll know what he's looking for until he finds it. He purchased the legendary Lost Boys' coin for far more than its value. My guess would be that the coin and where it was found are part of the puzzle."

"So, Joel, I'm curious... is there really treasure to be found in northern Wisconsin? What treasure would it be?"

Bolin laughed. "The same treasures we heard about as children. Buried pirate chests, lost gold mines, relics of Allouez, and more sunken ships than you can count. Following the tales of lost treasure in northern Wisconsin would take a lifetime. With all those stories out there, treasure hunters figure some must be true. For each treasure, there are legions of people who have invested time and money to find it, mostly with little luck. Occasionally, someone finds something or a piece of supposed evidence that supports the story of a hidden treasure. Then the race is on.

"Gold and silver were not uncommon forms of trade. Recently a vault was found in a river near here. It is my understanding that a heavy rainstorm had uncovered this safe. It was opened, and inside was a bag full of coins, several gold. It's said to have been on board a wanigan that followed the loggers. The log structure floated along, steered by a lone rudder, carrying a number of women with various things to sell. Their products were exactly what the lumberjacks were looking for after a long winter in the big woods. According to legend, the wanigan was piloted by a hardened river man who, among other things, protected the women. When spring came, they would ride the river south and take their money to the bank at Wisconsin Dells and invest the proceeds in a hotel they owned. They flaunted not only their riches to their best advantage.

"The next year they again rode a wanigan down the river. It was to be the last journey for them. The raft came to a ferocious set of rapids fueled by huge snowfall up north. Witnesses said the wanigan reared up like a wild horse and was smashed into the rocks. No one ever saw them again."

"Treasure. I never gave it much thought. I really appreciate your help, Joel. I'll let you know if we make some progress."

"Good luck, Sheriff Cabrelli."

I checked in immediately with my colleagues. Price was working with Sergeant Kruger and two deputies with metal detectors searching the area around where the body was found. I called Chief Delzell and told her I was headed out to see Dr. Schmutz.

"Do you think there is anything there?" she asked.

"I don't know, but I've got to keep at it," I said.

My next call was to Julie. "I'm driving to Ashland to visit with Dr. Schmutz. I've got to be back at the office for a debrief at five and will be home after that. How's the pup?"

"She's a sweetie. I applied the cream Dr. Kouper gave us on her shoulder, and she didn't move at all. I've got to tell you, John, we should give keeping her another thought. In fact, I took your long tape and measured out where we could put up a fence and doghouse when we're gone for the day."

I hadn't been home long enough since Stevens was murdered to spend any time with Julie or the dog.

"We'll talk about it if I ever get home."

"Sadie and I will be waiting," she said with a cheery voice that told me Sadie had found a new home.

Schmutz didn't answer his cell phone, so I drove directly to where he was staying and knocked. He opened the door.

"Sheriff Cabrelli, how can I help you? Have you ever thought about calling ahead?"

"No, Professor, I thrive on the element of surprise," I said. "Anyway, sorry for the intrusion. Dustin Stevens was killed. I need to have a heart-to-heart with you. I think it might be important, maybe lifesaving, maybe yours or mine."

"Consider me all ears."

"Here's what I think. Our investigations are heading in the same direction. Different end goals, maybe, but in the same direction.

It's not just following up on a few threads of information. It's much more than that. You and I are in pursuit, and I think we are further along than we thought. Here's the kicker: Someone is following us. I don't know who, but someone. Your robbery, Stevens' death, and you being in Musky Falls at the same time are all tied together; that's pretty easy to see. What else is easy to see is that person is dangerous, and you are not taking this as seriously as you should. Somebody already shot you once. They may do a better job next time. Professor, if you are going to continue with what you are doing, we need to work together."

"Sheriff, this is my life's work. I'm at a place that few will ever understand. I have no doubt that any number of people are following me. You have accurately described some members of my professional community. I'm always watching for someone raising the 'skull and crossbones' in my wake. Having said that, I would miss the ribbon cutting if someone were to shoot me down before we announced this to the world. Work separately on our individual projects, share and share alike?"

"To some extent within the constraints of a criminal investigation."

"Ha, reservations already from the start of this new partnership. I understand how embarrassing it would be if, at the conclusion of all this, the gun ended up in my hand. It would likely have a negative impact on your election. But we will work together, see where it goes. Right now we are going forward inch by inch. There is probably one big difference between me and others who are searching. There may be gold at the end of this rainbow, and for most, that will be the prize. For me, the mystery awaits. My treasure will be putting together a significant and valuable piece of history, which will undoubtedly lead us on yet another journey through time. I can't wait."

I spoke with Deputy Plums during my return trip. Dr. Chali had not yet successfully located Stevens' next of kin. They were still searching.

I finally found my way home. I don't remember it ever feeling better. I walked in and was treated with a vision of domestic bliss. Julie sound asleep in her chair with her feet up and Sadie curled up on the rug, nose tucked under her tail. Both woke at the same time. Neither seemed overjoyed to see me. Sadie went to the door, and I let her out. Julie gave me a groggy peck on the cheek and went upstairs. ❖

CHAPTER 14

I love morning, greeting every new day with new opportunity. I got up early and took Sadie outside. She sniffed and snuffled, examining her new territory, thousands of scent receptors feeding the canine brain. I worked with canine units and am repeatedly amazed at what those dogs can do. Sadie did her business and went back to the door to get her breakfast. Julie came down wearing her cute flannel robe.

"Good morning, you guys. Oh my gosh, it's seven! I stayed up late and was able to finish grading all the papers. I have some exceptional students, and some who are showing pretty strong indications that they may be facing some challenges. I am going to reach out to their parents through Becky Chali. Did you and Sadie have a nice morning visit?"

"We did. I've got to admit, she's a nice dog. I get the feeling you are leaning toward keeping her."

"John, she's got to live somewhere. Why not here? If she doesn't work out, we can always find her a new home. Come on, what do you think, honey? She would sure make our hikes a lot more fun."

When Julie was excited about something, she explained it

rapid-fire. I always got the impression that we had already agreed to her side of the issue at hand. In this case, it was easy. Sadie had a new home.

"What about when we're gone all day?" I asked.

"No problem. Bud is going to fence in an area and build her a cozy doghouse for when the weather's bad."

"Bud's pretty busy. When can he get to it?" I asked, trying to make sure the bases were covered.

"He can get to it about an hour from now."

"Today?"

"Today."

"I'm done with my schoolwork for now, so I plan to help him. He thought we'd have the kennel done by dinner. His payment is Aunt Rose's walleye fillets, cornbread, and Moose Tracks ice cream fresh from the dairy. If you get home in time, there might be some leftovers. Well maybe... you know Bud." She chuckled, knowing full well that leftovers with Bud often turned into after-dinner snacks.

Thoughts of a peaceful Sunday morning went as quickly as they came. A quick kiss and out the door.

Always wanting to know what's going on in the county, I tuned into the *Voice of the North* radio show on my way to town. The news started with "no arrest of anyone in the recent suspicious death." The Voice said calls to the sheriff and police departments were not yet returned.

I was jolted back to the reality that I was running for election when the next blast on the radio was a campaign ad for Scott Stewart:

In a growing community, we need to make sure that all of our services keep pace. Law enforcement is a priority. Scott Stewart is the man for the job. It's time to put offenders in jail where they belong. Vote Stewart.

The sheriff's race was a distant second to the sheriff's work. A homicide was priority two. Priority one was making sure there wasn't another one. I turned off the radio. Stewart was becoming an annoying distraction. I had a job to do, and I would do it. There was a killer in Namekagon County. There was also a victim. I was positive I was somehow on the right track and close to finding my way. No stone left unturned.

I checked in with Joel Bolin. "Joel, I have asked Dr. Schmutz to work with law enforcement on a regular basis. I am convinced that all that is going on is tied together. I was hoping you could help us with anything you might come across. This is still new territory for me. I don't want to miss something that would be obvious."

"Sheriff, as I've told you, there are plenty of rumors about lost treasures, mainly stashes of coins and even some bullion. This was wild country during logging years and many overnight millionaires. Banks were few and far between. It was not uncommon for someone to carry their savings in a backpack. In addition, people came to the pineries from all over the world carrying the currency of their country with them. Most of the people who came were honest, hardworking souls. Most, but not all. Post-Civil War people drifted, looking for the next opportunity. The war produced some dangerous people. It may be as simple as a rain event like the vault from the wanigan. Heavy rain showers have been more frequent. Water with velocity washes away a hundred years of sediment. A dozen coins—a logger's life savings—sees the light of day. Suddenly a new buried treasure has been found. Before you know it, the area is alive with treasure hunters. I will do what I can to help you."

I hung up with Bolin and immediately got a call from Ron Carver.

"John, I may be able to help you a little with your investigation.

We need to sit down and talk face to face."

"I can use all the help I can get... something needs to break." Before I got the next word out of my mouth, dispatch broke in.

"All units switch to TAC 1 and report 10-20."

I reported immediately.

"Sheriff, we have multiple silent alarms coming from 2244 Hatchery Road. What do you advise?"

Just in case someone came visiting Stevens' house, we wanted to know. The alarms were small and placed where they'd be hard to see. No lights, no audible, just a broadcast on a restricted channel that went directly to dispatch. Every cop with any experience knew there was always a possibility that the criminal, for assorted reasons, would return to the scene of the crime. Firefighters often will video the crowd at a fire scene trying to catch an arsonist admiring their work. Or the perpetrator who drives by a crime scene several times pretending to be a rubbernecker, when really, they are admiring their own cleverness. Or maybe, in Dustin Stevens' case, the person who tore apart the house was coming back to look for what they didn't find the first time. If that was the case, it wasn't a burglar we were looking for; it was a murderer.

"I am close. Who else?"

"Plums and Pave," the dispatcher replied.

"Send two more cars. This may be our murder suspect."

"WSP and MFPD also en route."

One of the most difficult jobs in law enforcement is communications. The dispatcher and the communication team need to remain calm when everybody around them has their pants on fire. It is essential they make good decisions when charged with coordinating the response of patrol units. Anyone who knows the truth will tell you law enforcement communicators save lives every day. They are that critical link between the citizens and those who are coming to their aid.

Cars were closing in on the Stevens residence. I ran black and quiet. The request a few minutes ago for the 10–20s of responders let me know I was the closest. The bad guy would momentarily be fully aware of the company he was about to get. My plan was a full-out assault to catch the visitor in the act. I was turning into Stevens' driveway when the dispatcher advised we had just received a 911 cell phone call from an agitated male reporting a murder at the Stevens' residence.

"The caller reports extensive damage to the residence and 'blood everywhere.'"

I drove up to the end of the driveway, parked in a shadow, and started to move toward cover.

Just then, a lone figure ran out the front door of the house right toward my position. I sidestepped as he ran past, sweeping his legs out from under him. He went down hard, landing flat on his chest. I heard a *whoosh* as the air was expelled from his lungs. Years of practice came into play; I grabbed my cuffs, brought one arm, then the next around, and in no time had him secured.

My knee in his back kept him down, but there wasn't much fight left in him. I lifted him by the handcuffs and dragged him toward my car. When he saw my squad car, he jerked around hard to see for the first time. His knees went out from under him, and down he went.

Then he looked up at me, smiled, and said, "Thank God you're here, Sheriff. I've never been so glad to see anyone in my life."

"Is there anyone else involved here? Anyone in the house or buildings?" I demanded.

"I didn't see anybody. I don't know. I just got here. I'm supposed to meet Dustin," he blurted.

"Dustin Stevens?" I asked.

"Yes, Dustin Stevens."

I kept ahold of my prisoner, and the other officers searched every square inch of Stevens' house and outbuildings. After a few minutes, Deputy Pave called the place clear.

I brought Hetland to his feet and let him catch his breath. It took a minute, but he suddenly realized I was not as excited by the discovery as I should be.

"What happened with Dustin? Was he hurt?"

"I'll answer your questions to the extent I can after you answer mine," I said.

"I've got nothing to hide, Sheriff. Ask your questions."

"Thanks, Mr. Hetland. What are you doing here?" I inquired.

"I'm supposed to meet Dustin here today. He got a really good job for us in Seeley. Six, seven months' work. I've got all my tools in the truck. Take a look if you want."

I nodded toward the conservation warden, who made a practiced visual examination of the back of the truck and cab.

"It looks clear," said the warden.

"Now, Sheriff, tell me what's going on," Hetland said.

"Dustin Stevens was killed. We believe it was an intentional homicide. I'm in charge of the investigation. We are pursuing several different leads, but we don't have a specific person of interest."

"Why would someone kill Dustin? He's about the nicest guy you'll ever meet," Hetland said.

"We don't know. You're the first person other than his neighbors that had contact with him. Hopefully you can help us figure this out."

"I'll do what I can. Can you tell me how he died?" asked Hetland.

"He was run over and died from blunt force trauma."

"Run over by a car?" he asked.

"Car or truck."

"Are you sure it wasn't an accident?"

"Right now, we are investigating this as a homicide. We have evidence to support that."

"I can't believe this. Everybody liked Dustin. He'd do anything to help somebody out. No way, this just happened. No way."

"That's what people have told us, but the fact remains that everything points to murder, and Dustin Stevens is the victim. Mr. Hetland, would you mind going down to the sheriff's office to talk this over?

"Of course I will. I want you to know that I'm pretty shook up here, but I'll do the best I can. Dustin was my best friend. To be honest, Sheriff, he was probably my only friend. I guess I better ask: Am I under arrest for something?"

"No," I replied. "You can ride with me or follow in your truck. Okay with you?"

"I'll follow you, Sheriff."

In the time it took to get to my office, I had several thoughts. I called ahead and made sure an interview room equipped with recording capabilities was ready.

He followed me in, and I showed him to the room. There was fresh coffee on, and I stopped to pour myself a cup and offered one to Hetland. He said he could use one. The tiny indicator light flashed once and disappeared. Recording was now in process. I chose not to tell Hetland he was being recorded. One-party consent is all that's needed, and I was one party giving my consent. I didn't want to inhibit the flow of conversation.

"Thanks, Mr. Hetland. I appreciate you talking with me. I am doing everything I can to catch Dustin's killer, and I need all the help I can get. Can you give me some general information about him?" Hetland nodded. "Do you know if he had any next of kin or other friends?"

"As far as family, he had nobody. Neither of us really had anyone. Dustin was an only child, and his parents passed away when he was eighteen or so. Up north here, there are all sorts of jobs in the backcountry for a carpenter. You know, cabins or lake houses. Sometimes we'd just camp out. Save traveling back and forth from town every night. We worked a lot of jobs together in remote areas. It suited us. At night we would sit around a fire and talk. It may seem strange, but we talked about family quite a bit. Those talks around the quiet campfire really meant something. If you can be a pair of loners, I guess we were. I can't believe he's dead." Hetland looked up to the sky, and tears ran down his cheeks.

"We know he was behind on his bills. Anybody mad enough to kill him?"

"Well, people were plenty unhappy, but it wasn't him who defaulted. They sued Dustin because he was easy to come after. Anyway, most of that's cleared up. I have been down around Stevens Point on a job since I was here last. We got an offer to do a big project up in Seeley, some rich guy. That's why I'm here. I tried calling him to tell him I was coming, but it went to voicemail."

"He had a couple of things to clean up before we packed up. The owner of the lodge required a clean record. Up until a while ago, that wouldn't have been a problem. But as you know, Sheriff, he definitely screwed that up. He told me he had a plan to fix it. I guess that doesn't matter now."

Hetland's story checked with Dustin's.

"Mr. Hetland, are you going to be staying around here for a while?"

"To be honest, I don't have any idea what to do. I'm kinda in shock. I was going to stay with Dustin at his house, but I can't do that now. I guess I'll get a room somewhere. Heck, I don't know. The other part of this is that I would like to help you anyway I can. Dustin and I were close friends, so if I can help you out, I would like to stick around to do that."

"What about I put you up in a hotel for a couple of days? You might be a big help. I am going to consider you a material witness, so we'll cover your room, meals, and so on. Just give me your receipts. We are investigating a homicide, and the fact that you are the closest connection we have with the victim makes you very important to our investigation. Don't get the wrong idea here. This is a homicide, and if you say you're sticking around, you'd better mean it. If you did take off, I'd have to put out a locate on you, then have someone haul you back here."

"Okay, Sheriff. You've got my word. I'll stick around."

I got all of Hetland's personal information, including confirming his and Dustin's cell numbers, and booked a room for him at the Moose Lodge.

"Get yourself something to eat. I've got to check on the jail then I'll come back. Maybe we can make some headway. Hetland, one thing you should be thinking about: Whoever killed Dustin may or may not have gotten what they wanted."

"What do you think they want?"

"For the minute, Dr. Schmutz's briefcase looks likely."

I was just about to show Hetland out when he stopped in front of me. "Sheriff, by the way… any idea what may have happened to Dustin's dog, Sadie?"

I filled him in. He thanked me for taking care of her.

"Dustin loved that dog," he said.

Hetland drove out in his pickup truck, heading south toward the Moose Lodge.

I returned to the interview room, took the coffee cup Hetland had used, and put it in a sealed evidence container. On my way out I secured it in an evidence vault and listed the contents and the fact that it could only be released to me or SI Price. I got him on the phone and asked him to send the cup for DNA testing homicide, priority. SI Price reported that he had reset the alarms and added a surveillance camera.

It was apparent that this murder had everyone on edge. I felt the same way. Something would break loose as long as we kept looking. Everyone agreed to meet back at the command center in the morning. We needed to consider a change of strategy.

I advised dispatch I was clear from the call, drove a little way, and pulled off at a roadside rest stop that provided parking for a trailhead. I put down my window and leaned my head against the headrest. Namekagon County needed a new sheriff. If I held a press conference today regarding the Stevens homicide, I would start out by telling the crowd that although I have a body, I don't have a suspect. I had no witnesses. In the old days, tough cops would sit people under a hot lamp and sweat the information out of them until someone broke.

CHAPTER 15

I drove out to my cabin, where Julie and Bud were both hard at work on the dog kennel. Sadie had a clean wrap on her leg and a bandage on her shoulder. She was comfortably reclining on her big pillow, attentively watching humans at work, and seemed to approve. There are dog kennels, and then there are dog kennels. Steel posts wrapped with wire were the least secure. These were stout wooden posts with fence secured around the perimeter. The entry door was set just right to allow easy entrance. Julie was securing shade and sun panels over an elevated platform. She and Bud looked sweaty. They took a break, and we drank lemonade at the picnic table.

Julie broke the ice. "How's the case going?"

"Well, a friend of Stevens just showed up. I talked to him a little, but I'm going down to get his statement as soon as I'm done with this lemonade."

"Are you coming home for walleyes and cornbread?" Julie asked.

"It's okay if you don't; that's more for me," laughed Bud.

Bud and Julie sipped their lemonade while I gulped mine.

"John, you are so on edge. Why don't you call in and do what you need to do tomorrow? You deserve a little rest," Julie said.

No rest for me. Minutes later, I was on the road again.

I pulled in under the large neon ungulate at Moose Lodge. I didn't see Hetland's truck in the lot and figured it was probably around back. I was wrong. The desk clerk at the Moose said he'd never checked in. In other words, Hetland was not where he'd said he'd be. I wondered if Len Bork still needed somebody to work at his gun shop.

At the sheriff's office, I sat down with one of our data people and put together a BOLO for Hetland. I contacted the DA, who gave me the go-ahead for detention as a material witness in a homicide. I walked down the hall past a set of interview rooms that were shared by the city PD and sheriff's office. Mary Delzell was sitting at one side of the table. Across from her was my missing witness, Hetland. I opened the door, walked into the room, and sat down in a vacant chair.

"Sheriff, I hope you don't have every law dog in the state looking for me," he said.

I didn't respond.

"I'm here to confess. I got about halfway to Illinois and knew I had to turn around. I got back to Musky Falls, and I saw the chief here and figured confessing to her is as good as confessing to you. She read me my rights already. I don't care. I am tired of carrying this burden."

Delzell and I stepped out into the hall.

"John, I have Jack Wheeler coming to represent him. He wasn't sure about needing a lawyer or not. Since it is a homicide case, I asked the PD's office for a legal representative. Wheeler is the man filling in today. He should be here any minute."

After Jack arrived, a city officer escorted him to the interview room. Attorney Jack Wheeler was a man who had integrity running through his veins. He and I were good friends, but when it came to the law, that and two bucks would get me a cup of coffee.

The first thing Wheeler did was send us out of the room. He admonished us for speaking with his client without him present. It was two more hours before they invited us back in. I envisioned Bud eating my dinner.

"Sheriff Cabrelli and Chief Delzell, we have a proposal. It should not be considered a point of negotiation. It is an agreement that will be mutually beneficial to all parties. My client is here voluntarily. He has information that may have a bearing on an ongoing case in this jurisdiction, a homicide to be exact. My client, however, is not involved as a principal in the homicide. Our only deal here is full immunity."

Jack Wheeler, my wonderful friend, was so skilled as a lawyer he had the ability to irritate me beyond belief. This time was no exception. In the real world of law enforcement, dealmaking was part of the process. The chief brought me back to reality and quietly reminded me that we were ready to work a deal with Stevens, and it might be what got him killed.

"We need to get the DA over here. You know we can't make any deals without him." I called Hablitch and explained the situation. Even though it was a Sunday, he said he'd be on his way promptly due to the exigent circumstances.

The discussion resumed before Hablitch finally put a stop to things. "Attorney Wheeler and I need to meet with Judge Kritzer. Chief Delzell, Sheriff Cabrelli, do you agree with what's proposed here?"

"I do," said the chief.

"Me too," I said.

The judge was not in the most jovial of moods when he answered the phone.

"Judge, this is DA Hablitch. We have a plea agreement that involves immunity from prosecution."

"Fine. You people get with my clerk and set a time for it to be heard next week in chambers," he said.

"It can't wait, Judge. It involves the ongoing homicide investigation."

The phone was silent for a moment. "I assume that we have everyone involved present for our discussion."

With Judge Kritzer's blessing behind us, we prepared to hear what Hetland had to say. DA Hablitch, Chief Delzell, Attorney Wheeler, Hetland, and I crowded into the larger of the interview rooms before we started. Jack Wheeler laid out the rules.

"My client has agreed to allow the DA, Sheriff Cabrelli, and Chief Delzell to be present during the interview. He wants to be very clear that he will only say what he's got to say once. So whoever the DA determines needs to be here should be. We will go on as long as we need to, but make it crystal clear that when we're done, we're done. Also, we agree to allow the whole session to be recorded. The DA's office agrees to give us a copy of the recording.

"We are confident that my client's exposure was limited, to begin with, in this situation. The immunity agreement will not cover any further issues. However, if at any time my client becomes dissatisfied with the direction of the interview, he may stop the proceeding. The information will come mostly as a narrative from my client. He is naturally somewhat anxious about the whole process and feels that might work to everyone's advantage. The rest of the details regarding this situation are thoroughly covered in the attached documents. Please take as much time to read them over as you need. I expect we should have a complete understanding, and we have no intention of rewriting this agreement during the course of the interview."

Jack Wheeler got things going. "Before we start, Mr. Hetland needs to get something from his truck," said Wheeler. "Sheriff,

Chief, or whoever is welcome to accompany him to his vehicle to receive the items."

Hetland grabbed an old leather briefcase from behind the seat in his pickup. He handed it to me, and I took it inside. I emptied the contents on the interview room table. There were five leather-bound journals and another much smaller one.

"Is this the briefcase that was stolen during the robbery?" I asked.

Hetland nodded and began his story.

"The way this all got started is pretty simple. Dustin Stevens and I have been friends over the last couple years. He and I are both carpenters, and I am a land surveyor as well. There are a whole bunch of cabins and lodges around here that are back off the road. Some of them are on inholdings in the national forest. A guy bought several of them for a low price. Then he hired us to fix them up so he could resell them for a lot of money. Each property also needed to have a certified survey. Dustin and I worked together.

"One day I was surveying a tract of land with the Namekagon River running through the northwest corner. I was wading through some real shallow water and saw something shiny on the bottom. I thought it was a fishing lure and picked it up. It was no fishing lure; it was a gold coin. I put it in my pocket and kept on with my survey.

"We met back at the cabin at the end of the day. The property was vacant, so Dustin and I set up camp and built a little fire. After supper I remembered the coin and showed him. He figured that it might be worth a few bucks. I was going to take it in to see if it was worth anything but didn't get to it right away. Then Dustin got in that car chase and landed himself in jail. So I went to the jewelry store and showed the woman at the counter the coin. She asked me what I wanted to do with it. I told her I wanted to know if it was worth anything. She told us that she would have to call someone who was familiar with coins.

"What I didn't know was there had been a robbery where some coins were involved, so the clerk called the law from the back room. That's the first time I met Sheriff Cabrelli. Then Cabrelli called in another guy who could tell us if the coin was one of the stolen ones. He said it was solid gold and from France. The expert said it was the real thing and worth quite a bit of money.

"Dustin and I aren't rich; we've made good money on some jobs. Working on cabins out in the bush suited us just fine. No houses of ill repute tempting us, we were paid by the job so we could work as long as we wanted. We were rebuilding a screened-in porch and sitting room that overlooked the water. Sometime in the past, the cabin we were working on must have been a real dandy. Timber frame, with hand-rubbed red maple cabinets throughout. It was a pleasure to work on. One day we were working on resetting, squaring, and retightening the large beams. I was sitting on a cross beam, and Dustin was using the truck winch and pulley to raise the next one into place. It's the kind of project you've got to watch what you're doing, so we didn't notice when this guy we'd never seen before pulled up.

"He walked over and was all smiles, friendly sort. He introduced himself and said that he was from the Cities, and a guy at the Musky Falls Lumber Company had recommended us. He asked if we could show him what we were working on. We agreed. Dustin and I were both pretty good at our trade. The guy knew quite a bit about construction and didn't hesitate to tell us he liked our work a lot. Then he got down to business. He had a project that involved two large condo buildings on the water that needed to be rehabbed. Some of the work had been done, but the contractor just picked up and took off one day. He took a flatbed straight axle truck loaded with construction materials with him. Anyway, that put this guy in a spot, and he needed to find someone else to finish the job. He said he'd heard good things about us.

"The problem was he needed us to start right away. Dustin and I would never jump jobs. Once we agreed to a project, we were on it until it was done. So, we thanked him but turned him down. He came back two weeks later. We were just finishing the timber frame cabin. He was smiling ear to ear and said he had good news. Seems he had buyers for the two condos once they were finished. If we could fit it into our schedule, he'd give us a solid 5 percent of the sale price of the property on top of our regular charges. That night, sitting by the fire, we figured out that would be more money than we'd seen in a long time.

"We'd made lots of progress on our current job, and if I do say so, those cabins were looking pretty good. I went to see the guy we were working for, and he told me that we could split our time between the projects as long as we agreed to come back. So that's what we did. Things were going real good for us. Long hours in the backcountry was still to our liking. Then one day I took the truck and trailer into Musky Falls Lumber. I hand selected the lumber, got it loaded, and headed for the front gate. I didn't get very far before the yard boss stood in front of the truck. He told me that I needed to pay cash for my load of materials. We had been on credit, so I didn't know what to do. The owner of the lumber yard told me that we were behind payment on our last two loads. Those loads had been signed off by Dustin. Anyway, we tried to get ahold of the guy from the Cities, and he was gone to who knows where. It didn't take long before people found out they couldn't find him, but they sure could find Dustin and me. Before you knew it, everybody in town was after us.

"We split up and wanted to work on getting our feet underneath us. I took some surveying work and Dustin took a job at the Cedar Inn. Slow but sure, we were trying to make things right with everybody, but it wasn't happening. We finished the cabin project, and it looked great. The owner paid us and even threw in a bonus. The next day the lumber yard filed against us on the condo project.

"I came back to town for a couple of days. Dustin and I went to the Fisherman for dinner and a beer. There was a newspaper lying on the counter about the robbery on the front page. I told Dustin that Namekagon County was turning into crime central. He didn't have much to say. A few days later he's in jail. I went to visit him, and he told me the whole story.

"A guy approached him one day as his shift ended at the Cedar Inn. Dustin had never met him before. He knew everything there was to know about Dustin's financial issues. He told the guy to take a hike. As he started to walk away, he turned around and told Dustin he had a chance to make real money for a few minutes of work. Holes in his pockets, he couldn't help himself from listening. The guy laid it out for him. There were security cameras at the Cedar Inn. Four of the cameras would need to be disabled. When they found the cameras weren't working, Dustin would just do what a good maintenance man does—fix them. No one knows he has anything to do with anything. Dustin walks away with a bunch of cash. No one gets hurt. He agreed to do it and cut the wires on the right night the following week.

"The day before he was supposed to cut the cables, the guy who was paying him for the job drove past the motel and gave Dustin a hand signal to follow him. He drove his old truck, and they met at the edge of town. The plan was not going like it should. A guy was supposed to exit the motel carrying a briefcase. Someone would run past him and grab the briefcase and run with it. No guns, no knives, no violence needed. But there was an issue. The guy who was going to grab the bag had backed out. The man offered Dustin a pile of cash to put the cameras out of commission and make the grab. He went for it. I mean, what would you expect him to do?

He's getting ready to face bankruptcy."

"There are all kinds of people facing financial troubles that don't try and solve the problem by committing armed robbery," I said.

"Sheriff, I'm not saying that what he did was right. If I had known what he was planning, I would have tied him up to a tree, but I didn't. I knew his luck had gotten worse. His ex-wife's lawyer sent Dustin a letter demanding that he make the last two payments she said she had coming. All the while, Dustin said she was living with a rich guy."

"Do you know where we might find her?"

"I definitely do not, nor do I care to."

"You're going to need to tell me everything you can about her."

"It won't be much, Sheriff. But I'll tell you what I can."

"We'll come back to that. Let's continue with the robbery and Dustin," I said.

"Anyway, Dustin was told where and when he was to get the briefcase. Dustin sure didn't have any experience in robbing people, so he came up with one of those 'shouldn't have done that' ideas. I guess he was thinking he was Jesse James or something. Anyway, he put his grandpa's old pistol in his pocket, just in case. He wasn't figuring on shooting anyone, just scaring him.

"The guy with the briefcase walked out into the hallway, and Dustin grabbed it. The man was stronger than he looked and was putting up a real fight. Dustin pulled the gun, the guy gave him a shove, and the gun went off. The guy let go of the briefcase, and Dustin took off with it.

"He used his master key to open a vacant room and stashed the bag and ski mask. It was one of the rooms that the cameras would have covered if they worked. Then he went down to where the robbery had occurred and called the police and attended to the victim. He jumped in to help the police.

"The deal was someone was supposed to make contact with him to get the case. It didn't happen and he was worried. Dustin said there were cops everywhere. The last word I heard from him was where I could find the case. It was hidden in the lodge we were working on. He said I should leave it there until I got ahold of him. I guess that's never going to happen."

"Mr. Hetland, do you have any idea about why this case and its contents would be so important?"

"Well, I was hauling a load of materials out to the lodge, and when I got there, curiosity got the best of me. It was right where he said it would be. I didn't read the diaries. I didn't want anything more to do with the whole mess. He got himself arrested, and I helped him out best I could with that. The judge let him out on bail, and he went back to work at the Cedar Inn. Don't get me wrong, Dustin and I were close and everything, but I needed to get out of town, get a little space between us. I packed up and headed out on a survey a couple hundred miles south of here."

"Mr. Hetland, there are some big questions that need answering. The first is who hired Dustin to rob Harold Schmutz? Did he give you anything to help us out with this?"

"I don't know, and I don't want to know. Dustin Stevens needed money. He decided to turn to crime for a quick fix. I decided to keep working. He made the wrong choice, and it had a bad ending. Dustin was no criminal, but he was desperate. Now he's dead. The answer to any more questions went to the grave with him. To be honest, folks, you have about wore me out."

Attorney Wheeler spoke up. "I would like to take this opportunity to make sure everyone understands that Mr. Hetland has more than met his part of the agreement. I would also question whether or not there were any charges that could be brought against him. I ask that, at this point, you agree to an unconditional release regarding this case."

"He covered up a crime and was not forthcoming with information," Hablitch said.

"Maybe, but in reality, he gave the investigators more information than they had. He had nothing to do with Dustin Stevens' homicide and, in many regards, is a victim, having lost his best friend and business partner. He called 911 to report a possible violent crime and remained on the scene until law enforcement arrived. I can go on if I need to. Hetland will be more of an asset to your investigation than a hindrance. Let's not forget he chose not to take off when he had the choice."

I took the floor. "I think that we need to regroup. We have a dead man, and that means we have a murderer. This case is not over. My thought is we don't even know what's going on here. Mr. Hetland, we need your help. It will be instrumental in helping to find your friend's killer."

"Sheriff, I will do whatever I can to help. I would ask you to let me return to the timber frame lodge we were working on. The owner liked our work and has decided to build a timber frame shop addition. I would need to hire a couple of helpers. There's enough work to keep me busy, and I hope far enough away from anyone who might want to shoot me."

The group adjourned.

CHAPTER 16

The only thing I could do was bring the investigators back together, so I scheduled an emergency meeting for the next morning. Chief Delzell and I personally called each member of the homicide task force and involved first responders. Sergeant Kruger agreed to join us and share their investigative findings. I called the *Voice of the North* on my way home and asked for five minutes on the morning show before my task force meeting. He agreed.

I was getting agitated to the point of distraction, agitated and angry. I tried to hold it in.

Julie was changing Sadie's bandage. Her gentle hands cleaned the surface, and although healing was well on its way, any pressure elicited a squirm. Sadie was walking and enjoying her new home.

Dr. Kouper and Professor Newlin had not yet returned from their cougar exploration, although several pictures of an adult cougar had appeared in the most recent issue of the *Outdoor News*. The trail cam pictures were taken forty miles south of where Kouper and Newlin were looking. But the photos were telling. The cat was walking along a fence line. Newlin and Kouper measured and scaled the animal's size using the fence and the photos. The cat was about eight feet from nose to the tip of its tail and thirty inches at the shoulder. A big animal by anyone's estimate.

I said hello and told Julie I'd be back in a minute, which turned into more like an hour. On the spur of the moment, I grabbed the paddle and launched *Sweetheart*. There was a little breeze, and it slowly pushed me out toward Hannah Bay. I went past Tommye Heinemann's cabin, and she waved from the shore.

I considered using the paddle but knew I just needed to drift. I took a couple of PFDs and laid one on the bow and used it as a pillow. I watched the sky as the clouds and *Sweetheart* seemed to move along together. The late-day sun was perfect.

A tall tree on a small island had become the preferred perch for one of nature's keenest predators, the osprey. Professor Newlin had given Julie and me a high-power spotting scope mounted on a tripod just to keep tabs on the eagles and ospreys with whom we shared Spider Lake. We could see our osprey was a male because it lacked a brown bib. He was very determined, catching a fish about one out of every four tries. Today he gave me quite a show. Only a few feet from *Sweetheart*, he launched a successful attack on a northern pike and flew off with his prize. I couldn't help but wonder if I would be as successful.

I picked up the paddle and slowly made my way back toward our dock. As I rounded the point I saw another boat heading for me on a direct course. I left my gun in the cabin when I got home and was now armed with only the paddle. It is funny how a police officer's mind works, moving quickly toward assessing threat potential even when the risk is low. It wasn't long before I recognized that the approaching craft was commanded by one of the potentially dangerous creatures I knew. The cedar strip canoe came along side without a bump, my wife at the helm.

"I was looking for you and noticed *Sweetheart* was gone. I could see her approaching the bay but couldn't see you. I looked with my binoculars and saw you lying flat. So, I came out to check on you and am glad you appear in good health."

I took a line from *Sweetheart's* gunwale and secured it loosely to the canoe's thwart.

We floated gently, quietly on Spider Lake. No one around, no roaring motors. The call of a loon told us they knew we were there. I thanked the Lord, for I desperately needed this moment of peace.

We paddled back to our home, our place, where we would cherish our time. Back inside, I told her what I intended to say on the *Voice of the North* morning show.

She locked her eyes with mine. "Aren't you chasing a murderer, by definition, a person that has already killed someone?"

"Yes."

"How do you know that you won't be the next victim?"

"I don't know. I do know that there is something strange going on. I also know we have a dead man in the ground and a killer roaming free. Probably until the election is over, the job of finding him falls to me. After that, Scott Stewart can chase him down. Julie, don't worry. I promise I'll be careful."

"That, John Cabrelli, gives me all the faith in the world."

I drove to the radio station the next morning instead of calling in and risking spotty cell service. Inside I saw the Voice in all his glory in a soundproof booth, headphones on, and a microphone in front of his face. He was listing the events and meetings that would take place that day, emphasizing those issues that had or would generate a significant amount of public interest. He even played a wolf howl before reminding people that the DNR was hosting a wolf management meeting at seven o'clock that evening at the county building meeting room. Tom cut to commercial and waved me in.

"Have a seat, Sheriff, and put these on," he said, handing me a set of headphones. "We'll be live in ninety seconds. Now sixty... thirty... and we're on." The Voice introduced me. "We have a special guest this morning who has asked for a few minutes of your time. Sheriff John Cabrelli is currently running against Scott Stewart, county executive, to keep his position as the Namekagon County sheriff, and it has been a very heated election. Sheriff Cabrelli has not told me what he intends to talk about this morning. If it strays too far into politics, we will, as soon as possible, allow Scott Stewart the chance to rebut the sheriff's comments. In addition, there will be no questions. So now, without further ado, Sheriff John Cabrelli."

"I want to thank Tom and the station for allowing me this time. I will be brief. I am no longer going to be actively running for sheriff. I have enjoyed engaging with people who care enough to be involved in the political process. I am dedicated to all the citizens of Namekagon County, and I am proud to serve you. In some ways I am new to this community. In some ways I have been here all my life. But I am not confused that this is my home. This is the place I will hang my hat for the rest of my days. My job as sheriff asks... no, demands... that I step up to whatever challenges face the people I serve. No matter the risk, no matter how dangerous.

"I know you have heard about the recent killing of Dustin Stevens. By all accounts, he was a good man who helped his neighbors and community whenever he had something to offer. He had no next of kin, as far as we can find. We have to speak for those who can't speak for themselves. We have much to learn about what happened to him. We—you and I—have a responsibility to find his killer. Wherever we have to go, whatever it takes, as long as the killer is on the loose, he or she is a danger to our small community. I am as certain as I can be that someone else will die before this is over. How do I know? Because he—and

I believe it is a he—is not done with what they started out to do. I think Dustin Stevens either stepped in the way or became a liability and simply was taken out of the picture for the sake of convenience.

"Your law enforcement teams have been working night and day to find this person. Starting this morning, we are redoubling our efforts. I have requested additional help from the State Division of Criminal Investigation. Our anonymous tipline is open twenty-four hours a day, seven days a week. Absolutely every tip we receive will be followed up on. This effort will require my complete attention. The homicide occurred in Namekagon County, which is in my jurisdiction. Please don't be offended if I can't make it to an election forum or if I don't respond to my challenger's most recent statement. My only job is to catch a killer and keep Namekagon County safe, and that is what I intend to do. I think that one of you knows something we need to know. Your confidential tips could help us figure this out.

"To the person or persons we are looking for, I hope you're listening. If you don't hear anything else, hear this. I think you already know my name, but let me refresh your memory just in case. My name is Sheriff John Cabrelli, and I am coming for you. I am going to unravel your plans. We are getting closer every minute."

The sole applause came from the Voice as I left the studio.

My colleagues were more than ready for me when I showed up.

"Before we get rolling on our assignments, we got a call from DA Hablitch," I began. "He wanted to know whether we intended to push on Hetland anymore. I told him that I thought we were squeezing blood from a stone on him. He seems more interested in covering his own butt than anything else. A records check has come back with nothing of interest so far. SI Price sent his coffee cup off for DNA. I don't think he's our man, but that doesn't mean we are going to forget about him."

We went over what we learned from Ken Hetland. It helped us close the loop on the Schmutz robbery, but we still had a killer on the loose. The consensus was that he helped us cover the same ground but with more detail. If anything, it reinforced what we thought.

Then SI Price stepped up to deliver what they had come up with so far. It was connected and confusing. "I'll repeat myself to cover any ground, old or new. Preliminary firearm information has a gun involved in both the armed robbery of Dr. Schmutz and murder of Dustin Stevens. The professor received a leg wound, and Stevens was shot in the elbow joint. After in-depth, albeit preliminary, comparisons it is almost certain that the two recovered bullets were fired from the same gun. The bullets, live cartridges, and the firearm were sent to the crime lab. They will capture a fired round from the Colt Police Positive thirty-two. Then a comparison with the bullets will be made. Thanks to Commander Malone, this process has been expedited. Any evidence that can be captured from the firearm and cartridges will also be entered. It appears likely the firearm was at both scenes. It appears as if the gun was owned by Dustin Stevens, and that it was hung on a wall rack in the Stevens' house. According to Hetland, Stevens took a gun with him to rob Dr. Schmutz. They struggled, and the gun that was in Stevens' hand went off, the bullet striking Dr. Schmutz.

"In one case, the firearm was brought to the robbery by Stevens. In the other case, Hetland said the gun was stored at Stevens' house. It seems likely that Stevens knew the perp, and there may have been some discussion. In both cases, it appears as though the perpetrators were looking for something specific."

Next up was Wisconsin State Patrol Sergeant Kruger. His experience putting cases together was immediately obvious. "We received the report of a motor vehicle versus pedestrian accident at the intersection of Hatchery Road and State Highway 77. The accident was called in by a part-time school bus driver heading toward Musky Falls to fill in for an in-town route. He came up on the scene and, from a distance, observed what appeared to be red taillights swerving back and forth on Highway 77. The lights straightened out and took off west on 77. He pulled over and activated his flashing lights and stop bar. He got out and, with his flashlight, looked around the area. The bus driver saw the victim and immediately called it in through his dispatch center at 6:02 a.m. EMS was dispatched arriving at 6:25 a.m. Due to darkness and distance, the bus driver cannot provide a vehicle description, but it appeared to be a medium-sized vehicle.

"At this point, I would like to switch gears," Sergeant Kruger requested. "All of the reports, times, etcetera are available right now, and I suggest we move to the results of the evidence we gathered and our conclusions. Anyone feel free to interrupt with questions. In our opinion, this was an intentional homicide. Fortunately, the first responders, as well as the bus driver, respected the scene, and that allowed us to reconstruct significant elements. We photographed, scaled, and cast both footwear and tire impressions. The perpetrator made an aggressive attempt to run the victim down as he tried to get away. That is likely what he was trying to do when the bus driver saw him swerve back and forth. Just before impact, the vehicle likely accelerated. It is our opinion the vehicle was traveling between fifty and sixty miles per hour when it made contact with the victim. Stevens went forty feet in the air before ending his flight, slamming into the trunk of a white pine tree. In Dr. Chali's opinion, he was dead on contact from having suffered significant blunt force trauma. After the victim was transported, we, along with the sheriff's personnel, searched the area with metal detectors and found nothing of significance. Everything we did find has been placed into evidence. "In summary, the vehicle involved clearly pursued the victim, Dustin Stevens. We believe the tires are significantly worn Goodrich Mud Terrain T/A KM3 tires—a very popular off-road tire. We found one small area of soft mud that had an almost perfect tire impression. It showed that the tread depth was about 4/32nds. The outside edge of that tire had some wear that was not detected in other impressions. We have also downloaded the traffic cams and did a run down on every plate we could. The one that wasn't local was a preacher visiting Reverend Redburg. Our reports are available to anyone in this task force. Any questions?"

There were none. Everybody was mulling over the information.

"In that case, I do have a request," the sergeant continued.

"Go ahead, Denny," I replied.

"We have gotten some basic information about who distributes or sells this particular tire. We can identify the general area. A trooper from a different district is on his way here to start tracking down who bought or sold these tires. I would like to have someone assist him."

"Officer Good, can you help him out with this?"

"Absolutely!" she said.

Ah, youthful exuberance is an amazing thing, I thought.

I gathered up my stuff and headed to the squad. I decided to pay another friendly visit to Ken Hetland just to see if anything new had occurred to him. My call went right through. He was at a private mill loading timbers on a trailer. He said he would be there for at least the next couple of hours. The mill was a short drive out into the county.

Milling trees into timbers or lumber had been going on in Namekagon County since before its founding. The first mills in Wisconsin were run by harnessing the abundant water and the power it could produce. Machines like the turbine-driven Muley pit saw and steam-powered mills built the country. Huge circular saw blades turned logs into lumber. Some antique steam and water mills are still in operation today.

The mill where Hetland was working was a large portable band sawmill run by a diesel engine. Hetland and another guy were using cant hooks to roll the logs onto a lift that would put it in position for sawing. They lined them up and moved them until they were just right. Hetland and his partner stepped back, and I recognized his partner, Bud.

"Looks like you guys are hard at it," I said.

"Hey, John," said Bud.

"Hello, Sheriff," said Hetland.

Next to the saw were squared-off timbers. "Are these for the building you're working on, Bud?"

"Yup. Ken and I both needed some custom-cut stuff and partnered up to get the mill over here."

Hetland stepped out of the way and into a light breeze, knocking a coating of sawdust off his clothes.

"As soon as Bud and I measure up this first batch of timbers for the sawyer, I'm all yours. Your brother-in-law is just the kind of guy we need on an operation like this."

I watched the sawyer square up some boards. He cut them all square to 5/4-inch thickness. He explained that the wood that went into and came out of the saw belonged to the customer. So, part of his job was to make slab lumber usable. Bud and Ken measured up four sets of timbers. Most were 10x10 and milled to two different dimensions, with some select cuts eighteen feet long. The sawyer said he specialized in the bigger stuff, and he'd use a long flatbed trailer to deliver it to his kiln, which could take a twenty-four-footer. Once everything was set in the kiln, the inside temperature would be raised slowly to about 170 degrees. It would take at least two months to dry. The moisture and characteristics of any given timber were closely watched as it went through the drying process. These pieces were structural components of the buildings they worked on and were expected to last for at least a hundred years.

Hetland finished up and said he was ready to talk.

"We're just working through things and back-checking. I was just wondering if anything else came to mind."

"Believe me, Sheriff Cabrelli, if anything comes to mind, you'll be the first to know."

I arrived back at the sheriff's office in time for SI Price and Dr. Schmutz to go through the contents of his briefcase. To work productively together required some understanding of the documents. The professor found Price to be an able student. One of their first steps was to go over each manuscript. Schmutz had a very detailed but incomplete inventory, and they worked for hours cross-referencing. Everything was there except for a one-hundred-franc Napoleon gold coin and one of the journals—the one most difficult to work with. It included twenty-five pages of text that appeared to be missing every other page. Price and Schmutz discussed at length why this particular journal may be gone.

"As is our procedure, we photocopied each page when we received the journal," said Schmutz.

"Any theories regarding the significance of that journal?" asked Price.

"Actually, yes. Nothing for sure, but some idea. I think the journal is half of a puzzle. By itself, it doesn't lead anyone anywhere. The other half would confound the possessor in the same way. Their half would not get them anywhere. Put the two halves together, and you complete the puzzle. A set of directions and more likely than a map that will lead you someplace.

"There are known examples of this kind of activity, Jared. A sort of a code to find your way back to what were likely ill-gotten gains. Whoever took it must think they can complete the puzzle. I would hazard a guess that it is a 'treasure map.' Co-conspirators—of one ilk or the other—found this a good way to find their way back to hidden loot. It was especially used by seagoing marauders. They covered a lot of territory, and knowing where X marked the spot was a way of recovering their treasures. Many a phony treasure map was sold in the back corner of a dark tavern after too much rum. I have a couple of dozen examples in my files. However, someone went to a great deal of trouble to hide the location of this possible treasure.

"The journal did have some interesting words written on pages that would have followed or preceded those removed. I was able to make contact with a student working on an Ojibwe English dictionary. She was very helpful. If you're interested, I have a list of the words, with translations from Ojibwe to English, though the translations are not perfect. In my opinion, they are a significant part of the journal. Here, take a look."

SI Price read each Ojibwe word and the corresponding English translation:

Namkaagong-ziibi – place of the sturgeon
Mesconsing – Wisconsin, Red Stone River
Naabikwaan – ship
Jiimaan – boat
Bezhigoogzhiik – horse
Waasewizaawizi – gold
Gichigami – Superior
Ajijaak – crane

"Some of these words seem straightforward. For example, the "place of the sturgeon" is likely the Namekagon River, a one-hundred-mile-long tributary of the St. Croix. That doesn't give us an X, but it does start to narrow down a location. Add new pieces to the puzzle, and we get closer and closer.

"We begin to follow these new threads, but just as importantly, the remaining missing pieces become much better defined. In the right situation, we can create the answer to a question based on other known factors. I don't know, of course, but it is highly likely that whoever took the journal from my case now is under the assumption that they have all the puzzle pieces. They have some, but they are wrong," Schmutz said confidently.

"How can you be certain?" Price asked.

"I am because I believe in my heart of hearts that I am the only person alive who knows the rest of the story. I am still missing a few pieces but aren't even close to giving up."

"May I ask, Dr. Schmutz, why are you going through all of this if you already know the story?" asked Price.

Schmutz began to pace as if he were giving a lecture in front of a crowd. "Let me explain. I have willingly taken on the most difficult cases. My people and I have chased history across the world, only to find mostly dead ends. I say mostly but not all. Some go on to become the keystones of history. This project is one like no other. I know I'm right and will not stop until I can prove it to the world.

"You see, there is nothing else like it. It is the story to end all stories. The story I have chased all my life. We really need the trail, and to find that, we will need to recreate history, and that is exactly what we'll do. To us, a seemingly useless artifact that we find on the trail may be as valuable as a gold coin. We are doing what others have failed to do."

CHAPTER 17

I got a phone call from Ron Carver, who said he needed a favor. Kind of a rare circumstance because Ron was more a grantor of favors than a recipient. He asked to meet at a table outside at the far back of the coffee shop. I was just early enough to run into Scott Stewart.

"Sheriff Cabrelli, how are you today? Any progress on the Stevens murder? I understand that you have been successful in stirring up the community. Confidentially, John, I should tell you I had lunch with a group of local business people, and they shared their concerns about a murderer running around Namekagon County. I don't think I'd expect the support of that group if I were you. I'll let you go, but just a piece of advice before I do. This coffee shop is a great little place to while away the time. I don't think it is a place to catch a killer unless one comes in, identifies himself, and orders a latte. Just a suggestion."

Ron Carver came up behind Stewart and said, "Hey, Stewart, I take it you were just leaving."

"Ron Carver, ever your defender."

Ron and I sat. The air was just cool enough to make our coffee steam.

"I need a favor, John."

"What can I do for you?"

"Do you remember meeting Marie Bennet at her shop on the Superior shore?"

"Of course I do. Julie and I joined her for dinner and some of the most pleasant conversation I have had in a long time."

"Well, she would like you and Dr. Schmutz to join her for coffee tomorrow morning at her home on the Namekagon River."

"I'd be glad to visit with her, but right now I am really up to my ears."

"Please, John, it's important to Marie and important to me."

"What does she want to talk about?" I asked.

"I guess you'll find out when you get there. Dr. Schmutz has already agreed."

Dr. Schmutz and I pulled up to Marie's home at the same time. What appeared to be ships' lantern hung by the door. Marie welcomed us in with a warm smile. She wore a colorful long dress with a swooping neckline, one that would be at home whirling and twirling across a Spanish tile patio. A pearl necklace with a large emerald at the center topped it off.

We followed her to a sitting room. While she retrieved coffee from the kitchen, I looked around. A large window overlooked the river. The room's walls were adorned with Marie's paintings and Hugh's ship wood art. It would have been polite and simple to compliment the works, but it wasn't necessary. They were incredible. Each piece stood on its own. Marie invited us to sit, pointing at two antique chairs. She sat in a large high-back chair facing us. There was a regal air about her, and it was easy to see that Dr. Schmutz was quite taken.

"Thank you for coming, gentlemen. I knew this day would

come. Hugh and I discussed this for many years. I do not know what the outcome will be. I do know that I have reached an age where I can no longer serve as the gatekeeper for a very important piece of history. It has remained part of my family for generations. I believe you to be men of integrity. I need to ask a favor. You can say no, and I will understand, but I must ask. I wish to place it in your hands. First, I must share my secret. Without knowing the truth, you could never be able to complete the task."

She was silent. Schmutz began to speak, but she silenced him with a finger in front of her lips.

Then Marie stood up in front of us. "To those who know me today, I am Marie Bennet, a somewhat itinerant artist, but the blood of a hero and pirate queen runs in my veins." Marie slowly unfastened the two top buttons of her dress, revealing the same blazing sun tattoo on the upper part of her left breast that I saw in the drawing at Schmutz's townhouse. "I am a direct descendant of Maria Fuentes Trevain. It is like a breath of fresh air for me to speak those words." Dr. Schmutz gasped.

It was impossible not to feel the power of the moment. Marie rebuttoned her dress, walked over to a shelf on the side of the fireplace and removed an ornate box. She handed it to Dr. Schmutz. His hands were shaking so badly he could not open the latch.

"Go ahead, Dr. Schmutz. Open it. If I am not mistaken, it is just what you have been looking for."

He set the box on a side table and managed to open the hasp. Inside was a leather-bound journal exactly like the one taken during the robbery. He carefully went page by page. The pages would correspond with those in the other journal. Native words also appeared in places that would match. Many meanings from each one. There could be no doubt that this was of historic significance.

After a few minutes, Dr. Schmutz finally spoke. "What do you want us to do?"

"Dr. Schmutz, I need you to join this journal with the one you have. I suspect, but am not certain, of their significance. My family was meticulous in keeping up with written accounts of their journeys. Some that we still have are in archival storage. I hope you will then choose to tell the story of William and Maria Fuentes Trevain to the world. I believe it will be spellbinding."

"Marie, when my briefcase was recovered, one journal was missing. It is the journal that would join with yours. To complete this puzzle, we will have to make do with the photocopies we made."

"We'll make do, but in order for this to work, I need to be available to help Dr. Schmutz fill in the blanks. I'm afraid I cannot do this if I am dead."

I was taken aback, automatically assuming she was ill.

"How can I help you?" I asked.

"Catch the killer that is stalking me before he is successful. We must find him before he destroys the truth and me along with it."

"Why would he want to kill you?" I asked. Marie got up again and walked to the shelves on the opposite side of the fireplace. She retrieved another box and handed it to Dr. Schmutz. Inside was a leather pouch. Inside the pouch were a dozen gold Napoleon 1862 one-hundred-franc gold coins.

"He wants the treasure. He has been looking for it all his miserable life. I believe he is the worst kind of marauder. He may be driven by some sort of honor. I don't know. Dr. Schmutz, you are probably the only person alive who can tell this story. Please share it with me and Sheriff Cabrelli."

The lecturer, world-renowned orator, as much as he tried, could not make the words come out. His eyes were locked on Marie. She gently encouraged him, and soon he spoke.

"There are few lost treasures that have sparked the imagination like the lost treasure of Poverty Island. In 1863, the South was struggling in the Civil War. Cotton was one of the most important items, the production of which was critical to the French. Napoleon III secretly sent French aid—gold coins and bullion—to bail out the Confederacy, determined the South must prevail. Legend says the gold was transported by wagon through Canada and put on a ship in Lake Michigan. The ship sailed toward and through the Potawatomi Islands archipelago by Poverty Island, the burial site of many shipwrecks. This is largely due to that area's ability to brew up, without warning, the most vicious storms that join treacherous currents. Anyway, the ship never arrived in Chicago. There are many stories to account for its disappearance. The two most common are that the Confederate ship was attacked by a Union ship and sunk or seized, or that it became another victim of a Poverty Island storm. Rumor says that the ship had four chests of gold that the crew chained together. To prevent a Union ship from getting it, they were thrown over the side near Poverty Island. There has been no confirmed sign of the lost schooner. Many accomplished historians and researchers have sought the ship with no success. There have even been nationally broadcast television documentaries.

"During this period of time, each seaport was rife with spies from the Union, Confederacy, and various pirates watching for opportunity. A mystery ship would certainly draw the attention of these spies. One ship is thought to have sailed to Poverty Island, but the French and Confederates aboard knew that Union ships and privateers were everywhere.

"Here is what my team and I think may have happened. The gold was divided between the main ship and another schooner, hoping to cut their losses should a ship be lost. The main ship sailed for Chicago and, choosing a course around Poverty Island, was lost. The other ship headed north with its cargo. The captain of that ship could, in 1863, take full advantage of General Winfield Scott's weakness in what was called Scott's Great Snake, or the Anaconda Plan. The idea was to squeeze the South out. Instead of trying to make their way through the blockade, they would sail north to the Soo Locks and into Lake Superior and connect there with active Confederate sympathizers. There was no evidence to suggest that the second ship was successful—at least until the last three years. There have been many finds of interest along the St. Croix and Namekagon Rivers, including French gold coins all dating before 1863 with the same proof marks."

"What is the value of the gold?" I asked.

"Value is hard to determine. From a historical perspective, it's priceless. From a dollar perspective, it's estimated to be worth somewhere in the neighborhood of four hundred million dollars."

"Four hundred million, that is plenty of motive. Also, plenty of incentive to try and locate the ship. Why do you think it hasn't been found?" I asked. No one spoke.

Then Marie said, "They are looking in the wrong place. I think the story that everyone believes is only partly true. I believe William Trevain was the captain of one of the gold ships."

"Take a look at this, gentlemen." Marie walked over to an umbrella stand and pulled a sword out.

Schmutz identified the weapon from across the room. "Oh my goodness, it's a CS & Star Foot artillery sword. Where did that come from?" From what I could tell, it was like the one he showed me at his townhouse.

"I've had it all my life," she replied. "Ironically, we used to play pirates with it. Sheriff, if you wouldn't mind, could you bring the seaman's chest out from under the window seat over there.

The trunk was heavy. She again invited Dr. Schmutz to do the honors. The chest contained Civil War uniforms neatly folded, separated by a wooden divider. Union blue on one side, Confederate gray on the other. Marie laid the gray uniform first, the blue next to it.

"The bars and loop and the three stars are the insignia of a Confederate sea captain. The other uniform wears the silver fouled anchor and two braids. The uniform of a Union sea captain." Below the uniforms were two flags, the Confederate Stars and Bars and the Union Stars and Stripes.

Schmutz asked Marie if he could look through the rest of the contents.

"Of course, Dr. Schmutz. That is why you are here."

The next layer had several journals, well preserved. But the greatest treasure of all was a waxed folder sealed on the edges with what appeared to be pitch tar.

"I have never opened any of the documents in that envelope. I think now is the appropriate time." Schmutz asked Marie if she had a hair dryer, a thin-bladed paring knife, and two pairs of tweezers. She quickly retrieved the items.

Schmutz laid the packet on a cutting board. We watched silently as he plugged in the hair dryer on the low setting and began to carefully heat the pine tar seal. It took quite some time before the packet was opened. Schmutz used the tweezers as if he were doing surgery on a living being. He pulled back one side of the envelope at a time, lifting one corner, then the opposite, using the thin-bladed knife to separate the edges. Soon the folder came free and was gently folded over to expose the contents. Inside were two pieces of parchment paper.

"Oh my Lord," Schmutz exclaimed. I thought the professor was going to faint.

The packets contained letters of marque and reprisal, one issued to William Trevain and signed by Jefferson Davis, president of the Confederacy, and one to Samuel Benson, signed by

Abraham Lincoln, president of the United States. "This is a truly remarkable find."

Schmutz continued, "Let me explain. In response to aggressive attacks on Union ships, Abraham Lincoln issued Proclamation 81. The proclamation deemed Confederate-issued letters of marque to be pretend as the United States did not recognize the Confederacy as a legitimate nation. In the proclamation he warned all persons attacking Union ships would be tried and sentenced as pirates. This only served to fuel the Confederate fire. The Confederates had few ships at the beginning of the war. The Union had many and access to the vast pineries which provided lumber for many more. So at any opportunity, the South boarded and took the Union ships and pressed them into Confederate service. The uniforms in the trunk are those that belonged to a privateer. Not just any privateer, but a man of the sea who, with his loyal crew, became the scourge of those who challenged him.

"It all makes sense. William Trevain was part of a secret mission. I believe he was part of a bold plan to save the Confederacy. In a matter of minutes, he could turn his ship and crew from a Southern marauder to a Yankee ship. Change of uniforms, hoist the right flag, and they were given free passage. They probably found the uniforms on a Union ship they took. He was a wanted man. The Union offered a ten-thousand-dollar reward for his capture. He stopped being William Trevain, sailed through the Soo Locks flying the Stars and Stripes, guided by Confederate spies disguised as Union soldiers. Once on Lake Superior, he was gone."

"Okay, Marie, let's talk about why you think there is someone out to kill you," I said.

"I went down to our storage locker one afternoon. The padlock on our unit was lying on the ground. At first, I thought nothing was taken, but when I looked more carefully, I found some things missing: a trunk full of old papers and, sadly, some of the captain's logs. I'd never had any problems with theft before. I called the manager, and he replaced the padlock.

"Then last year we had heavy snow. It knocked off my rain gutters. I left them lying in the yard until I got around to hiring someone. Hugh was so handy with all these things. Well one day, I was sitting on a bench in the front yard. A fellow pulled up in a truck and got out. He approached me and took off his hat. He was a handyman and noticed the gutters had fallen down. He offered to fix them. It needed doing, so I said yes. In an hour or two, the gutters were back where they belonged. He asked if I needed any other work done. I asked him if he could look at a leaky faucet in the kitchen. He said it was an old type of faucet, and all it needed was a new washer. I left him to his work, and before you know it, he was doing all sorts of little projects.

"It was late afternoon when I remembered that I needed to drop off a package a mile down the road. I told him I would be right back. When I got to the end of the driveway, another neighbor stopped to visit, and she offered to drop off the package. I know how foolish it was leaving a stranger in my house. He obviously expected I would be gone longer than I was. I walked in, and he was going through papers on my desk. He glared at me, said, 'No charge,' and walked out."

"Did you call it in?" I asked.

"No, I didn't. What would they say? Most likely that I was a foolish old woman who let a stranger in her house."

"Anything else happen?"

"Never saw him again. As you know, I don't have many neighbors, but I told all the ones I do have."

"Marie, other than your neighbors, who knows about this?"

"You two, my attorney, and a consultant I work with."

"I don't know exactly what is going on here, but there is

something. If I come across someone of interest, do you think you could identify the person who was here with a picture?"

"I could do you one better. He had distinctive features, things an artist notices. I can draw him for you."

While we waited, scenes of firing cannons and sword fighting on the deck of a three-masted schooner flooded my head. Dr. Schmutz's energy was infectious. After all his efforts, he now knew for sure he was on the right track. His best researchers would be ready to jump to the task. They would work day and night putting together pieces of the puzzle. His scheduled presentation at the university would be much different than the one he would have given yesterday. I couldn't help but wonder if they would have enough chairs.

After about five minutes, she handed me the drawing. Alarm bells went off in my head.

"If he shows up again, I want you to call 911. I'll have cars flying your way."

"Thank you for your concern, Sheriff, but just so we are clear, I am not totally helpless." ❧

CHAPTER 18

I headed right for the sheriff's department. Cell service was spotty at best in this part of the county, so when my phone rang the voice on the other end was hard to understand. It sounded like a highly agitated SI Price. The call dropped, and then my pager went off. My squad radio commanded me to switch down to TAC 1. SI Price came through but was unwilling to transmit any of what he wanted to tell me.

Dispatch said, "Sheriff, Price is waiting for you in your office. He said it is critical. We have spoken to Chief Delzell. She will meet you there."

SI Price met me at the door, his face beet red. "Sheriff, I just got the DNA results back from Madison. The cup you ran for Ken Hetland definitely didn't come back to Ken Hetland. It came back to Andrew J. Benson who has a sheet a mile long, which includes several violent offenses. This guy is bad news."

"Did you ask the lab to confirm their finding?" I asked.

"Yes, they confirmed it. Benson's DNA is in the databank. It was used to tie him to a manslaughter case. His prison picture came over. Hetland is Benson." Price kept going rapid-fire. "I was able to pull up lots of information on him. He's a bad guy who escaped from a Georgia medium security correctional facility where he was doing time for aggravated battery, fraud, and burglary. During the escape, he beat a correctional officer almost to death. Two months after the escape, Benson was the chief suspect in the theft of archival files from the document room at a Savannah maritime museum. Fuzzy security camera photos match with Benson. Fingerprints were retrieved from a glass case. The real Ken Hetland is listed as a missing person. He was last seen two years ago. Safe bet he's lying in a cold grave somewhere."

I handed Marie's rendering to Price. He immediately recognized the likeness to the prison picture.

"Where did you get this?" he asked.

"A woman who lives up on the Namekagon River near the county line just drew it for me. It is the image of a man who she believes will try to kill her." As I filled Price in, the pieces of the puzzle started to fall into place. Hetland had been cooperative in every way. He described Dustin Stevens as his only friend. It was almost sure the last person our homicide victim ever saw was Hetland/Benson. They were partners working together in rural Namekagon County. My last contact with Hetland/Benson was when he and Bud were loading timbers together. Not the behavior of a wanted criminal, unless he was a very smart one. Hetland/Benson and Stevens were involved in something together. Stevens didn't survive the partnership.

SI Price and I made a priority conference call to Bear. Price briefed him on what we had as well as the sources. Two other voices joined the call from Bear's end. No more than ten minutes had passed when Bear said, "We're on it. Where are you going to be, Cabrelli?"

"As soon as I hang up, I'm going to start running this guy down, as quietly as I can. I would love it if I could keep an eye on him until we're ready. Maybe try to watch him in plain sight. I think I know where he's working right now. I am going to get a couple of my people together and see what we can come up with. If this guy turns out to be Benson, he's dangerous. That could change things fast. We need a positive ID. Can you get us a mugshot, Bear?"

"Okay, John. We'll run the ball and find out everything we can on this end. I need you to make sure you've got people working with the incoming data. Somebody filed a missing person report or something else with law enforcement. I've got a feeling about this guy, nothing for sure, just a feeling. We need to know what kind of case we've got. We'll build our case from this end." As quick as he'd come, Bear was gone.

SI Price and Chief Delzell took the job of running the information intake. It appeared to be a complicated process, but both were very familiar with how it was done. Information was received from whatever source and entered into the computer database and automatically cross-referenced. A single word would generate millions of responses. We searched using a different input system that removed useless choices. The computer started to create a profile, supporting that profile with known information. We needed to run down Andrew Benson and any known associates. Malone's team contacted Ken Hetland's next of kin. They also got a copy of the missing person's report. Hetland was a carpenter and worked at a gun shop two nights a week. He had disappeared after a day of work. The shop owner said two firearms disappeared as well.

The first piece of information came in. Hetland/Benson had been issued a parking ticket at the Museum of the Great Lakes three months prior by Superior police. He had not paid the ticket, and Superior wouldn't pursue it. They did what most departments did; if he was stopped for something else, the ticket would show up.

We needed to be ready to move in on Hetland/Benson at a moment's notice—no waiting for a tactical team. We'd have to hide in plain sight and hope Hetland/Benson was unaware that we'd identified him. If we played our cards right, a small group may be advantageous.

Bear made contact with the Georgia Bureau of Corrections. They were glad to send over everything they had, including photographs that positively identified Benson. The corrections officer Benson battered was permanently disabled, and they were hopeful Benson would be returned to their facility. The cell inventory listed several books with titles about marine history and the Civil War.

All the intel in the world was not as important as knowing where Benson was. I shared the location of the sawmill where Benson was last seen and advised everyone that Bud Treetall was unaware that he was working with an escaped convict. We'd proceed to arrest Benson on outstanding warrants instead of trying to build a new case on Ken Hetland's disappearance. Benson wouldn't surrender; he would fight.

We brought up a large map. We needed to move in and take positions that would keep us out of Benson's view but have him clearly in ours, and that would cut off his escape. Everyone was somewhat familiar with the area, but trapper and hunter Deputy Pave knew it like the back of his hand. He showed us locations that would give us the best advantage and, hopefully, a clear target. Some places had room and cover for a squad. Others required hiking in. Once in position, I would give the direction to my people. Earbuds kept things as quiet as possible; communication was to be kept at a minimum. SI Price suggested that we send up his drone to gather current information. That was vetoed. Prisons had begun using drones to watch prison yards, and a drone overhead could tip Benson off.

Backup units from other departments were directed by dispatch to meet us at an off-the-road vacant lot. It was critical that we be able to get our people in position without alerting Benson.

After the briefing, our small team moved quickly and quietly into position, adjusting location based on site-specific situations. When everyone advised they were where they needed to be, driving two squads, Pave and I moved to where the sawmill was to make the arrest. Two men, the mill operator and his assistant, approached us. Neither was Benson.

"Where is the rest of your crew?" I asked

"You mean Bud and Ken?"

"Yeah, I thought they needed a bunch of sawing done."

"They do. These timbers are ready to be moved. In the meantime, we got this big saw ready to go."

"Where are they going?"

"Once we're done with the smaller timbers, we are going to move to Ken's job site with the big saw. He needs two ridge beams that were too big to be sawn with the smaller mill. Ken, Bud, and a couple of our guys went ahead to level the ground where we want to set the saw."

The job site was in the backcountry. Pave knew the location and recognized an opportunity when it came his way. He winked at me. "I know that road. Are you going to be able to make those curves? It's a pretty twisty two-track."

"I think so, as long as we don't meet an oncoming car or need to back up," I replied.

Pave offered to give them a police escort, allowing us to hide in plain sight. The mill boss accepted immediately. No siren, just flashing lights.

Pave casually asked me if it was okay with me.

"Okay with me, Pave. I'll advise dispatch."

I called in. "Pave is giving a police escort to a lodge at the end of

Deer Run Road. Ken Hetland hired a sawyer to bring his sawmill to the project site. The saw owner is going to be hauling a big band saw rig in on these two-tracks and asked if Pave would use lights to lead them. I'm taking a parallel fire lane, coming up a little behind and out of sight. According to the mill owner, there are several workers on site, including Ken Hetland. It is about two miles from our current location."

That radio communication set everyone in motion. Backup units were needed to close the two miles to the new location. The tactical wheels started turning, preparing to engage a wanted criminal. Rifle magazines were slapped home, rounds chambered.

The dispatcher, the data center, and the backup knew exactly where Pave was headed. It was anybody's guess what would happen; it was Pave's hand to play.

The sawyers started moving at a reasonable pace, making sure that all the safety rules for wide load escort were followed. Pave met only a couple of vehicles coming the other way during the escort. Both were pickups that had to back up to let them through. The road curved so sharply, the saw made it by inches.

I drove in, leaving my squad to block the road, and began to bushwhack my way in. Pave reached the destination and advised dispatch of the situation. Our person of interest there was working with Bud Treetall and two members of the saw crew to prep the location where the saw would be set up. Pave recognized Bud's truck parked next to a pickup that he guessed belonged to Hetland/Benson. The last vehicle was a four-door truck with the name of the company doing the millwork. All the men were busy moving equipment and tools out of the way. The crew waved at the incoming vehicles but continued to work, making sure the place where the saw would be set up was just right.

The big logs were laid out about thirty feet from where the saw would sit. A skid steer with a grapple on the front looked like what they would use to position the logs. Heavy, exacting work, just the kind of thing people like Bud were made for. The sawyer and his crew measured, leveled, and moved the saw into the exact spot. The work was fascinating to watch, but Pave wasn't confused about his purpose. Benson showed no signs of suspicion.

After the saw was set up, everyone took a breather before the work started.

"Thanks a lot for suggesting that escort, Deputy," the sawyer said. "I'm afraid that big rig of ours is just not made for these narrow two-tracks. Once it's in here, it's fine, but there to here takes some maneuvering." He looked at his crew. "Well, let's get to it, guys. Ken, get that skid steer squared up."

Benson jumped onto the skid steer and began to position it, then stopped. "Hey, Deputy, could you move your car over a bit? Don't want to ding county property."

Something told Pave he'd been made, but he kept going. He got in his squad and started to move it when two giant jaws came smashing down on the driver's side of the car. The grapple dropped down and flipped the sheriff's unit onto its roof. Benson bailed off the machine, ran to his truck, jumped in, and tore off down the road.

I heard Deputy Plums call on the radio, "EMS 10–33. Officer down, requesting JAWS. Deputy Pave is pinned in his vehicle." I ran as fast as I could down to the two-track. I made it to about fifty yards before Benson passed me. I brought my rifle up and fired as his truck smashed my squad out of the way.

When I got to the scene, Plums was on his stomach, inched in as far as he could into Pave's driver's side window of the smashed-up squad on its roof. Pave was pinned inside and covered with blood, but he was still talking and conscious.

Using his immense strength, Bud tore at the passenger's door like a madman. The saw boss suggested we try and pull the door off with the machine. Bud looped a chain around the door frame and slowly backed up to take up the slack. The door screeched, metal against metal. Inch by inch it started to pull away from the rest of the body. Just when it looked like it was going to work, a tension point held in place on the roof of the driver's side popped like a gunshot, and Pave moaned.

The last thing I wanted to do was step away from the rescuers, but getting information out on the air was critical. Every minute put Benson farther away from us. I asked dispatch for a clear channel and gave all the information I could give to anyone listening. The best I could do was describe his vehicle and direction of travel. Next came the data center with photos, date of birth, and any other information.

Then everyone stopped; their blood ran cold. The rescuers backed away as gasoline began to run from what looked like a fuel line or maybe a puncture in the tank, a continuous fuse to the tank. Pave was trapped, and any further efforts on our part might just be what generates the spark that burns my deputy, my friend, and the father of two girls alive. I ordered everyone to turn off their radios and the incoming units to go silent. Minutes later, the fire chief came puffing down the drive.

"Which squad does Pave have?" he yelled.

"The new four-door pickup," I replied

"Bed storage over the wheel wells?" he asked.

"Yes."

"There is suppressant foam in those storage compartments. Can one of you guys get at them?"

Plums pulled out of the window and ran to the rear. I pushed on the pop lock, and it wanted to go but wouldn't. Bud came over with a crowbar, its end wrapped in a big shop rag, and told everyone to back up. He drove a wrecking bar with his bare hands under the top edge. He put all his muscle into it and slowly pried the top open. Once Bud had room, he reached in with his bare fingers and ripped the top completely off. He handed me the foam cylinder, I ran around the truck, opened the nozzle, and was rewarded with a white blast of fire retardant.

The fire unit with the JAWs came around the corner, followed by the unmuffled exhaust from a first responder's vehicle. The fire crew disembarked, quickly assessing the situation and realizing what the foam meant. Jimmy the Jeep rendered aid the best he could through the window and encouraged Pave to hold on while waiting for the rest of the EMS crew to arrive with the ambulance. Another firefighter recruited Bud to help remove pieces of the truck. Jimmy covered Pave with a heavy protective blanket as chunks of metal flew off.

It took only minutes for a highly trained crew to get him down, slide him out on another heavy blanket, and transfer him onto the stretcher. I tried to assure him that he would be okay. He had nothing to say about his state of affairs. He did, however, want to know if he'd really been hit with a skid steer. Pave was adamant that he would be part of the arrest team when they got the guy. I promised to call his daughters and get them to the hospital. One of his daughters was studying criminal justice at the local tech school, and the other was in culinary school in Duluth. Pave was loaded and on the way. It was hard to determine the extent of his injuries, but it looked bad.

The chase was now on. I spoke with Bear and brought him up to speed. My overwhelming urge was to run this guy down. Do what real cops do—get bad guys off the street—but my first responsibility was to get to the command center. When one of our own is hit there are no holds barred. Everybody wanted to put the crosshairs on Benson.

Things were moving faster than we were. Every cop, every parking attendant, every postal delivery person now knew what

Benson looked like. I had perforated the side of his truck with my AR, so every repair shop was watching for bullet holes. BOLOs were sent out to radio and television stations. I knew the task before us would require all we could muster. Andrew Benson was out there and getting more dangerous by the moment. Our meager force needed to operate with purpose; everything we did needed to be focused on catching Benson and taking him out.

Pave was a popular guy in this community, coached baseball, and volunteered with Northern Lakes Academy and Fishing Has No Boundaries. Med Flight was waiting in the football field. As soon as they lifted off for Duluth, I started to get things in order.

Blame for what happened was swirling around my shoulders. I had taken a chance to capture a killer, and he was on the loose again. People were pitching theories like horseshoes. Pave was one of the best people I knew. He was fearless, ready to take on any challenge. I was feeling pain, but there was no room for that.

I flew into Musky Falls lights and siren. Everybody made way. I bulled my way into the office, and those people who weren't on the road quickly gathered around, asking me what our plan would be.

Just as I began to speak, the meeting room door swung open and banged hard against the door stops. Scott Stewart blew in and shouted at me. "So, another one of our finest law enforcement officer's life hangs by a thread because of Sheriff John Cabrelli. Enough is enough. Death follows in his footsteps. Cabrelli, you are a dangerous failure. Hiding in this conference room will not bring this killer to justice. It was a horrible thing I had to do, Sheriff, but I've made a formal request to the governor that you be replaced immediately. I have recommended that Chief Mary Delzell take over command of both the Musky Falls Police Department and the Namekagon County Sheriff's Department. I suggested that the appointment be effective immediately."

The room was quiet.

"What was the governor's response to that request, Mr. Stewart?" Chief Delzell asked.

"He hasn't got back to me yet, but I expect to hear any time now. It is important that we don't wait until the last minute to move on this thing. So, I am taking over with Chief Delzell effective immediately."

Silence resounded.

"Chief Delzell and I will go across the street to have me sworn in by Judge Kritzer right now. When I return, I will lay out my plan to capture Benson."

One of the older senior deputies spoke up from the back of the room. "You might want to call over there before you and the chief go to the courthouse."

"We have no time to waste. Chief Delzell, are you ready?"

"I don't know if I'm ready, but I intend to go with you." Stewart crashed out the door with the chief trailing along at a slightly less dramatic pace.

I used that moment to speak to everyone in the room. "Whether or not this government appointment thing goes through has little to do with what we're called to do. We continue where we left off. Just for the record, I don't intend to step down as sheriff. However, I can understand that there may be people in this room who are not interested in working with me. We don't have people to spare, but we can spare anyone who is not 100 percent up for the task. So, let's get this over with. Any of you who want to go are good to go. I will require that anyone who does go becomes part of the intel team, effective immediately. So, let's get this over. Who's going?"

From the back of the room came a gruff but pleasant voice. It was a guy known as Schultze. Schultze had retired at age seventy, unwilling to do things any other way than his own. Scott Stewart was instrumental in using age discrimination against Schultze without anybody noticing. He retired before I took the sheriff's job.

His retirement lasted about twenty-four hours. The day after he retired, he applied for the new part-time bailiff position and got hired by Judge Kritzer.

"Well, Sheriff Cabrelli, the stupidity of what's going on here is a little bit hard to understand. But I'm old, so maybe I've shifted into low gear. You know, this thing is too complicated for my old brain. I'd be willing to bet you will have your answer from the judge any moment now."

It was as if it had been scripted. Stewart burst back into the room, pained by indignation, followed by a laughing Chief Delzell. Unwilling to give up the floor, Schultze asked, "What did the judge have to say, Stewart? Should Sheriff Cabrelli start packing his kit and caboodle?"

Chief Delzell saved him from himself. "Sheriff, we didn't talk to Judge Kritzer. His clerk told us he couldn't be reached. It seems that he had warned everybody with plenty of notice that he had a new pup and was going to spend the week at his cabin up by Seeley chasing grouse," the chief reported.

"I told you ya shoulda called," said Schultze.

"You should have told me, you old fool," barked Stewart.

"You should have asked me, stupid." No one chose to leave except Stewart.

Whether they supported me or not, everyone was on board and ready. ❖

CHAPTER 19

We'd requested air support from the Wisconsin State Patrol and the Blue Hills Flyers, a local club flying out of the Namekagon County Airport, coordinated with the State Patrol and ground searchers looking for Benson's truck. The county lines were as secured as those counties could make them.

I've never been much for sitting on my hands, and this was no different. The chief, SI Price, and none other than Schultze himself took over the command center. As tense as I was, I couldn't help but laugh when Schultze walked in wearing a long-barreled Smith and Wesson revolver.

He smiled back. "K-38 Smith and Wesson, the finest wheel gun ever made. I won six Barney Awards in a row with it. Made of steel, not Tupperware. Got to be ready. Six rounds where they belong is a lot better than seventeen in the Hinterlands. By the way, Len Bork is coming down here to give us a hand. I expect he'll be toting his 1911."

Before I went out on the road, we talked things through. "We have a direct line to Commander Malone. He has support people on the way. We suspect that Benson, an escaped convict, has killed two people and attempted to kill Deputy Pave. He is also wanted for a burglary of a museum in Savannah, Georgia. He got a parking ticket at the Museum of the Great Lakes in Superior. His behavior has a pattern; I think he has a goal. Let's just say that he did burglarize the maritime museum in Savannah, then he disappears for two years before he shows up again. Then maybe his next step is Namekagon County, and he builds himself a life here. He does construction with Dustin Stevens, working out in the open—buying supplies, bidding jobs, visiting local restaurants, becoming a member of the community, even helping us on the Stevens homicide. There is no way I believe Namekagon County is his final destination. We need to know where he's headed, and wherever that is, we need to be there waiting when he shows up. Commander Malone has detailed agents to find out what specifically was taken from the museum. When the Georgia Bureau of Investigation or the Wisconsin Division of Criminal Investigation have anything, they will report it to you. At that point, work with the field agents to pick up the next lead and combine relevant information. I don't think I'm wrong. He's not in the wind; Benson is headed somewhere."

"We're on it, John," said the chief.

It was a relief to hit the road. I started at the beginning with Bud, who was still at the construction site. He glanced up at my car and quickly looked back down. I approached him but didn't say anything. I just waited until he spoke.

"Is Pave still alive?" he asked.

He's in intensive care in Duluth. They are dealing with the most critical issues right now. I am expecting an update when they can. A trooper took his family to the hospital. Bud, I need to know everything you know about this guy. We think his real name is Andrew Benson. We also think that he killed a man in Georgia, Ken Hetland, and assumed his identity. We also suspect he killed

Dustin Stevens."

"How could he have fooled me like that?"

"He fooled us all. How did you meet him?" I asked.

"We ran into each other at Musky Falls Lumber. I was working on that timber frame reconstruction. I rented a long trailer from the log home guys. I could get most of my timbers on it, but I knew I would have to figure out something for the real big ones later. Ken, or whatever his name is, was arguing with Shorty. He saw my truck and trailer and came up to me. He was all sorts of friendly. He had some timbers, too, and needed them hauled. Shorty wouldn't do it, which is why I rented the trailer I was using. Hetland asked me if I would haul his and split the moving cost. I knew he was the guy whose partner had been killed, and taking a little bigger load wouldn't be much of a big deal, so I did. He told me he had some solid paying projects and wondered if I could help him out. I felt sorry for the guy, and the truth of it was that I needed the help. Well, it turned out he was a darn good carpenter. I'm ashamed to say that I liked working with him."

"Did he say anything about family, friends, or anyone else?"

"Not that I remember. I guess he mentioned an elderly aunt he planned to visit one weekend. I think she was in an assisted living place. But I don't know that he ever did. He liked staying out in the backcountry. I know lots of nights he just slept outside by the job he was working on. He was friendly enough, but I could tell deep down he really didn't like people much."

"What about Dustin Stevens? Anything about him?"

"I already told you everything I know about him. Like I said before, he was a good guy who got tied up in a bad deal. I know the whole thing really bothered him. He was definitely happy about having a work partner."

"How do you think he knew we were on to him?"

"When Pave showed, he started acting different. We had that

monster skid steer for the week, and it was costing quite a bit. When the saw rig pulled in, I was pretty happy about Pave lending a hand, but Ken started looking around. He started greasing the machine, tightening up the tracks, testing the grapple. It took us a solid hour to set the saw and level it. Ken said something to Pave, and Pave jumped in his squad and started moving in reverse. I think you know the rest."

"Bud, I want you to pick up your tools and get out of here. I don't want you to come back until I give you the all-clear."

"There is a lot to do here. I can't just pack up and go."

"It's by order of the sheriff. I'll help you pick up the stuff that's easy to grow legs."

Thank goodness for Canada geese honking as they landed on the water and the quack of a hen mallard, because without that, there wouldn't have been any sound at all. We loaded the tools, and Bud started the truck to go. He drove ahead a few feet, then backed up. With a look of pure sadness, he said, "I'm sorry, John. I didn't know he was a bad guy," and drove away.

I started a thorough search of the job site. Cutoffs, scrap lumber, and rotten boards had been piled up on an area of cleared ground ready to burn. I was ready to pull out when dispatch connected me with the task force and one of the Blue Hills Flyers.

"Sheriff, I think I have a positive on the truck you're looking for. Anyway, it is a truck that meets the description. What do you advise?"

"What's the location?" I asked.

"It is in the national forest just over the county line near Birch Road. It looks like it is on the shoulder. The truck is hard to see if you're coming from the south or west. Looks like maybe there's some brush piled on it. I just caught a view of it when I was taking an east loop. I'm trying to look like someone taking flying lessons. I haven't seen anyone. Should I stand by?" he asked.

"Do the best you can to keep your eyes on the truck. Switch down to the emergency frequency and transmit through the com center," I said.

"Sheriff, we aren't able to monitor or transmit on that channel," said the pilot.

"Ten-four. Keep your eyes on him."

Then the dispatchers did what they did so well: coordinating units heading for a threat.

"Still no activity, Sheriff. No... wait... a truck is heading north a mile or more behind the pickup. Stand by a minute. It looks like a contractor's quad cab. Probably someone cruising timber. He's going to run smack into the truck."

The pilot gave us play-by-play from the air while units moved in. When the oncoming truck reached the possible suspect's vehicle, it stopped, and the driver and passenger got out. The driver of the truck full of bullet holes was waiting. It appeared he first clubbed the driver to the ground with an axe handle or something and then turned on the passenger. They didn't see it coming. He used the contractor's truck to push his own pickup off the road. He stopped the truck and took out something.

"He's doing something, Sheriff," said the pilot. Then he yelled, "Fire! His truck is on fire!"

"Air support, go again!"

"Fire! His truck blew! Must've been gas he had in the can." A dry fall had left pockets of very flammable prairie cordgrass, reed canary grass, and big bluestem. "Sheriff, send the fire department before that grass starts burning," the pilot said.

"Fire is on the way, and so is EMS," the dispatcher responded.

Then another call from air support. "I can see one of the people he attacked lying on the road."

"Follow the truck," I said. "Our people should be there soon."

"I hope it's real soon. I'm low on fuel."

Benson absconded with the truck, put the pedal down, and turned off at the first forest road. The pilot had to pull off, and another small plane came up and took his place, but they couldn't locate Benson again under the canopy of trees. The Chequamegon-Nicolet National Forest, put aside by Theodore Roosevelt, had a little over a million and a half acres. Lots of room to hide. Grab a powerboat from one of the Superior marinas and add twenty million acres of water.

Things were getting more complicated. Thirty percent humidity, plenty of fuel, dry conditions, and gusty wind are a rare combination. Benson's truck had started a rip-roaring grass fire that was running down the road shoulder like a racehorse. Big bluestem will get eight or more feet tall. Prairie cordgrass loves to burn. When your back door is the national forest, a little breeze gives flames plenty of room to wander.

Grass trucks from the surrounding fire departments hit Benson's fire hard. Things looked like they would spread, but the conditions and time of year let the experienced firefighters stay ahead. Still, the fire had done its job for Benson; we lost track of him.

The ambulance transported the two loggers to Musky Falls. A stout tree branch had been Benson's weapon of choice. Both men would survive, but Benson had dished out some vicious licks.

My rifle shots had punched a hole in the gas tank on Benson's truck. A trail of gas came up to the point where the truck quit, and it became the fuse. He must have used a metal gas can on the road to supplement the fire.

The search would continue unabated, with units from several different jurisdictions pitching in to look for the Sande County Forestry Consultant truck. Photos of Benson were being circulated and, as might be expected, he had made contact with many of the locals.

I knew that Benson wasn't hiding. Maybe short-term he was, but he was going someplace. He covered over a thousand miles from Savannah, Georgia, to Namekagon County, injuring and killing people to get here. He had made his way into the community. There had to be a reason. I needed to get ahead of him, put this puzzle together. When the time came, Benson would surely resist, and when he did, I would kill him if I had to. He would not get away again.

CHAPTER 20

I spent a sleepless night in the command center. The chief, the former chief, and SI Price went home. Bailiff Schultze announced he would find a spot in a chair. He warned me that after all the years in law enforcement he no longer kept his 38 revolver on the nightstand—too jumpy when somebody or something woke him up. He kept it on a dresser a few feet away from his bed. That required he take a couple of steps before he picked up his hogleg (as he called it) and decided whether or not he was going to shoot someone. The top of a file cabinet would serve dresser duty tonight. Didn't take him long, and he was snoring away in a chair with his feet propped up on another.

For the first time that day, no one was talking to me. My heart begged for a few minutes of family time sitting by the fire. But I didn't deserve it. The mantle of guilt weighed heavily on my shoulders, again. Pave was lying unconscious in the hospital, burning up his family time by the minute, with a tube allowing him to breathe. A tooth on the grapple punctured through one lung and did plenty of ancillary damage. I could envision his family sitting by the bed holding the red call button, an intensive care lifeline. The priest from their church praying with them, hoping miracles really happened.

It was a mistake to have taken Benson so lightly. He attacked at the first opportunity. Now he was gone, leaving only a path of maximum destruction.

Beyond the command center walls, the searchers were still searching. I was of little help right now, but I would be ready when I needed to be.

I fell asleep twice reading officers' reports. At five o'clock in the morning my cell rang. It was Bear. It wasn't unusual for him to call this time of day. He was known for staying awake all night. We used to tease him that he operated best under the cloak of darkness.

"Bear, what's up?"

"No rest for you, Sheriff. Didn't anyone ever teach you that you had to be ready twenty-four seven? Seriously, though, what's the report on Pave?"

"He's holding his own. The hospital may Med Flight him to Mayo. They're going to evaluate him in the morning."

"Tanya and I are praying for them."

"He's a good man, Bear."

"He's also an experienced law enforcement officer who knew the risks when he put on the badge, and he's lived in that environment for a long time. I know you, Cabrelli. Anything that happens to your people falls on you. You're a good man, John.

"Now down to business. Tell me how we are going to play this, and that's what we'll do. The Georgia Bureau of Investigation agent who caught this case from us is the perfect choice. His daughter did an internship at Atlantic Shipping, where they are getting ready to open a Savannah maritime museum. She and the other undergraduate students were tasked with inventorying documents, diaries, ship logs, and all sorts of other stuff. She remembers the theft well. She knew the thief by the first name of Kenny. She saw him every day; he was one of the temporary workers clearing out junk from an old warehouse. She was interviewed by the Fulton County Sheriff's Office. Of course, after being talked to by the cops, her next call was to her dad.

"The GBI agent and his daughter will be available for a video call at seven. Before the call you will have a copy of the report and her statement. Finally, it turns out that the records, files, and the like were all scanned before the theft in the section where his daughter worked. As always, I have delivered important information to you. No need to thank me. Now wake that new SI I got you from his beauty sleep. He'll need to set this all up. I'll see you at seven." Bear signed off.

I called SI Price, who answered immediately. "Jared, we may have something. I need you down at the command center as soon as you can get here."

No complaint, no whining. "I'm on my way, Sheriff."

Ten minutes before seven we received the scanned documents. The computers were set up, and a GBI techie handled the virtual meeting. Schultze was up, had the coffee going, and joined us to watch the monitor when we started.

GBI Agent Brown sounded like a gentleman with a smooth Southern drawl. "First, let me tell you, Sheriff Cabrelli, this guy you're trying to run down is a genuine desperado. I have some intel that I need to share. Andrew Benson was never really known to us until the last few years when he was arrested for burglary. A patrol officer in Savannah caught him coming out the service door of the museum library in the middle of the night carrying a three-ring binder. When the patrolman tried to search him, Benson attacked and took off. Patrol units searched the area with a dog but didn't find him. The next morning a couple of detectives went to the library to follow up. There was no evidence of forced entry, no alarm, but a custodian had lost his ring of keys a month or so prior. When the chief librarian started looking back in the restricted area, meaning an area where things cannot be checked out of the library but used in-house, he found several files missing.

"The library has a pretty extensive collection of historical documents regarding ships, especially Southern ships during the 'War of Northern Aggression.' It's not uncommon for people, most often history students or maritime history buffs, to use the material in-house. Unfortunately, those files that were taken are irreplaceable. That made them close the barn door before all the cows got out. They hired students to inventory and catalog every page. In addition, each document was scanned into a master database with a backup. That is where my daughter Emily comes in," he said.

Emily was a Georgia beauty. "Thank you, Daddy. I am pleased to be able to help you in any way I can. I was a history major in my sophomore year and was given the opportunity to work directly with the archivists. An anonymous donor was funding a major effort to protect these things as part of the remodeling of the Savannah Maritime Museum. A group of three students were assigned to each archivist. We had one day of briefing. A great deal of time was spent going over security measures. Dr. Schmutz, who was leading the archival process, explained how they intended to prevent any further loss. He also made it clear that any theft or other violation would be punished to the fullest extent of the law. Then we went to work.

"It was a wonderful experience. I completed my yearlong internship, and I was searching for new opportunities. The archive coordinator approached me and asked if I might stay on for another six months. They needed someone to work on a special project. It was fascinating. All of the information involved the war between states and how that played out on the Great Lakes.

It was when I was working on this that I first met Kenny. He was a cleanup man and did not work in the archives. Kenny did come past us several times a day, wheeling a trash bin. Kenny's trash bin, as well as several others, were emptied onto a conveyor belt, and the trash was slowly moved to a disposal bin, but this final inspection was done in case something of interest was swept up or thrown out.

"It was during my time on the Great Lakes archives that the issue came up. I had some very interesting documents, including a well-preserved captain's log. This captain had sailed the Great Lakes for the South during the Civil War. The documents filled two boxes. I asked permission from the director to work through both boxes. He looked at what I had and quickly agreed. He directed Kenny and another man to bring me one of the lighted examining tables and set it up. Other than a brief hello, that was the first time I ever engaged Kenny in conversation.

"Kenny, in a very casual way, asked me what all the excitement was about and what I'd come across. I was so excited that I told him everything about the history of the Great Lakes ships. He told me that he had taken some history classes and remembered hearing about one ship he thought was called the *Andrea*. That was exciting because one of the captain's logs included time on the *Andrea*.

"I never thought much of it after that day. I finished putting things together and took them over to the museum director's office. I was very surprised when the next day Dr. Schmutz asked to meet me in his office. I gave him a briefing about what the files contained, and I could see he was excited. Then he told me that the following day some of the principals of the project were having a luncheon at the museum to raise funds. He asked if I might give a presentation about the findings. I quickly agreed. The next day I spent the morning getting ready for the presentation, using the scanned versions to prepare. I asked Dr. Schmutz if he could bring the originals to the lunch area.

"I was in the reception area, and many of the guests were people I had only read about. I was talking with someone when the museum director approached me. The original file had been misplaced, and he asked if I had any idea where it was. I thought that maybe Dr. Schmutz had it. The director was getting nervous in front of his colleagues, and Schmutz confronted me about the files. The police were called, and the theft was reported. The next day Kenny didn't show up for work."

"So, Emily, did Dr. Schmutz actually know Kenny?" I asked.

"I'm sure they saw each other every day. I don't think they were friends, but I don't know."

"Emily, thank you for your information. SI Price is going to show you ten pictures of possible suspects. One may be Kenny, or none may be Kenny."

Jared showed her the pictures, and without hesitation, on the third one, she picked out Kenny. She was 100 percent sure Kenny was Andrew Benson.

The history student and I talked a while more, and she was trying to be helpful, but she was very involved with her work.

"Just out of curiosity, Emily, now that you're almost done with school, what are your plans?"

"Well, Sheriff Cabrelli, I just finished sending out my resume and application."

"Where are you looking?"

Her dad shook his head, and she laughed. "Georgia Bureau of Investigation."

"Law enforcement, I'm not surprised. Often in law enforcement families, the apple doesn't fall far from the tree. Emily, we've got some openings in Namekagon County."

"Sounds nice. Dad told me it was beautiful country, but it's an up-and-down place to live. Snow up to your butt, temperatures down to twenty below zero. That doesn't really work for a Southern girl. If y'all get tired of the chilly weather, you're welcome down here come February or March. Redfish are just coming out to the flats. Until then, see y'all later."

"Thank you for your help, agent, and good luck to you, Emily."

Everyone signed off but Bear, who piped right up. "Okay, Sheriff, this sounded complicated before; now it's different. I think we're on the road to clearing things up a little. Two people that are connected. Two murders across state lines, maybe more. If we can connect Benson to the murders, it will help us with the Feds if we need it. There is no way that it's coincidental that Dr. Schmutz and Andrew Benson are both in Atlanta at the same time. Now they are both together in Namekagon County, a thousand miles away."

"Eventually Benson is going to show up. We put a national BOLO out yesterday, and our media partners were having a slow week, so they've been playing it up. We got a couple of solid tips but came up empty both times. We're still getting plenty of positive IDs on Benson, but no one has seen him in person since the attack on Deputy Pave," I said.

"I have some available agents that should be here around noon. Put them to work," said Bear. ❖

CHAPTER 21

After our meeting broke up, I studied the map of Namekagon and our border, Sande County. Deputies and police officers were assigned to cover backcountry cabins—two officers to a car, full gear.

I tried calling Dr. Schmutz several times with no success. He mentioned he would shut off his phone when he was working, and I assumed that was the case. I drove up to see him at the lake house in Ashland. His Mercedes was gone. I left a note attached to his front door with evidence tape. I was getting ready to leave when Chief Delzell let me know Bear's people had arrived and were gathering at the area behind the sheriff's office.

Delzell was briefing the agents when I arrived, a mix of a field search team and techies. In the past, drones had been very effective working in the dense Northwoods. They believed in going with what worked in the past. Using a combination of ground searchers and drones allowed an area to be covered quickly and efficiently.

To be honest, I was whipped. I needed a break. The escaped killer made national news. I called the hospital before I went back at it. The considerate nurse explained that the family designated me as someone who could receive condition information on Pave, who was breathing, being fed, and medicated through tubes. Progress was slow, and there had been no decision about transferring him.

SI Price burst into the room and told me there was a problem brewing in the parking lot. I walked out the door and was greeted by Scott Stewart and at least two dozen armed men dressed in various forms of outdoor clothing, from blaze orange deer hunting coats to military surplus, everyone armed.

"Sheriff Cabrelli, we are here to help with the search," Stewart announced.

I didn't respond immediately; I was full up. Volunteer searchers were not an unusual part of life in the north country. Deputy Plums had a great deal of experience with organizing searches. I told both to come over to the sheriff's office. They were both Namekagon County born and raised. Adding a few searchers didn't put them off at all.

Plums stepped up and faced Stewart's group. "Listen up! This is a law enforcement led effort, and that's how it will stay. I know several of you guys, and with all your experience in the backcountry, you could be a real help, but this is not tracking a wounded deer. This guy is a killer, and given the chance he will kill you. We don't know where he is, but we think he might be hiding out in a backwoods lodge. He worked as a carpenter restoring and remodeling them. He stole a four-door truck with a bed full of forestry gear. The truck is red and white with Sande County Forestry Consultants on the side. For the record, he took this truck from two crewmen after knocking them unconscious with a tree branch. Get careless with this guy, and you could be next. We're starting with some inholdings on gravel roads off Highway 77. One team will go south, the other north. We're going to stay in sight of each other, and each team will have a drone providing a bird's eye view. For right now, everybody into the meeting room to coordinate the search areas."

Searching the wild country of northern Wisconsin was tough going, but with drones and feet on the ground using a grid pattern set up by the State Crime Team, it could happen. Everyone was given a photo of Benson.

Plums addressed the volunteers once more. "I'm not trying to scare anyone away. It is likely that Benson is wanted in at least two states for homicides. He will not go easy, but this doesn't mean we can shoot him on sight. The law requires we use the 'minimum necessary force to effect the arrest.' Benson lives by no such rules. I know some of you folks have younger kids. If you choose to go home, no one is going to say a word. I would advise it. If you stay, there is going to be plenty to do."

"I was planning to use my extensive training to stay here in the command center and coordinate efforts. They are welcome to stay with me," Stewart said. No one responded. They didn't have to; his bravery was shining through for all to see.

"Just so we are clear, Scott, if you stay here, you will be working at the direction of law enforcement," I said. "Any issues with that let's get them out on the table now."

"I can find plenty for you to do, Stewart," Schultze said.

I stayed out with the searchers while we ran our first grids. We came upon two cabins. The first one had the front door nailed shut from the outside. Also nailed to the outside were two-by-fours with nails driven through, sharp points keeping bears from tearing open the door or windows. We pried the door open, and the empty place gave us the chance to practice cabin clearing.

Everybody was on high alert. A mile and a half out, we found a cold but fresh campfire. Someone had relieved themselves on a downed log nearby. We radioed the drone operator who flew over us and looked ahead. He said we had a clear trail and recommended a dog. We waited in a huddle to give the dog the best chance. An experienced canine handler showed up within an hour. The dog was ready and took the trail with intensity. It ended at a stream, Dead Creek, where the handler waded in and walked up and down each bank. At one point it looked like the dog hit scent again. Nothing doing. The dog and his handler were called back again for another possible location of the suspect.

In fall, dark comes early in the Northwoods. It was time to turn around, move east, and start south. If our plan worked, we would meet the other team at the road, maybe even pushing out Benson.

No such luck. A school bus waited at the road for us. As dusk creeped in, we arrived back at the sheriff's office. Several news teams were set up in the parking lot. Chief Delzell was keeping them happy. I slipped into the meeting room relatively undetected. I was relieved to find the retired chief running the inside show.

"John, we just got a report from the hospital. Pave is improving. They may have him breathing on his own tomorrow afternoon. Any luck with this Benson guy?" Len asked.

"No, nothing really. Where's Stewart?"

"He's working the press. What a jerk."

I hung my head, and when I did, I almost passed out. Len grabbed me by the shoulder and straightened me up.

"John, you're exhausted. You need some sleep. I'll call Julie, have her come and get you, or get a squad to take you home. If you don't take a break, you'll be no good to anybody."

He was right.

"I'm going to go out the maintenance door."

"Before you do, Officer Good wanted to make sure she got a word with you."

The retired chief called her on a portable, and a few minutes later she came in.

"Hi, Officer, how are you holding up?" I asked.

"I'm fine. Jared Price and I have been following up on potential sightings. No success, but we plan to keep on going until ten or so. I wanted to pass something on. Before we knew you were looking for Dr. Schmutz, I recognized his car ahead of us in traffic on Highway 63 moving along, when for no reason I can figure, he slammed on his brakes and swerved into the oncoming lane and quickly back. We almost hit him. I thought about pulling him over, but we were on the way to check on a Benson sighting and thought that was more important."

"Samantha, thanks for telling me. At least he's alive."

I got home, and I did not actually know for sure I was at the right place. Julie met me at the door with Sadie. I got a hug from one and a tail wag from the other. Apparently, Len had given her a heads-up that I was on my way home. Venison stew, homemade biscuits, and apple cider were on the table. I offered to help her with the dishes, and she shooed me off to bed. I don't remember even walking up the stairs.

My sleep was tortured with dreams that took me back to places I didn't want to go. Around midnight Julie gently shook me awake. I got up with a start and asked if Pave was alive. She slept in a spare room for self-preservation.

My pager woke me at three o'clock Thursday morning. I called in immediately. The truck had been found neatly parked next to other similar trucks in a construction site in Ashland. I threw on yesterday's uniform, splashed cold water on my face, and started to run out the door. In the doorway I stopped. I asked dispatch for and received a call from the Ashland County officer in charge (OIC).

I asked where the truck was found in relation to Schmutz's condo.

"Sheriff Cabrelli, I am at the truck and can see Schmutz's condo."

"Lieutenant, I need you to see if Schmutz is home or if his car is there." It was probably not necessary, but I needed to know for sure. The lieutenant got back to me five minutes later.

"Sheriff, no one home, no car in the driveway. A red piece of evidence tape stuck to the door asking Schmutz to call you."

Ashland County agreed to impound the stolen truck. The keys were in the ignition. At my request, the OIC gloved up and tried the ignition. The truck started right up. This told me that where the truck was found was a planned destination as opposed to a place where one may have happened to run out of gas.

The OIC had been around the block before. As far as he was concerned, he now had a killer on the loose. Anything I needed from him would be a distant second unless it involved locking up the suspect. Until then, his people would keep looking until they found him, or he moved on to the next jurisdiction.

I drove faster than my lights could cut through the darkness. How did I miss the connections? Schmutz was the common denominator in all of this. His fingerprints were on every piece of the puzzle. Schmutz and Benson were working together. The dignified professor out front, Benson coming up from behind doing the dirty work. But why the robbery? All that brought was a lot of public attention to their covert treasure hunt.

I swerved to avoid a deer, and the answer hit me. Marie. Schmutz, becoming a victim while searching for the truth, earned her trust.

I had communications put out an "emergency attempt to locate" on Professor Schmutz and his car. I requested that Schmutz should be detained if located and to notify the homicide task force.

I soon found myself within sight of Marie's driveway. I parked my squad in a wide spot on the road out of sight from her house. I let my eyes adjust to the dark and started my approach. Even though it was predawn, all the lights were on in the house.

Visibility was hampered by river mist. Schmutz's car was in the side yard. I could see at least two people in the sitting room but couldn't make out who. I had gone with my gut and now found myself where I didn't want to be. Backup squealing in at this moment would only raise the body count.

I needed to make my move. Clear identification and then a clear shot. Schmutz's Mercedes was my best chance for both cover and concealment. I slowly moved toward the front of the car and the big front window.

Marie walked past the window toward her kitchen, if I remembered the layout correctly. She returned with what looked like a white cloth. She bent down out of sight. I inched forward, straining to make out what I could. Benson appeared and looked to be towering over someone while holding something.

I had to live with the choices I had made. I knew better than to rush off alone in the dark to try and capture a murderer, especially one with a potential hostage. A shot now would be through window glass that could deflect it. The sky was lightening. I moved to where I thought I had my best chance. I needed to take him alive if I could, so I waited.

A piercing scream came from inside the house, and I made my move.

My mistakes compounded themselves. As I was coming to, I found myself on the floor of Marie's sitting room, my hands locked behind me in my own cuffs. The dispatcher on the radio was calling my number and attempting to find out where I was, providing last known information as heading to Ashland at three o'clock.

I looked up, and Benson kicked me hard in the guts. Then he laughed. Schmutz, beaten to a pulp, lay on the floor near me.

"Sheriff Cabrelli, so nice of you to join us. I had a feeling you would eventually try to spoil my plans. I have waited a long time to get all of you together. You have been as elusive as my ultimate goal. Finally, we're here, and it's so nice to have you. Two of you are necessary; Sheriff Cabrelli is not. Finding his way here in the darkness on a hunch, just a possibility. He is such a clever, clever man, and I want you to know that if everyone plays along with me, it won't make any difference. I'm going to kill him anyway. He is way too dangerous to leave alive. Is everybody ready to listen to what I have to say?"

He took his own place in a captain's chair looking down at us, smugly smiling. Clearly a man pleased with what he had accomplished. He had a pistol tucked in his belt; in his hand he held Marie's short sword. To make sure everyone was paying attention, he slammed the edge of the sword on a small end table, splintering it.

"I am now the captain of this ship, in the noble tradition of our family. Here are my rules and what I wish to accomplish. I want my share of the treasure, plain and simple. Professor Schmutz led me down a trail that ended here. I was so excited when I first realized how close I was. Do you remember the handyman who fixed your rain gutters and faucet? Almost caught me there. I would really like to visit, kind of an impromptu family reunion, get to know Aunt Marie. But I can't. I just don't have the time. So, the four-hundred-million-dollar question is this: Where is the gold? I am so close I can smell it.

"I want to start out by introducing myself. You may think you know who I am, but I am someone different to each one of you. To Cabrelli, I am a violent criminal that he needs to catch and put in a cage. In days long past, a noose, a broad sword, or plank would have been more fitting. Your instincts about me were not wrong, but you far underestimate the evil in my heart.

"Schmutz, lying there, saw me as a work-a-day carpenter and

land surveyor. By the way, I am a land surveyor. I learned the trade in prison. It has helped me a great deal. It was he who confirmed I was on the right track and closer than I'd been before, much closer actually.

"I am Andrew Trevain Benson. This lovely woman over here is my great-aunt. She has my inheritance, and I am anxious to get it back.

"So, you and Schmutz are the two most important people in the room. Professor Schmutz, you are truly an amazing researcher. I was fascinated with your appearance on *Mysteries Unsolved*. I watched it time and time again. Whenever you got to this one part of the show, when the interviewer asked about other plausible theories, you blinked and didn't stare at the camera. I could tell you were holding back. You have put together one half of the puzzle, and then you found dear, sweet Aunt Marie, who has the other piece. Professor, you first. Let's start out on the right track. What do you think I am talking about here?"

"Napoleon's gold."

"Bravo, Professor! Napoleon's gold. My gold. Now comes the tricky part. I will ask you a question, and because of the secretive nature of your business, you will be inclined to either not answer or lie. There is absolutely no time for that. I will torture you until you tell me what I need to know. Now I hope everyone was listening for I won't repeat myself. So, Professor, the obvious question is this: Where is the gold?"

He answered, "I don't know, exactly."

"What does that mean?"

"There have been individual coins, like the Lost Boys' coin and the Fisherman's coin, found in the Namekagon over the last few years."

"How about you, Aunt Marie? Where do you think the gold is? Now remember, no lying. That would be a bad example for your great-nephew. And I do have something to tell you. I did hesitate telling you this secret, but what the heck. I intend to kill Cabrelli with this sword. Dustin Stevens could have really made out on this deal. His ideas about this and mine just didn't work out. Then Cabrelli sticks his nose in and won't go away. I could have gone on a long time before anybody figured out who I was."

I was coming around enough to keep myself upright. Nausea was subsiding. Benson kicked me hard in the ribs, then stood over me with the sword. I watched from my spot on the floor as Marie Bennet became dark-eyed Maria Fuentes.

"Touch him with that sword, and you will never see the gold," she shouted. "I will die first. You will leave empty-handed. Do you understand, Andrew? No answer? Then kill me, you coward. Go ahead and kill me. I do not fear death, but I do fear the evil blood that runs through the veins of our people. Not all, you see, but some. Somehow, when you escaped from prison, a law enforcement officer showed up at my doorstep looking for you. He told me what a dangerous man you were, but for some reason, I was not afraid. I knew that you would find me, somewhere sometime. When you came to my door offering to do repairs, I knew it was you. You stared at me with those mean eyes, but I was not afraid. I have the gold, more than you could ever spend. I will give you every coin, every ingot. Hugh and I tried to do something good with the money we got from the coins, so we started a scholarship program. The only thing the gold ever brought that wasn't trouble."

"Where is the gold, Marie?"

"I will give you proof of its existence. It is not the great fortune the treasure hunters have been looking for. However, what we have left is still significant. Take it all with you." She walked over by the fireplace and retrieved a key from the bookshelf, removed a woven throw rug, and unlocked a hidden compartment.

"See for yourself."

Benson reached in and brought out a heavy bag of coins. He was mesmerized.

"I have more over here." She said and opened another compartment. "Come and see what I have here. You can have it all."

He turned to look at her. Her left hand held out another bag of coins, her right a Colt Navy pistol. He charged her with the short sword, swinging wildly. I launched myself into his legs, knocking him down. He swung the sword as he got up and came face to face with Maria Fuentes Trevain. She stood stone still, the cocked revolver in her hand. She smiled, said, "Go to blazes, you devil," and pulled the trigger.

The Colt revolver, over 170 years old, proved again it was deadly in the hand of someone that was able and willing.

Marie lowered the Colt's hammer, set it down, then took the cuffs off me. We helped Dr. Schmutz up. He looked like he had gotten the bad end of a barroom brawl. I checked Benson's vitals; he was dead. The shot from the pistol hit him dead center in the forehead. There was no sign of exit. ❖

CHAPTER 22

I got out my cell to call Chief Delzell. Marie took the phone from my hand.

"Please sit. I know you must alert your colleagues immediately, but please give me just a minute. Andrew won't be going anywhere. I am in a dilemma and don't know what to do. I was certain that someone like you, Sheriff, would kill Andrew before he got to me. Instead, I have killed him myself without remorse. No one can refute what happened here. He abducted the good professor who would have been the next victim and then would have killed you. I saved your life and granted you one more day to spend with your wonderful wife."

My radio squawked, calling my number. The world around us was still in search mode. They could not have known that minutes before it had ended.

"The world is waiting. But the gold cannot be part of this; it is not necessary. I have no idea where most of Napoleon's gold is, be it Poverty Island or elsewhere. What has been passed down in our family is a small fraction of the lost treasure. Professor Schmutz, you have already benefitted from the gold through the anonymous donor who continues to fund your brilliant work. We use the gold to support those things worth supporting, all with a minimum of bureaucracy. When I shared with you the other day, I knew you were men of integrity. Now prove it." Marie put the bags of gold back in the hiding place and handed the pistol to me.

"Do you cash the gold in at the local pawn shop?" I asked.

"No, of course not. A mutual friend, who is a bit of a clever pirate himself, has been able to convert the gold to a more usable form of currency. A very skilled attorney-at-law aided him, and both found that there is absolutely nothing illegal."

"Might I know this particular attorney-at-law or maybe his cohort?" I asked.

"Possibly so, it is after all, a very small world," Marie replied. "Help with this. Bring some goodness to the world."

I called Chief Delzell and told her Andrew Benson had been killed. "Chief, I need EMS, the ME, SI Price, two of the state agents already on loan to us, and you at Marie Bennet's place. Everyone should get free from where they are with as little notice as possible. Stay off the radio cell phone only. No lights or siren."

"Ten-four, Sheriff."

It was not long before the little house was packed with people. ME Chali pronounced Andrew Benson dead. He was positively identified by the chief and me and was loaded and transported to the morgue. The other EMS unit treated me and the professor. They decided that Schmutz should be transported to the Musky Falls hospital. The Colt pistol and the short sword were secured and tagged.

This investigation was going to go high order. The policy manual must have missed the chapter about shooters, and I needed to make sure Marie was out of the line of fire. I told the chief that I was going to move her to a safe location and asked for

Officer Good to be detailed to me. Marie got into Officer Good's squad, and I followed with mine with no fanfare or extra attention. We passed two TV remote vehicles on the narrow road.

Julie opened the door for us. Sadie was immediately interested in the company. We sat around the table, and I explained my strategy while Julie took care of yet another one of my wounds. The press presence in town would be driving the town into a frenzy. Marie would stay out of sight at our place with Officer Good or another officer with her twenty-four seven. She was reluctant to stay at first but finally relented.

I had much to do in short order. I told Julie as much as I could about when and where I might be. I put on my cleanest uniform and came downstairs to head for Musky Falls. Officer Good and Julie quietly prepared something to eat, while Marie sat in a chair staring out the window at Spider Lake. Sadie was snuggled up on her pillow.

I got back on the radio and was advised that the number of reporters was increasing. I needed to get to the hospital to see Dr. Schmutz regardless. A call to the emergency room nurses' station let me know the press had already swarmed the exits and entrances, so a nurse let me in through the back door. Dr. Schmutz was sitting up in bed when I walked into his room.

He looked at me cross-eyed. "Sheriff Cabrelli, how unsurprising it is to see you standing there and me lying here wounded."

"I know how it may feel that way."

"What can I do for you this time? I mean, it can't be much. Seeing how other than during a brief period of unconsciousness, we were both present for pretty much the entire event."

"Professor, I would like you to stay at my cabin. You are going to be besieged with people who want a piece of you, and it would be best for you to hide out until things calm down."

The same doctor who had treated Schmutz before and so

graciously kicked me out of the hospital came into the room. "Ah, Sheriff Cabrelli, here to torture another one of my patients?"

"No, the same one as before."

"I really don't find that funny, Sheriff."

"Please excuse him, doctor. He has a weird kind of police humor," said Schmutz.

"Well, what do you want with him?"

"I want to move him out of the hospital to a secure location until this is over. That is, if you think he is able."

"Where?" he asked.

"An undisclosed location, secured by law enforcement. This case is complex. Several suspicious deaths are connected, and they have tried everything to add the professor here to that number. I would like to avoid that."

"Dr. Schmutz, what do you think? Do you feel well enough to care for yourself? Just for the record, normally I wouldn't consider this, but..." the doctor gestured out the window to the growing number of media vehicles.

I called Ron Carver. He picked Schmutz up at the back doors and drove him out to our cabin.

Dr. Chali called. "John, the pressure of this investigation is mounting. We need to make a public statement. We have a body in the morgue, and everybody in Namekagon County has been looking over their shoulders for killers because of this clandestine mission you've been on. I am going to go ahead with a formal coroner's inquest. You need to be with me, calm things down."

"I'm just leaving the hospital," I said. "I'll meet you in the big conference room."

Dispatch advised me to call in. FBI Special Agents Huffaker and Swenson from the Superior office had just arrived and were parked in an unmarked car four blocks from the building. I picked them up, explained the situation, and we pulled into the "Law Enforcement Only" spot. We came in at the back of the room to find ME Chali at the podium was with none other than Scott Stewart.

Chali was to the point. "I am going forward with a coroner's inquest to positively identify the deceased and determine where, when, and how the person died. We're using available information and an intensive scientific data collection process to determine if there are connections to other people missing, living or dead. The results of our tests will determine any further steps we may take. For now, we will continue our investigation."

People shouted their questions from the audience. Scott Stewart stepped up to the podium.

"I am Scott Stewart, the Namekagon County executive. The question I just heard was regarding whether or not there are still dangerous people out there. I'd like to say no, but it wouldn't be true. Namekagon County has become a dangerous place to live."

ME Chali came back to the podium and ended the meeting. I went out the door, fully aware that Stewart had planted a seed in those at the meeting. There were still bad guys out there. Same as almost anywhere else. But he strongly implied that I hadn't finished the job.

Dr. Chali pulled me to the side in the parking lot. He took a small flashlight from his pocket and shined it in my eyes. A pupillary light reflex test. I knew what he likely would find.

He turned off his light and said, "Sheriff, get in my van. I'm driving you home. One of your deputies can pick your squad up later. For now, you're going home until Dr. Krump or I clear you."

Friday morning, I felt like I had been dragged through the woods behind a mule. Dr. Krump showed up at about seven o'clock and walked me into my room for an examination. I had a couple of different knots on my head; one was extremely ugly. My general condition report was that I would survive and would be back at work long before any doctor would approve it.

A call into Delzell got me a croaky hello.

"How are you doing, John? Dr. Chali called and told me he sent you home to bed."

"Yeah, he did, only attesting to what many others have already found—I have a hard head."

"Let me tell you there are newspeople everywhere looking for Schmutz and Marie. At least three major networks. Len Bork, Schultze, and a couple of others used the Great Timber Lodge as a decoy. The lodge is vacant at the moment, and the owner was glad to help out."

The media paid attention when a black suburban with flashing lights cut through the crowd headed for the fancy lodge, but they didn't move fast enough. The closest news crew almost made it before the two iron gates closed the front entrance, and an armed law enforcement officer wearing a hogleg stepped in front of them. Within twenty minutes, the media camp was set up outside the wrought iron perimeter fence.

Two days after the event, I gave a formal press conference to give them what I could. An investigation with many jurisdictions and cases tied together is almost impossible to follow. The case against Benson in our county was as straightforward as any could be: armed robbery, two aggravated batteries, attempted murder, first-degree murder. Marie Bennet had no choice but to use deadly force to protect herself, Dr. Schmutz, and me from the perpetrator who clearly stated he fully intended to kill me and Dr. Schmutz. Wisconsin law allows the use of deadly force to protect yourself or another, and the Castle Doctrine allows you to protect your home. Marie Bennet saved our lives. The world was rid of Andrew Benson; it was good for all.

Bill Presser, our local reporter stood in front and gave me a smile.

"The perpetrator was using the stolen identity of Ken Hetland listed as a missing person in the state of Georgia. A DNA sample was taken, which identified Hetland as Andrew Benson, a man with a long criminal history and several outstanding warrants. Benson was a suspect in at least four homicides, maybe more, in continuing investigations with the FBI, Georgia Bureau of Investigation, and the Wisconsin Division of Criminal Investigation. The degree of difficulty is significantly increased when crime scenes stretch from the state of Georgia to Namekagon County, Wisconsin.

"Two of his victims are part of our community. The evidence led us to conclude, beyond any doubt, that Benson killed Dustin Stevens. Benson broke into Stevens' house and there confronted him, shooting him in the arm. Stevens ran out the door to escape. Benson got in his truck and chased Stevens, who was found dead at the scene from excessive blunt force trauma. The Wisconsin State Patrol reconstructed the scene and determined that Stevens was running away when he was struck by the truck. The vehicle was traveling in excess of sixty miles an hour.

"A camera at the Walleye Wash got a picture of Benson next to his truck putting money into the meter. The time clock on the photo showed it was taken three hours after Stevens was run down. After the truck was in custody, the WSP recovered hair and other potential sources of evidence. Amazingly, even after the carwash and vehicle fire, hair fibers caught in a headlight trim piece matched Stevens."

Chief Delzell and I laid out the entire sequence of events, ending with the gunshot to Benson's forehead. As we finished telling the story, I felt a pressure valve inside of me release. There was a lull, and I announced we would answer any questions we could.

Bill Presser went first. "What is the status of Deputy Pave?"

"As most of you know, Namekagon County Deputy Robert Pave was severely injured in the attempt to capture the suspect. I am thrilled to tell you that he is resting comfortably at home, with his family. It is expected that he will be sitting with his feet up for several more weeks watching hunting and fishing shows," I said.

We were about to wind up when a reporter from the back of the room shouted out a question.

"In just two weeks the citizens of Namekagon County will be going to the polls to elect the sheriff. It has been no secret your opponent has been very critical of your performance, most recently, your handling of this case. He gave a press conference yesterday afternoon calling for your resignation. Has this caused you to rethink running for reelection?"

I took a breath and said, "I have nothing for you. It's up to the citizens of this county."

Then I just stepped down and walked away. I had done my job and paid my bill.

Home was a sight for sore eyes. Sadie, Marie, Harold, and Julie were waiting for me. ❧

CHAPTER 23

Television producers, treasure hunters, and historians swarmed to Namekagon County. Taverns served pirate food rum buffets, and episodes of *Mysteries Unsolved* and a Green Bay TV show about the sunken treasure of Poverty Island played on their big-screen TVs. Long forgotten, previously out-of-print books about the lost treasures of the north were now flying off retailers' shelves. Clever entrepreneurs at Northern Lakes Academy had a special run of sweatshirts printed with gold coins and treasure maps.

Professor Harold Schmutz had been robbed, shot, and severely beaten, all in the pursuit of tracing history. He was no Hollywood explorer; he was the real thing. The release of his book was now so anticipated the publisher doubled the first order, and he hired someone to manage his schedule. The network that had been so quick to send him down the road was even quicker at offering him a lucrative television series, which he turned down.

Julie had purchased our reserved seating tickets weeks ago for the event at the Harbor Convention Center in Ashland that was now standing room only. Dr. Schmutz was backstage. Marie and Chief Delzell sat with us, and we were ready for the history that laid the foundation for the events we had just experienced. The lights dimmed, and the crowd became silent. A stage light shone on the podium, and the Voice of the North spoke to the crowd.

"Tonight, we are honored to welcome world-renowned historian and author Dr. Harold Schmutz. His research project is like no other than he has ever undertaken. He was shot and attacked, yet was unwilling to give up on his quest. Sitting among you are some of the top professionals in their field, waiting just like you to hear this story for the first time."

The lights again dimmed. There was movement on the stage, and when the lights came back on, there was a high-back chair. Dr. Schmutz limped from the wings and sat down. The crowd's applause was deafening. Pain or not, he could not, would not be restrained. He got out of the chair, walked to the podium, and held the sides. Then looked at the audience. The crowd was silent, so he began.

"There was a moment in the not-too-distant past when I thought I might not be giving this speech. There are many of you here tonight hoping for answers to the rumors swirling around about pirates' gold in the Namekagon River, Civil War spies, Great Lakes ships, and lost treasure.

"Tonight, however, we are not here just for answers or theories. I invite you to join me in the tale I am compelled to tell, a tale of peace, war, and great change. A tale that nearly got me killed. In over three decades of following history, we have never come upon anything like what I will introduce you to tonight. The story seems impossible, yet its roots are intertwined in the very founding of the north country.

"For twelve thousand years, indigenous descendants of the upper paleolithic communities moved northward, hunting and gathering along the glacial margin. They established their camps where rivers flowed into lakes. Land close to the water but high enough in elevation to avoid flooding and dry enough to distance themselves from the dreaded mosquitoes.

"They followed the glacier north, carrying the seeds of the white pine with them. Over generations, these trees grew until they reached hundreds of feet into the sky. The white pine established itself on the landscape and became an important part of these indigenous peoples' habitat, culture, and storytelling. The cadmium bark was harvested to make flour. People found that white pine was resistant to fire, and they learned to use controlled burning as a tool to manage the land to their benefit. The people of the forest flourished. Their journey across the land was unknown to them, molded hundreds of years in the future yet to come. They explored vast areas, living not off the land but with it. Taking what they needed, but no more. These first peoples set the stage for the gold rush yet to come. Millions would be made, and the landscape would be changed forever.

"When scouts and fur traders first explored the land that would become northern Wisconsin, they were awed by what they saw—millions of acres of virgin pine forests. It was some twenty years before entrepreneurs and the U.S. government realized the potential. Trees hundreds of years old. Sixteen to twenty mature trees to the acre, thousands of board feet of lumber. What is thought to be the largest of these giants was noted in the 1875 *Ashland Press*. A tree taken down the Totogatic River yielded four eighteen-foot logs, the smallest one measuring forty inches at the top end. The four logs scaled 7,300 board feet.

"White pine was the wood of choice for construction, as well as ship building, fueling a national demand. Water-driven mills were set up on the rivers and streams to mill the logs into lumber. Land was free or cheap. Experienced loggers, sawyers, river pigs, cooks, and blacksmiths came from the East Coast to northern Wisconsin's seemingly endless forests, and so began the logging boom in northern Wisconsin.

"Hardworking settlers spent their winters in the lumberjack camps, first felling the white pine giants, then moving them onto the ice to then float downstream with the high water and raging rivers during the spring thaw. When logs reached their destination, lumberjacks received their pay. Most of the hearty men, and yes, some women, walked or, if they were lucky, rode a horse to their homestead, usually a piece of land that had been cut over where a family tried to eke out a meager backcountry existence. They hunted, fished, trapped, and grew hardscrabble gardens. Logs that were not suitable to be harvested and sent downriver became single-room log homes. Hand-split shingles kept out most of the rain."

A photo was displayed on a large screen behind Dr. Schmutz. It was the same one I had seen at Schmutz's townhouse. "Ladies and gentlemen, now I would like you to meet Samuel Benson. This is one of the few photos we are sure is Benson. He was a wealthy, successful businessman who came to stake his claim in the pineries. At the height of his success, he owned two large sawmills, thousands of acres of land, and several logging operations. He also owned a Great Lakes schooner. It was an able craft that could be at home on these large inland seas or the great Atlantic. No one knew where he had come from. People said he just appeared one day with two Navy Colts tucked in a sash around his waist and began to buy large tracts of forested land."

Another picture flashed onto the screen, and the crowd was instantly quiet. A detailed ink drawing depicting a stunningly beautiful woman with long black hair and deep brown eyes. The now familiar blazing sun tattoo was impressive on the big screen.

"I can see that she has the same effect on my audience as she did on others many years ago." The next image showed writing on the back of the drawing. "Maria Fuentes Trevain Benson was drawn by Jean Paul Fibido, a well-known artist who traveled with pen and ink, capturing images of the people who lived and worked in the north country. Some remembered when Samuel Benson first arrived in Namekagon County with his wife on the wagon seat beside him. People wondered who they were, but no one looked too hard. The north country was a good place for people to start over. Where they came from mattered less than what they brought to the table.

"Men, especially those in the logging camps, found Maria's beauty irresistible. By all accounts, Maria was an incredible woman known to possess a strong spirit and proved herself to be a canny businesswoman. The Bensons established themselves in the community, contributed to local causes, and paid good wages. But just as suddenly as they appeared, they were gone. The accounts of what happened are many and varied. To find out, we've got to understand as much of the past as we can."

A new image appeared. It was a drawing of a man resembling Benson but with a heavy black beard. The poster was dated 1864 and offered a reward for information leading to the death or capture of William Trevain.

"Please come with me as we go back in time. Pirate, merchant, sailor, war hero, murderer, and legend are all names that have been used when talking about William Trevain. To find Trevain's roots, we must begin our journey many miles from Namekagon County."

Dr. Schmutz wiped his brow and took a sip of water. He turned the pages of his notes, looked out at the audience, and continued.

Trevain was a man born to the sea. His family owned the Atlantic Merchant Company, and in 1856 he signed on as first mate on their three-masted clipper under Captain Honus Wellstone. They carried a variety of cargo: lumber and logs from the pineries in the north, sawblades and ironwork from the South and central Atlantic. William could both read and write and took over keeping the captain's log. A few days out from port, Trevain noted in the log that Wellstone was a drinker and not the least bit hesitant to use a club or lash.

One day, Wellstone told Trevain to alter course toward a deepwater harbor. Suspicious of the change in direction, William approached the captain who assured him they were picking up a small load of cotton cloth for a short run. They came to the harbor and the captain ordered Trevain to fire a rocket and lower the jolly boats. William's was the first boat ashore, and his worst fears were realized. Several groups of black men were chained together. Wellstone was a "blackbirder," taking on a cargo of slaves to be sold like cattle. The company had a strict policy against blackbirding.

The young first mate ordered his crewmates not to load the chained men. Unsure if they should defy the captain's orders, the crew sat on the beach and waited. Soon the rum-soaked captain came ashore with a lash in his hand, charged with fury. He ordered the chained men into the boats. They did not move. Wellstone moved to strike one of the men with his lash, but Trevain blocked the captain's arm. Wellstone stepped back and struck William with a vicious blow, ripping through his clothing.

"What happened after that is noted in great detail in the ship's log, but we will not get into the details here," Dr. Schmutz explained. "Several crewmen attested to a notation in 1857 where Captain Wellstone is listed as deceased and buried at sea, with first mate William Trevain listed as captain. The next we hear of Trevain is when he is recorded as the captain of another clipper: the *Andrea*. The ship was 197 feet long and weighed 500 tons."

The *Andrea* had a crew of thirty men, experienced sailors who knew their jobs. They sailed primarily in the Atlantic, running close inshore, dropping off everything from nails to giant saw blades.

Sailing north one full moon night for a Georgia merchant, a favorable stiff breeze was blowing which would put them at their destination ahead of schedule, resulting in a bonus for Captain Trevain. Dawn came and Trevain sent his mate up to the crow's nest to survey landmarks. The mate advised the captain of a schooner at full sail on course to intercept the *Andrea*. Pirates. Trevain pushed his ship hard, squeezing out every knot.

The pirate ship was not large enough to carry *Andrea's* full load. They likely intended to capture the clipper and kill the crew. Or capture the crew and put them to work.

Andrea had only a few rifles, pistols, and swords on board. The pirate ship was ready to fight, and a blast from its stern sent a cannonball that splintered the base of the foremast, sending it crashing to the deck. The pirate ship then swung starboard to protect two small boats full of men attempting to board the *Andrea*. As the pirates climbed the cargo nets, they were met with all the rifle and pistol fire Trevain and his crew could muster. Trevain's crew took heavy losses, and their only choice was to go over the side, for to stay on board was certain death. William and his remaining men reached one of the small boats now abandoned by the pirates and headed for the beach.

After burying their dead, they decided to row the small boat south, hoping to reach a town or settlement of some sort. On the tenth day they saw smoke rising and pulled their jolly boat to shore. They crept to the top of a sand dune and saw the *Andrea*, anchored off shore. It was the pirates, not good Samaritans.

They surveyed the pirate camp. From a low building came the laughter of many men. A woman ran out of the building toward the water. One of the pirates started to give chase, but was stopped by a brute of a man who stuck out his foot and tripped the crewman, slugging him when he tried to get up.

Trevain knew they were no match for the pirates and decided they would have to leave the *Andrea* behind. But before dawn the next morning, the woman with long black hair and fearsome dark eyes found them. Her name was Maria Fuentes, a prisoner of the pirata who planned to sell her. She pleaded for Trevain's help in exchange for information.

In two days the pirata were going to set sail and return with another crew to man the *Andrea*. The woman did not think they would leave many at the pirate camp. Trevain decided to try to reclaim his ship.

It happened as she said it would. The second day most of the pirates sailed away, and those who were left sat around a fire that night and drank until they passed out.

Trevain and his men snuck into the pirate camp by the light of a half-moon. Maria showed them the magazine where rifles and pistols, along with powder and balls, were stored. The door was standing open, and a drunken pirate was sleeping on the ground. William quickly passed guns out the door to his waiting crewmen. On his way out, he tripped over the unconscious man. The pirate yelled and a close-pitched battle ensued. Shots were fired at arm's length; men fell to the ground.

The brute Maria called Diablo used his sword with brutal effectiveness, charging Trevain sword held high. But then the sword fell from Diablo's hand as a hole appeared in his forehead, and he crashed to the ground. William watched the smoke rising from Maria's pistol and saw that her shirt had been ripped, exposing a blazing red and yellow sun tattoo over her left breast. She pulled her shirt back up and covered it.

Seven of William's crew and Maria remained, injured but standing. Three pirates were left alive and without a second thought, Trevain hung them by their necks. The next day the weather was right, and the crew maneuvered the *Andrea* toward the open sea.

With recovery of his ship, William resumed hauling cargo and sailed to a port he had worked before. "Y'all loaded heavy by the looks of your ship," said a man on the dock with a growling Southern drawl. "What are you carrying?"

"Mostly sawn lumber, two sawmills, hardware, and tools."

"Too bad y'all didn't get here a month sooner. Now you got to pay the tax."

"What tax? There's no tax," said Trevain.

"Where you been, boy? Ain't you heard? They's a war on."

"What are you talking about? There's no war."

"Well not right at this spot at this time, but there sure is one. We took over Fort Sumter in Charleston harbor. Took all them Yankees prisoner. Ships coming here flying the Stars and Stripes are now property of the Confederate States of America. I reckon I got to seize your ship and cargo. Name is Buck, quartermaster of this port. But I gotta tell you, boy, you happen to be in the right place at the right time. Instead of losing your cargo, maybe we can make a deal that works for both of us."

"What do you mean?" Trevain asked.

"What I need you to do is turn that ship around and run it up the coast to a deep-water bay. I got a chart that'll show you the way. There'll be a fire burning on the shore. That'll be my men. Once your cargo is off, head right back here. We'll have another load for you."

"How do you know I won't just keep sailing and take my load to a Yankee port farther north?"

"'Cause this here war is goin' to be short. You might just come out of this war a rich man. I know everybody that needs knowing. But I ain't got a ship like yourn."

"When do we go?" Trevain asked.

"Tonight. If the wind stays right, you can set sail. Are we in business?"

"I don't see I have much choice."

"You keep up your side, and I'll keep mine. By the way, I got two different papers here. One's from the Union, one's for the Confederacy. They are letters of marque and reprisal. When you're runnin' in Union water, fly the Stars and Stripes, and if they come alongside, show them your letter from the Union. Southern water fly the Stars and Bars and show them your letter from the Confederate States of America. These here papers make you a privateer. Make sure you know you got the right flag flying. They string pirates up without askin' any questions."

"What's a privateer?"

"A pirate that's workin' for the government. Somethin' else. We get paid in gold, not worthless paper. We kin spend that no matter who wins."

If there can be honor among thieves, it is certainly based on mutual gain and gold. The partnership between Buck and Captain William Trevain flourished. It was said by many that Trevain and his crew provided all the white pine lumber needed to build the Confederate Navy. A simple merchant clipper, seemingly unarmed, delivering cargo back and forth, north to south and south to north, flying whatever flag was needed. William Trevain had become a man of the times.

Trevain's log dated June 10, 1861, notes two ships flying the Stars and Stripes following the *Andrea*. During the night, a crewman changed the name placard from the *Andrea* to one that said *Maria* and raised the Stars and Stripes. In port they offloaded their cargo and a Union gunship came alongside, the captain and two armed soldiers boarding the *Maria*.

The Union captain produced a document and gave it to

Captain Trevain, whose ship and crew were now conscripted into service to take Union troops down the coast. Uniformed soldiers loaded the *Maria,* and Trevain was given a chart for their route. He immediately recognized the drop-off location: Buck's pirate camp. Buck's men were able fighters, but when outnumbered five to one in with a surprise attack, they'd be slaughtered.

"Our mission is to raid a pirate stronghold and capture a merchant ship that has been working with them," said the Union captain. "I will give orders on how we will handle the assault. We expect armed resistance. If we come upon the merchant ship, it will be surprised to find our fastest gunboat lying in wait. No merchant tub will outrun her or her guns."

Trevain knew they would not find another ship, as the merchant ship they were looking for was his.

After five days, Trevain came to shore a mile down from the pirate camp and the soliders disembarked. With Union troops unloaded, Trevain quickly caught the wind in *Maria's* sail, picked up speed, and ran hard to put distance between them and the Yankees, firing several rockets to warn the camp. Come morning, the crewmen manning the tower saw what appeared to be the gunship. The merchantmen struggled to gain speed as the ship grew closer. They would be overtaken in a matter of hours. Trevain turned the helm over to the first mate and went down to the hold. He and two crewmen emerged with special cannon loads.

The gunship fired a cannonball that struck the starboard side but glanced off without any real damage. Without cargo, the clipper towered over the faster gunship, providing a slight advantage. Then without explanation, Trevain ordered the ship to stop and seemed to be dropping sail to surrender.

It must have confused the gunship's captain, who tried to swing his ship hard to the port to change direction. Then, Trevain yelled, "Fire." The cannon roared and bucked like a mule against the thick ropes that held it in place. It was reloaded and fired again. The captain ordered the rest of the crew to fire with rifles. The third shot from the cannon was devastatingly perfect. Two cannonballs linked by twelve feet of chain swept the deck like a broom. The next shot of ball and chain finished the job, taking the mainmast.

The *Andrea* had taken many ships during the war, most without a fight. Tales spread about William Trevain, the "Southern marauder." They came into a northern port and were greeted with posters and handbills with a crude rendition of Trevain wanted for murder and piracy, offering a five-thousand-dollar reward. It also said that he was in the company of a woman believed to be a "pirate queen." Trevain's attack on the Union ship would soon have everyone flying the Stars and Stripes looking for the *Andrea* or the *Maria*. It was time to part company from his crew before he was recognized, and they all paid the price.

CHAPTER 24

Trevain contacted a local he knew was a spy for the Confederacy.

Engle Knurser looked him in the eye. "Captain Trevain himself. You were a fool to seek me out. Five thousand dollars is plenty to turn a patriot into a traitor."

"Ah! It appears you have seen my poster. I find myself in a difficult position, and I don't doubt many would hunt me down like a dog. However, there are pockets of our supporters doing important work. I have little time and must be on my way soon."

"You are a true son of the South, Captain, and you have nothing to fear from me. The battle is moving around us. General Scott is launching a massive land and naval attack along the Atlantic and Gulf coasts as well as the Mississippi, trying to split the Confederacy in half. 'Scott's Great Snake,' as it is called, will strangle the Confederate troops.

"They have seized control of much of the Great Lakes—lakes as large as oceans. The land surrounding them has forests full of giant trees that are being milled into lumber and turned into ships that will strengthen the Union's blockade. We need to fight the battle of the Great Lakes from inside the Snake, and you're the man we need for the job. It will be a long trip, and there are many robbers on the way. I am sure you are prepared to defend yourself."

It would be an overland trip, Knurser loading their covered wagon with supplies. Maria dressed in men's clothing and carried a derringer in her pocket. Trevain's two 36-caliber 1851 Navy Colts would be a deterrent to any robber.

"William, Maria, go quickly and don't look back. Take the right fork off the main road. You'll come to a bridge over the river tended by a guard in a Union uniform. He's one of us. To make sure, look for a nasty scar from the top of his head to his jawline. Ask him if he has seen a 'black horse running loose.' He will help you. Don't tell him who you are."

After weeks of nonstop travel and avoiding Union patrol threats, they came to the bridge blocked on each end by two stout rails. A Union soldier stepped out of a small cabin with a rifle in his hand, a pistol on his belt, and a scar from the top of his head to his jaw. He demanded to know Trevain's business.

Trevain responded, "Have you seen a black horse running loose?"

The bridge guard asked William his name.

"I don't have a name," he said.

The guard asked if he was a sailor. Trevain didn't reply. Then he asked if he had a woman traveling with him. Sensing danger, Maria had already slipped out the back of the wagon and crept up behind the guard, pointing the derringer at the back of his head. She warned him that all the questions he has been asking would be the death of him, and she intended to see to it.

The guard looked at her and said, "The pirate queen. Just as dangerous as legend said."

He asked no more questions and told William and Maria to take a road to a spot in a valley where they should wait for a man to meet them.

The small valley provided much-needed rest. After dark, one of the horses stirred, warning of a visitor. A travel-worn man came out of the cover.

He invited himself to a cup of coffee that Maria had on the small campfire. After a minute, he said, "I know who you are, Captain Trevain, and I'm honored to meet you. I'm the captain of a bushwhack guerrilla unit. We've been making strategic strikes, attacking Union troops and freeing Confederate prisoners in the Great Lakes. I've traveled day and night to catch up with you.

"The Union Navy controls the pineries and sawmills. Their well-armed ships are hunting for ours, adding them to their fleet, sinking them, or just burning them to the water line. We need you to join others and attack Union ships. It is too risky for you to continue on this route. I have maps that will take you where you're needed, and my men will protect you. A shipping agent by the name of Johnsson will meet you. Give him this note signed by President Davis. Sleep well tonight and leave before light. God Bless the Confederacy."

It rained for days. The canvas cover on the back of the wagon was the only thing that saved them from being soaked to the bone. After almost two months of travel, they reached Parry Sound on Lake Huron.

William was anxious to seek out Johnsson, but Maria was wagon-worn. She wrote in her journal that "travel by any way but the sea is uncivilized." Maria spotted a boarding house that advertised a "hot bath" and told Trevain that if he didn't stop, she would jump.

The next day, William set out to find the shipping agent. William walked into a small building sporting a large, freshly painted placard that said, "Anders Johnsson Shipping and Supplies." Inside sat a man with a gray beard and a huge head of gray hair.

"Are you Anders Johnsson?"

"I am, and who might you be?"

"William, ah... Smith," he grinned.

"An endless number of Smiths come through here," Anders chuckled. "Well, what can I do for you, Mr. William Smith?"

Trevain gave him the letter.

He read it over several times and looked up at Trevain. "I, too, would trade my name if I were you. Have you come a long way?"

"From Maine."

"Wagon or horseback?"

"Wagon with my wife."

"Where is she?"

"At the boarding house."

"The hot bath gets them every time," he laughed. "Well, pack up your gear, and I will pick you up at dusk. You'll stay with me for now. I have a big enough house that we won't be bumping into each other."

"We can't impose," Trevain said.

"But I insist. Besides, I could use some help." He got up and grabbed a crutch. "Broke leg. It's on the mend but has slowed me down some."

Within hours of making his acquaintance, Johnsson put Trevain in charge of a small crew to deliver several shipments destined for different parts of the lakes.

Parry Sound was, by all accounts, a peaceful town, and William and Maria started to settle down for the first time in their lives. Much to Trevain's chagrin, Union soldiers were commonplace and walked among the people. Maria went to work at the boarding house and often served drinks to the very men who would kill her if they knew who she was.

The war was not over, and word of mouth from residents, travelers, and other sources (mostly Union) proclaimed that the

South was in trouble. Johnsson approached William, his jolly composure replaced by a most serious demeanor. They sat on a bench at the wharf looking out on the lake.

"The salvation of the South is at hand, and you and I are destined to be a part of it. If you wish to hear no more, you can walk away, and I will have every expectation that you'll keep my confidence. It pains me to say this, William, but I must. Should I suspect that you have betrayed me, I will kill you. Too many of our brothers have died." Johnsson reached inside his coat. His hand came out with a gun, but not fast enough. One of Trevain's Navy Colts, cocked and ready, was pointed at his midsection.

Johnsson offered his gun to Trevain. He declined.

"You would not take the life of a friend casually," William said.

"I would not, and it would pain me to do so. Some months ago, a Confederate operative came to my house in the middle of the night. I was told to expect someone. I did not know when or where, but they would identify themselves by handing me a French one-hundred-franc gold coin. You see, my disguise as an honest ship's captain shipping cargo from a single port allowed me to take supplies to where our brothers in the South needed them."

"Go on," said William.

"Cotton production is critical to the French, so Napoleon III is sending millions in gold to support the Confederacy." He reached into his vest pocket, extracted a gold coin, and handed it to Trevain who studied the coin with an embossed image of Napoleon III's head.

"Anders, tell me how we are to be involved."

"We'll receive and transport part of the gold. A previous attempt was made to come from the South. But the Snake captured the ship disguised as a merchant with no means to defend itself. The possibility of detection is far less this way. The gold has been loaded on wagons in Canada and is being moved by land to locations on Lakes Michigan and Huron, where it will be loaded onto two ships. One will be our new schooner, which appears as a merchant ship but can travel quickly and defend herself."

"Who will be at the helm?"

"You, William. Your skill is legendary. No doubt this will be a difficult mission. Every possibility will be covered to ensure success. Still, there is great danger. You will have a small crew, ten men, but men who can be trusted and depended on."

"Make that eleven—I will be taking Maria with me. Any idea when we might be going?"

"Soon. We will make it known you are headed North to pick up a load of white pine, including some suitable for masts. No one will ask any questions. Good lumber is hard to come by, what with the Yankees taking every board I can produce. We'll take orders just like always. Until then, keep a bag packed and inspect your ship daily."

A month passed. Trevain was on deck inspecting his ship when a man dressed in seaman's clothes approached.

"I heard you were hiring for a trip North. I'm looking to sign on."

"Sorry, I've got a full crew. Try one of the others down the wharf."

"Anders Johnsson was sure you needed help. I have money to invest." He handed Trevain a French gold hundred-franc coin.

Two days later Trevain and his twelve-person crew set sail. The schooner handled like a dream, and though it was able to be fast and responsive, they moved slowly and took advantage of quiet bays to assemble and mount four cannons on the deck. The stern cannon was mounted on a swivel to wreak havoc with any pursuer, a familiar tactic that had made Trevain so despised by the Union Navy.

A week out of port, they were sailing west of Manitoulin Island. It was dark when a rocket arched over Trevain's ship. Trevain and crew rowed a dinghy ashore and were met by four armed crewmen and a fully dressed admiral of the French Navy.

The admiral shared the plan only with the captain and first mate. The gold coins and bars destined for the Confederate forces would be carried across land to a hidden bay on Lake Michigan where they would meet the main ship and load most of the gold. Trevain's schooner would be loaded with the remainder. The strategy was twofold. If the main ship was in imminent danger of being sunk or captured, Trevain could sail his ship away from the action and follow the east coast to Chicago. If the main ship was under threat, Trevain's fast ship would come to its aid and engage the attackers.

The two ships were to sail at least a day apart. Spies would be watching from shore and fire three rockets if attack was imminent, at which point the ships were to take whatever action deemed necessary. The mission was clear: get the gold shipment to Chicago, one ship or two.

Trevain was to cross the Straits in full daylight, flying the Stars and Stripes and wearing Union uniforms. "If you need to," the admiral said, "run west to avoid capture. Our spies will make sure to get you through. Then head due south, sailing in full view of any adversaries that might be waiting. If you are positive they are in pursuit, head to Poverty Island near Green Bay and let them follow you. Your schooner should be able to cut closer to the island than their gunship. The man who joined your crew knows the shallow rock shoals that surround the island. Take the right course, and you will pass through; your pursuers will crash onto the rocks and sink. Your ability at the helm and our man's information will allow you to avoid capture and turn the attack on the gunship.

"In the meantime, the main ship will go through the Straits, hugging the east shoreline of Michigan, heading south at full sail. If the gunship runs aground on the island, you can disengage. If they make it past the islands, just keep them busy."

The shipment of gold arrived three days late. Crews were anxious, but the loading went smoothly. The amount taken aboard Trevain's ship was significant, but less than the four large chests chained together on the main ship.

Trevain sailed up the middle of Lake Huron with favorable winds. They would be crossing through the Straits of Mackinac sooner than expected and assumed the main ship would not be too long behind him. In his log he noted that once clear of the Straits, they were hit with a vicious storm. Giant waves were driving his ship into the west coast of Michigan. It was all he and the crew could do to make headway toward the Wisconsin shore, hoping to get some relief. Visibility was poor at best, and when a faint orange rocket burst in the sky, Trevain barely saw it. What fool would wage warfare in a sea like this?

Conditions worsened. Then out of the howling wind and waves, a ship loomed large at Trevain's stern, running for cover if there was any to be found. It was almost certain that the two ships would collide, but the wind blew them apart, and the bigger ship passed by close. Trevain realized it wasn't a gunship at all. It was the main ship, and it was running a wild course that was certain to put them aground on Poverty Island. The ship was quickly lost from view, and Trevain needed to quickly take a hard port tack to save his ship.

The storm abated as quickly as it had come. Trevain and his crew found themselves banging against the rocky shore, but not aground, in the Green Bay passage. Huge trees along the shore had been torn from the ground. Just before they lost control of the ship, it had risen and come down hard. He and his crew began an inspection and found the rudder was mere scrap pieces of wood hanging by screws and nails. It was a miracle they had made the passage past Poverty Island.

It took two days to repair the rudder before setting sail for Chicago. They flew the Stars and Stripes, hoping it would give them some advantage. But a Union gunship began pursuit a mere hour after they set sail. Trevain lowered the sail and waved. The gunship had cannons fore and aft, starboard and port. It was also moving toward Trevain in a way that would allow a broadside attack. They had no chance of surviving should the gunship let loose.

Trevain moved his ship into position. Union sailors were ready to board, lowering small boats. Though not in perfect position, Trevain's crew uncovered the cannon and fired iron shot when the Union crewmen were halfway down. They pivoted the stern cannon, firing ball and chain and ball and chain again. The foremast crashed to the deck.

Trevain and his crew ran for open water. Cannons and rifle fire roared from the gunship. The cannoneers were skilled, and Trevain's crew and ship suffered damage and casualties. But with rigging intact they sailed at full mast and were soon hit with yet another storm.

Schmutz displayed a journal page on the screen. "'The mates worry they are doomed,'" said Schmutz, quoting the log. "The storm finally blew itself out, and not a ship could be seen on the horizon. Even today, legends of the gold ships abound. Most believe, if they ever existed, they are resting on the bottom of one of the Great Lakes.

"The Civil War ended, and people wanted to return home. For the most part, what happened in the war was put behind them. Unfortunately, William Trevain and Maria, the Pirate Queen, were still wanted by the government, and posters offered big rewards for information that led to their capture. William and Maria, however, had disappeared."

Samuel Benson arrived at the town of Musky Falls in the 1870s. The north county had free land with white gold and a place where the past was past. People were not judged on what they had done but what they could do. A man with an axe and a saw could make a good living. A man with an eye for business may find prosperity.

A prosperous businessman, Sam let it be known he was looking for investment opportunities. Musky Falls was not yet a city, but the endless forests were where fortunes were being made. He was only in town a few days before he was approached by a man wearing a wool plaid shirt and well-worn boots. He introduced himself as Arden Jones.

"I understand you're looking to invest some money in good ideas," he said.

"I am," said Sam.

"Look no further, Mr. Benson. I got everything you're looking for."

"So, what would I be looking for?"

"Well, that kinda depends on you. I guess we should start with whether you want to make big money or little money."

"Explain."

"Well, Mr. Benson, I got big plans and little money. But I know everything anybody needs to know about how to make it here. I've been thinking about this a lot, and I'm a little leery of someone stealing my ideas."

Sam Benson laughed. "Well, Mr. Jones, we are at an impasse. If you won't tell me your plans, how will I know whether I want to invest?"

"That's simple, Mr. Benson. I'll give you my word. It's not going to be a problem, though, because once you see what I'm thinking, you're going to wonder why you didn't think of it."

Benson thought for a minute. "Okay, Mr. Jones. Let's see what you've got."

Arden and Sam took two saddle horses from the livery and started to wind their way through the giant forests. They came to a fast-flowing river not too far out of town.

"This is the exact spot where we're going to build a sawmill. That water's moving plenty fast to power a big mill. We'll saw our own lumber and cut out paying somebody downstream pickin' our pockets. We'll haul the boards and load them."

"Sounds like a good idea, Arden. Who owns the land here?"

"I do, Mr. Benson. I do. I also own ten other tracts. I would buy more land if I had more money."

Sam Benson got down off his horse and listened to Jones. They shook hands at a time when that meant something and became partners.

With Sam's investment, they traveled south with three wagons and bought a sawmill. Two sawyers were hired to supervise construction, although he knew as much or more than they did. Another crew was hired to build a lumber camp located close enough to the river so hauling logs would not be a problem. A makeshift dam allowed them to raise the water for a winter staging area. Eventually the dam would be replaced by one with gates that would move and channel logs down the Namekagon River.

Other loggers did not warmly welcome Benson and Arden's partnership, and Benson further aggravated things when he repeatedly paid top dollar for the best land. Sam ran the business, and Arden handled the mills and logging operations.

Maria was not involved in the logging business but bought an abandon saloon and boarding house for the balance of an unpaid note and hired local carpenters to turn it into the Black Horse Inn. Her boarding house provided bedbug-free rooms, served an honest drink, and simple but good fare among other things. Sam and Maria lived on the top floor. When Sam wasn't out at his camps, he could be found at the Black Horse.

They became welcome citizens in Musky Falls and Namekagon County providing good jobs for good pay. Maria added a room to the back of the Black Horse Inn, offering free use to anyone who needed a place to meet, and even hired a traveling preacher to come to town on Sundays. It was rumored that Maria had a vault built into the floor.

Their names began to appear on property deeds and other documents and opened a small office next to the Black Horse. Time passed along with the restlessness of life at sea. The Bensons found a beautiful spot up on a hill that overlooked a lake and built a timber frame lodge with the best logs available.

One day when Benson was returning from filing on a piece of land, a boy ran out in front of his horse and gave him a message from Arden Jones. The Union had not forgotten William and Maria Trevain. A team of federal marshals were combing the town distributing handbills with drawings of Trevain and his Pirate Queen. The handbill said that Captain Trevain and the crew of the *Andrea* were criminals, as prescribed by President Lincoln, accused of ambushing a Union gunboat and piracy, with letters of marque from both the Union and Confederacy.

William Trevain, $10,000 reward for his capture.
Maria "Pirate Queen" Trevain, $5,000 reward.
Other crew members, $500 each.

Dr. Schmutz paused, looked out at the crowd, and said, "You can imagine how much they must have wanted William Trevain to offer that sizable reward, almost $200,000 today." Then he continued.

Behind the inn Trevain's stable hand, Andy, held his best four-horse team and a covered freight wagon, which Maria was feverishly loading. Some say they watched Sam and Arden struggle to lift a chest into the wagon bed. They were ready to go when Union marshals came around back of the Black Horse. The troops raised their rifles, and Benson fired his Colts several times into the tight group of soldiers. One wounded soldier started getting to his feet with pistol in hand. Maria picked up a gun off the ground and shot him dead.

Arden drew his Schofield to cover their escape. Sam grabbed the horses and yelled for Maria to get on the wagon. With a slap of the reins the horses took off running hard into the night down the river trail. Maria held on in the back of the wagon, firing at pursuing soldiers and leaving dead bodies in their wake. Arden Jones stood his ground and died covering their flight.

That night, Samuel and Maria Benson, thought to be William Trevain and the Pirate Queen, disappeared into the darkness. Never to be seen again.

Local Sheriff Anthony Meany and his deputy were brave men but chose not to join in the chase for the Bensons. After the losses sustained in the aggressive firefight, Union marshals searched the Bensons' home and the Black Horse Inn, finding a small bag of gold coins from France.

An image of a gold coin with the profile of Napoleon came on the screen. "The coins in the Bensons' safe are long gone," Dr. Schmutz said. "Might these be the same? We'll probably never know. Ships' logs, diaries, and journals talk about a man to be reckoned with. Could Samuel Benson be the bold William Trevain who defeated the pirates and rescued his queen? A pirate, a sailor, lumberman, war hero, businessman, privateer, a seeker of justice.

"It is here, in the land of great forests, the land of inland seas, where hundreds of mysteries lie uncovered. It is where those bold enough will know the pleasure of waking up in the morning with frost on their nose and stars for their blanket. Paddle a birch bark canoe or walk the Anishinaabe Trail. Time for you to explore, put on your leather boots. The treasure of the north country is waiting for you to discover it. Thank you."

The crowd was silent for a few moments before the auditorium exploded in applause, followed by a wave of people standing wanting more, wanting to thank him. It was just after midnight when the crowd cleared out. Schmutz, exhausted, put his head back and was dozing before we were out of the parking lot.

CHAPTER 25

On the night of the election I would have been completely content with sitting at home by the fire, but no one was having it. We arrived at the Rich Ford Meeting Hall the Tuesday after the presentation just after six o'clock. A north country potluck was in full swing. My friends, my family, my community had come out to wish me well. I was a reluctant candidate, and win or lose I would spend the rest of my life in Namekagon County. It was then that my concerns and worries left me.

The Eva Zachery Band started playing Jake's rock music and switched to a lively country swing, which took folks to the floor. Pave parked himself close to the buffet tables. The girls waited on him hand and foot. Julie and Bud pulled me into a line dance. Later, Dr. Schmutz gracefully waltzed with Marie. She smiled for the first time in quite a while.

The polls were closed, and the final election results were rolling in. It looked like I'd serve another term as the Namekagon County sheriff. The energy in the room increased, and shortly after nine o'clock, the election results were officially called.

My supporters cheers quickly turned into a chant for a speech. I made my way up to the podium and looked out at this community I had grown to love.

Suddenly a hush fell over the hall. I looked around and was shocked to see Scott Stewart moving through the crowd, smiling and shaking hands. He stopped by the cake table.

All eyes were on Stewart. "I thought I'd come down here to congratulate you, Sheriff Cabrelli. Of course, I will be asking for a recount to make certain that the will of the people is well represented in this race. I've been very disappointed in the pack of lies that has been said about me when I am clearly the best choice for the job. I just want you to hear me out. Then I'll leave you to your party. I want you to know the truth. John Cabrelli is not the man you think he is. I have given so much to this community and certain members have just betrayed me." Stewart swiped his arm across the table, knocking plates and food to the floor. As I rushed him, he reached out and grabbed a long-bladed cake knife and pointed it a few inches from my chest.

Everyone froze. Stewart began to rant and rave, calling out accusations against individuals in the room. I could see people getting edgy. Then, before I could make a move, a hand grabbed Stewart's hand and, with a sharp twist, resulted in a snap that made him howl and drop the knife. Next a hogleg came down hard on Stewart's head, dropping him in a heap on the floor.

"Guess I'm not too old for the job now, am I?" Schultze said.

Samantha Good handcuffed Stewart, broken finger and all. The on-call EMTs were attending the event, so the ambulance was parked just outside. Stewart, pinned to the floor, again started yelling and cursing. There were plenty of volunteers to help put him on the stretcher, and he quickly found himself strapped down with a spit bag over his head on the way to the hospital and then the jail, where the deputies at the booking counter would be waiting for him.

As he was rolled out of the door, the crowd cheered. Schultze was the hero of the night. Finally, after lots of back-slapping he was convinced to speak to the crowd.

"I've only got one thing to say, and Scott Stewart and anyone like him need to pay attention. Namekagon County is our home, and there here is plenty of room for skunks or weasels as long they aren't running for office. Congratulations, Sheriff Cabrelli. We are lucky to have you."

Tonight, the chips fell my way.

The party went until midnight. When we arrived home, Julie and I sat outside looking at Spider Lake. The breeze was chilly. I went inside to get Julie a wool blanket and asked if she wanted a glass of wine. She smiled and said no.

Sadie came out to join us, lying contentedly at our feet. The moon was almost full and shone like only a north country moon can. Julie turned her head to me and whispered, and in those few seconds opened up a world of new possibilities.

I looked up and was sure that the man in the moon smiled at me.

EPILOGUE

The story of the Lost Boys and the gold they found was repeated time and time again, sometimes with the addition of a woodsman who chases children away from his strong box of gold.

The following summer a group of teenagers were wading and splashing in the Namekagon River on a hot day. One of the boys saw something on the river bottom underneath a rock outcropping. Soon everyone was on task investigating the find. A girl on the school swim team got a stout piece of rope out of her boyfriend's truck. She took a deep breath and dove into the depths. On her second try she was able to tie the rope around the mysterious object. On the count of three they all pulled on the rope. They dragged the object onto a rock. It was what was left of an old wagon wheel.

They showed the Musky Falls Museum curator where they found the wheel. He told the kids that the bend over the river at that point used to be part of the river road. The wagon wheel they found was well over one hundred years old and made for a freight wagon by a blacksmith. The kids got together the next weekend at the same spot on the hunt for more treasures. One of the boys had been tasked with taking his little brother along on the picnic. He was throwing rocks into the river when he noticed something in the water, shiny and gold. He told his big brother, and they mobilized to recover what they all could see was shiny and gold. It was just beyond the depth that any of them could dive. Finally, the swimmer gave it her all. Rope tied around her waist, she took several deep breaths and dove. She kicked herself to the bottom and, with one desperate grab, got the object: a Number Five gold Mepps bucktail.

The truth is always somewhere in the middle.
—Warden John Holmes • 1939–2017

AUTHOR'S NOTE

The mysteries held close by our great inland seas are countless. The greatest writer, the most eloquent wordsmith, could never do them justice. Yet we can walk barefoot in the shallows for a minute and are instantly captured.

Legend says that in the 1920s, a freighter ran aground on Poverty Island. Tugboats came to free it. During the rescue, the tug's anchors caught some wooden chests and chains. As the chests were brought to the surface, they broke free and once again disappeared beneath Lake Michigan's waves. Poverty Island, noted for extreme weather, as if on command from a higher power, conjured a wild storm, unwilling to give up its treasure.

NORTHERN LAKES MYSTERIES
Award-Winning Series

FIGURE EIGHT (BOOK 1)

After a career-ending event, John Cabrelli retreats to his late uncle's lake cabin where danger awaits—along with the truth behind his uncle's death in this award-winning first in series.

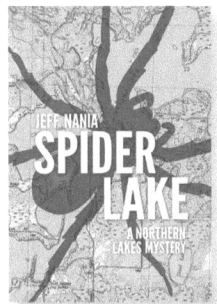

SPIDER LAKE (BOOK 2)

A missing federal agent, suitcases full of cash, a secluded cabin in the woods... *Spider Lake*, the award-winning second book in the Northern Lakes Mystery series, is an unputdownable crime thriller.

BOUGH CUTTER (BOOK 3)

Just as Namekagon County sheriff John Cabrelli adjusts to his new job, a body is discovered in the woods—and he must race against time to unravel the case when the lives of even more victims are claimed within the wilderness...

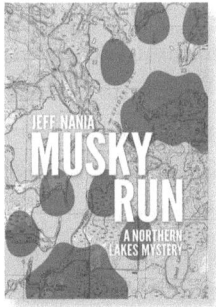

MUSKY RUN (BOOK 4)

Predators stalk the Northwoods as the Great Wilderness Race gets underway. Sheriff John Cabrelli and the new Musky Falls chief of police work to keep the community calm as they try to piece together the clues before it is too late.

ABOUT THE AUTHOR

Jeff Nania is a former law enforcement officer, writer, conservationist, and biofuel creator. He is the award-winning author of five fiction books, *Figure Eight, Spider Lake, Bough Cutter, Musky Run,* and *River Gold* in his Northern Lakes Mystery series. His narrative non-fiction writing has appeared in *Wisconsin Outdoor News, Double Gun Journal, The Outlook,* and other publications.

Jeff was born and raised in Wisconsin. His family settled in Madison's storied Greenbush neighborhood. His father often loaded Jeff, his brothers, and a couple of dogs into an old jeep station wagon and set out for outdoor adventures. These experiences were foundational for developing a sense of community, a passion for outdoor traditions, and a love of our natural resources.

Jeff has been recognized locally, statewide, and nationally. *Outdoor Life Magazine* named him as one of the nation's 25 most influential conservationists, and he received the National Wetlands Award for his wetland restoration work. The Wisconsin Senate commended Jeff with a joint resolution for his work with wetlands, education, and as a non-partisan advisor on natural resource issues.

Now a full-time novelist, Jeff spends as much time as possible exploring outdoor Wisconsin with his friends and family.

Read more from Jeff Nania and
sign-up for email updates at
feetwetwriting.com

@jeffnaniaauthor   @jeffnania

Made in United States
Troutdale, OR
08/10/2025